ALSO BY NATALIE D. RICHARDS

49 Miles Alone

Four Found Dead

Seven Dirty Secrets

Five Total Strangers

Six Months Later

My Secret to Tell

Gone Too Far

What You Hide

We All Fall Down

One Was Lost

PRAISE FOR *49 MILES ALONE*

2025 EDGAR ALLAN POE AWARD WINNER, BEST YOUNG ADULT

"A twisted and suspenseful story about survival in its many forms. You'll race to the end."

—Jessica Goodman, *New York Times* bestselling author of *The Counselors* and *The Legacies*

"Crackles with tension and desert heat. This pulse-pumping survival thriller is not to be missed!"

—Kit Frick, author of *I Killed Zoe Spanos* and *The Reunion*

"Genre vet Richards is no stranger to chilling and suspenseful stories, and this survival thriller earns a spot on the shelf with some of her standouts."

—*Kirkus Reviews*

PRAISE FOR *FOUR FOUND DEAD*

"[*Four Found Dead*] teems with rich character interactions and propulsive action as slasher-flick ambiance takes over the nostalgic setting."

—*Publishers Weekly*

PRAISE FOR *SEVEN DIRTY SECRETS*

"Richards's knack for blending exciting nail-biting plots with realistic and engaging characters results in yet another riveting page-turner."

—*Booklist*

"A serious thriller for readers itching for a good mystery, and also a cautionary tale about abusive relationships and how they can escalate into violence."

—*School Library Journal*

PRAISE FOR *FIVE TOTAL STRANGERS*

"A twisty thrill ride that will leave you breathless. I stayed up after midnight just to see how it all ended."

—April Henry, *New York Times* bestselling author of *Girl, Stolen*

PRAISE FOR *WHAT YOU HIDE*

"A taut, compelling mystery and a compassionate realistic fiction novel all in one."

—*Kirkus Reviews*

"A chilling small-town mystery… This page-turning story of teens helping each other through dilemmas will attract and inspire readers."

—*Booklist*

TWO PERFECT LIES

NATALIE D. RICHARDS

sourcebooks fire

Cover design by Ray Shappell
Cover images © Stanislas Desjeux/Arcangel, Tifonimages/
Getty Images, Wangwukong/Getty Images
Internal design by Diane Cunningham/Sourcebooks

Published by Sourcebooks Fire, an imprint of Sourcebooks
1935 Brookdale RD, Naperville, IL 60563-2773
(630) 961-3900
sourcebooks.com

Cataloging-in-Publication Data is on file with the Library of Congress.

Printed and bound in the United States of America.
VP 10 9 8 7 6 5 4 3 2 1

For Ian, my partner in crime
since the hassgropper days

ONE

I'm breaking the rules for the nerdiest imaginable reason.

My sixth-period Criminal Justice class is holding me hostage. Or at least it is for the next twenty-six minutes. I'm supposed to be reviewing the slide deck from Unit 6 and listening to Ms. Meek drone on, but instead I'm sneaking online for the nerdiest imaginable reason. To be fair, no one is listening. But most of my classmates are shopping for two-hundred-dollar leggings or checking one look-at-me social app or another. Whereas I'm stress sweating and obsessively refreshing my inbox waiting for a response—promised by 2:00 p.m. today in the application materials—from the John Carroll University Leadership in Chemistry summer program.

I check the clock. 2:02 p.m. Maybe it's a time zone thing?

No. John Carroll is in Ohio, albeit three hours nearly due northeast of me.

I refresh it again. And again. And again.

Maybe I read the time wrong? I could have sworn they said finalists would get their interview invitations today at 2:00 p.m. Maybe—

A new email pops to the top of my screen and I swear to God, my heart stops cold for a long second. My eyes lock on the sender. John Carroll University.

And then the subject line. Interview Request.

I jerk back from the screen in surprise. Then I open my texts before I even pull up the email, because if ever there was a best friend news emergency, this is it. Lily should actually be in this class, but she isn't back from her school office aide gig. God, I hope she's checking texts. She's going to flip.

"Let's talk about the process of placing someone under arrest," Ms. Meek says, in her trying-to-start-a-discussion voice. Of course I haven't been paying attention to the slide deck, but I have plenty of reasons not to care for this topic.

People around me begin to shift and twist in their seats. I look up and my summer program delight frosts over in an instant. Every pair of eyeballs in this classroom is directed at me and I'm pretty sure I know why.

"What precipitates an officer making an arrest?" Ms. Meek asks more directly.

A few hands shoot up around the room. Ms. Meek calls on Emma, but Jackson Collins takes the opportunity to lean closer to me, dropping his voice to a whisper.

"Bet you know the answer, Clara."

My cheeks go hot in an instant, and I hate them for the betrayal almost as much as I hate the Jacksons—because of course dickbags would come in pairs—for snickering. Out of the corner of my eye, I spot Henry Toussaint looking up. He is tall, dark, and so intimidatingly attractive, that even with my face on fire and my dignity sliding onto the floor I'm perfectly aware of his proximity.

"...an outstanding warrant exists or the officer witnesses you committing a crime."

"Which was it for you?" Jackson goes on softly. Not so softly that people near us can't hear, because now a few of our closest classmates are tittering.

I don't look directly at them, but I know it's all the usual suspects. Ava, Sloane, the other Jackson—key players in and hopeful applicants to the social group I orbit. But I'm not like Mars or Earth—more like Neptune, always included, but far enough away that no one pays me much attention.

"You're forgetting one other circumstance," Ms. Meek says. "Can anyone help?"

"Can you help, Clara?" Jackson asks, just a smidge louder this time.

Laughter erupts around me and two things happen concurrently.

"Knock it off," Henry says in a low voice.

At the same instant, Ms. Meek says, "Cool it, Jackson."

It's a half-hearted warning at best. We all know this forty-something teacher with her dark roots and tired eyes doesn't have the energy for enforcing anything.

But Jackson does stay quiet. Of course, he continues to watch me, staring with this shitty little smirk while Henry mutters another low warning and everyone else stifles laughter. Ms. Meek ignores it all, continuing to explain that an officer can also place someone under arrest if they reasonably suspect a crime. Kiasha—wicked smart and possessing zero interest in the social cage fight playing out quietly in the back half of the room—gets into a discussion with Ms. Meek about how reasonable suspicion is determined, and doesn't that feel too subjective to result in actual justice? All the while Jackson gapes at me, chin in hand, and I squirm furiously, hoping a fire drill will interrupt this nightmare.

How many minutes are left in this class again?

Twenty-one.

Fantastic. Might as well be twenty-one years with the way I'm feeling.

"Let's switch things up a little, class," Ms. Meek says. "I need three volunteers to join me up here."

My hand shoots up before I can stop myself. I don't know

what's motivating me more—the need to get the hell away from Jackson and all this giggling or the need to prove to them that I am not afraid of this conversation, despite the thing everyone in here is thinking about. Despite the fact that everyone in this room (minus Jonah, new to Tuskegee High this year) knows exactly what I did two years ago.

"Ava," Ms. Meek says and then, with the briefest shadow passing over her features, she nods at me. "Clara. And Jonah. Come on up."

My heart is pounding in my ears as I stand up. Walking to the front of a classroom always feels like being under a microscope, but it still beats out sitting there while Jackson stares holes into the side of my head.

At the front, our teacher holds out a crumpled grocery sack, lifting it high enough that Ava can't see what's inside. She gropes around in the bag, pulling out a gavel. Ms. Meek moves the bag to me and I reach inside. Something rattles at the bottom, but my fingers graze rough cloth. I pull out a brown burlap bag, turning it over in my hands. It's a round sack, tied at the top and sporting a big black dollar sign written on one side in permanent marker. The kind of loot a burglar might carry off in an old-timey movie. A few laughs sound out behind me. Fine. Whatever. I'm a bank robber. Ha ha, it's so very funny, isn't it?

And then the bag moves on, and Jonah takes the final item—the jangling thing. He pulls out something silver and metallic. He instantly turns pink from the tips of his ears down to the collar of his ratty flannel shirt. The class erupts, laughing and pointing at the pair of handcuffs he's awkwardly holding. There are waggling brows and leering too, because in high school, even in a criminal justice class, handcuffs are immediately the start of a dirty joke.

Ms. Meek claps her hands, and the room settles. "Okay, class, here's the scenario. A teller at Toontown Bank has called the police reporting the robbery of a single bag of Funny Money. Officer Jonah arrived and witnessed Clara exiting the bank with this bag, so he has reasonable suspicion..."

Whatever Ms. Meek continues to say is now lost on me. I can't hear anything other than a high-pitched whine in my ears layered over the soft laughter now rolling through the class. Some of that laughter is good-natured. Some isn't. Some of us aren't laughing at all. Me, for one. Jonah also looks miserable, and given the sex-joke fixation of the some of the people in the room, he probably knows he might as well be holding a dildo. Henry isn't amused either. He watches me with an unreadable expression.

I force myself to take a long deep breath as Ms. Meek gives Officer Jonah his instructions. I don't actually hear what she says or see Jonah move toward me. But I don't need to pay any attention to know what's going to happen next. I'm about to be arrested for a crime.

It won't be the first time it's happened. And that first time wasn't pretend.

TWO

Handcuffs are heavier than they look. They're cold too, though the last time I was placed in a pair of them, I was outside, so everything was cold. But this time is different than before. I'm inside a classroom that smells like pencil shavings and old carpet. Also, I'm not guilty of anything beyond a poor choice to volunteer.

Jonah has placed the cuffs on me so loosely that I could probably pull my wrists free, but I don't want to give anyone the satisfaction of seeing me react. He delivers some approximation of a police officer's arrest language, then stares at his feet, and now Ms. Meek is talking, and God, this is like one of those awful nightmares where everything is super slow motion.

"Clara?"

I jerk toward the sound of my teacher's voice. "Sorry."

"Can you tell me what's missing in the Miranda rights that Officer Jonah read?"

I look at my teacher. And then across the classroom where Lily's desk is still empty. What the hell, Lily? Get your ass in here and save me already. My gaze falls on Henry in the back, and we lock eyes for a fraction of a second. I don't want to get caught staring at him, especially while being humiliated in front of everyone, so I look at Ava instead.

She's a friend, if I get loose with the definition of the word, but she doesn't look inclined to help. Which is too bad, because she's probably one of the few people in this room who was following the Unit 6 slide deck. I was busy considering my exciting future as a promising chemistry major, not my past escapades as a small-time criminal.

Ms. Meek steps close to me. "Are you sure you don't remember?"

There is something behind her smile that isn't very nice. Something that tells me she isn't asking if I remember the lesson slides.

I smile back. There's something underneath my smile too, and it's a little like a middle finger. "I'm sure."

More laughter from the crowd. This time someone fake-coughs the word *convict* into the noise. Ms. Meek doesn't even pretend to give a crap about the jokes. She just keeps staring at me with that *I-remember-what-you-did* look all over her face.

"Well, since Clara doesn't seem to remember, how about the rest of you?"

"*Do you understand these rights as I have read them to you?*"

The voice rings through the classroom as sunny and sweet as the person standing in the now open doorway. I practically drop to the floor in relief. Lily Dalton. My best friend.

She's waiting with a sheepish grin and a hall pass. Neither are necessary because everyone knows Lily works in the office and everyone also knows she is the golden child of the school, that rare triple-crown student with the right grades, right attitude, and right social group. And she owns that social group. If I am Neptune to the popular crowd, then Lily is the sun.

"That's right," Ms. Meek softens as Lily walks to the front of the class to hand over her pass. The truth is, Lily wouldn't have to be right. People always believe her. Not just some people either. Everybody does. I used to hate her for it. She was a little rich girl, an only child like me, but the princess version with two adoring parents and an effortless warmth that people can't help but to love.

"Sorry I'm late," Lily says. The barest shade of pink colors her cheeks, though I know she's not embarrassed. Being Lily's best friend has taught me lots of things no one else knows, like the fact that she can muster a blush when she needs to, a skill which endears her to practically every school staff member. When Lily squeezes my shoulder in passing, Ms. Meek's obvious distaste for me thaws. It's like a Midas touch.

If Lily shows interest in or affection for anyone or anything, that person or thing is suddenly more appealing to all. Like the oatmeal cookies in the cafeteria that were almost discontinued, until Lily started claiming them as her favorite. Or like Ms. Bentley, a spindly, awkward science teacher universally loathed until Lily started the STEM Sisters club with her in junior high. Or like me. I was escorted out of the school in handcuffs in April of my freshman year, and my social universe imploded in an instant. But six months later, Lily was at my side, pushing all the doors back open for me.

"I'm certainly glad someone paid attention," Ms. Meek says.

Lily shakes her sleek, blond hair. "Actually I forgot to look this unit over. Thankfully Clara drilled me on the notes yesterday, so I can't really take the credit."

"Well, Clara is an expert in all things criminal." And Jackson Collins reenters the chat. I glance at him directly, now safer with Lily here. He's decent looking in a sharp-featured sort of way, with green eyes and tousled hair that is always styled to defy gravity.

Lily turns to him with a soft laugh. "You can't resist being small, can you?"

It's a barbed reply given Jackson's constant preoccupation with his slightly-less-than-average height. But even as someone else hisses at the burn, Lily offers Jackson a wink like she only means it in good fun. She doesn't. That's another Lily secret. Her best trick of all is the way she makes a person feel special, even if she thinks that person is a tool.

"I'm just pointing out the obvious," Jackson says, but he's looking scolded now.

Ms. Meek quietly unlocks my wrists, and Lily takes her seat. Our teacher walks us through the next part of the process, sharing that after an arrest, a prosecutor would decide whether or not to press charges, charges that will be heard by Judge Ava in Toontown Court.

Now that time is back to moving at a reasonable speed, it isn't long before the bell rings. The entire class surges into the hallway like a single organism, backpacks and hoodies jostling through the doorway. Lily brings me my bag and we walk together.

"Thanks for saving me," I say.

She doesn't look at me but laces her arm through mine, giving me a brief squeeze before releasing me. "That woman needs to unclench. Maybe I should give her a zap."

I laugh. Lily is currently obsessed with a stun gun she recently acquired. "Maybe that's why they don't allow stun guns at school."

She mock gasps. "It's not a gun! It's a personal protection device for my future college self, and it wouldn't really hurt her."

"Meek probably just needs to get laid." It's Jackson Towns (the taller Jackson with broader shoulders and a pretty-but-forgettable face). He nods to Lily and me in greeting as if he wasn't one of the instigators. "Ladies."

Henry Toussaint walks past quickly but, to my surprise, seems to change his mind, turning back. He is all cheekbones and smooth brown skin, and unlike Jackson, his face is seared into my memory like a tattoo. Being near him still makes me fluttery. God, do freshman crushes ever die?

"Okay there, Clara?"

He has the softest lilt to his voice, remnants of his Haitian accent coming through on the *there*. He moved to Ohio with his parents when he was eight, so it's almost imperceptible now. Almost.

I'm about to respond when Ava shoves in close to Lily, her hot pink backpack flung over one shoulder. She nods at Henry. "You better scurry unless you want an awkward convo with your ex."

We all glance up to see Mariana, small and striking with her cascading dark hair and petite features. Unlike the *awkward* Ava predicts, she and Henry share a decidedly undramatic wave before Henry moves on. Unsurprising since the breakup was nearly a year ago and ancient news at this point.

Mariana comes closer. Ava lives to publicly assert her friendship with Lily, but Mariana seems to be vying for a secret connection. She's forever pulling Lily aside or whispering about one thing or another. Lily routinely emerges from these liaisons rolling her eyes at me, but even if she's annoyed, she wouldn't show it to Mariana. Ava is insufferable, but Mariana is genuinely nice. Nervous but kind. She reaches for Lily's arm. "Hey, do you have a minute?"

"Hm, can it wait until later? I can't be late for French."

Mariana's face drops, but Ava absolutely beams. "We'll totally catch you later," she says as she tugs Lily away. It's an endless territory war, and Ava has won this round. Except for one fact that both of them conveniently like to avoid: *I'm* actually Lily's best friend.

Ava is chattering about the upcoming French test as she walks, but Lily clearly isn't listening. She's stopped to frown at the new poster on Mr. Droesch's door. *Congratulations, Daniel! International Exchange Program Selectee.*

"Ugh, who would want to live in Finland?" Ava asks.

Lily would. She doesn't say as much, but I remember the lengthy presentation she'd made to try to convince her parents to let her go if she were selected. I'm not sure on their reasons, but she was in a hell of a mood the week they refused to let her even apply.

I keep trying to remind her that she's about fifteen months away from college, where she'll have all the study abroad options you can shake a stick at, because Lily definitely has the grades to be choosy with her colleges.

"Shit, Lil, we need to book it," Ava says, and then she turns to Drishti. "Hey, you!"

"Shoot, Drishti," Lily says, touching her arm. "Do you have notes from history?"

"Yes," Drishti says, but she's clearly in a hurry. "Can I get them to you later?"

"Of course!" Lily waves. "You're a lifesaver!" Then she turns to me with a final wink. "Did you see that the chem test scores are up? There's a surprise in there for you."

"Really?"

"Come on, Lily," Ava says, pulling her by the arm.

Lily rolls her eyes and mouths: *My house after school?*

I nod in response.

Where else would I go? Home to watch my mom pull off her clinic scrubs only to squeeze herself into a ridiculous bow tie and miniskirt for another night slinging whiskey sours and Long Island iced teas? I respect the hell out of the way Mom works two jobs to cobble rent together without a *meep* of complaint, but it's hard to witness, especially since I can't do anything to make things easier for her.

The clock in the hallway informs me I've got less than two minutes to get to my last class. It might be enough time to check my chem test, and I'm sure as hell going to try. I pull up the classroom on my phone while I navigate down the hall and into the long, narrow stretch of classrooms that's nearly impossible to navigate—the Clogged Drain.

I move past a prom poster—gross—and watch my screen

slowly refresh. Finally, it's done. I spot the graded symbol on the right side of Test three and I freeze right there in the hallway.

Test one: 95%

Test two: 98%

Test three: 91%

Okay, not my best, but I was terrified of this test, convinced I'd fail. A 91 percent is so far beyond what I expected.

I check my class ranking at the bottom, stunned to find that I wasn't the only one who struggled with the test, because I am still in the number two position! Now, my shoulders slump in relief. I knew I wouldn't overtake Hiba Chaudhry, of course, but I did worry that Vera Johnson or Henry Toussaint (who've been trading three and four all year) might pull into the lead and knock me down a notch. Hell, I had so much trouble with this unit that I thought Lily (landing at number five) might have pulled up a few spots.

But number two is still mine. I grin to myself. Chemistry is still my ticket, and I intend to ride it all the way to a pharmacy degree and the chance to make sure my mother never works another night shift again. I hike my backpack higher and decide my day is taking a good turn. I pull up the email from John Carroll, figuring I can read a little more about the interview before I get to Mr. Cooper's room. He's an old-school teacher and a stickler about having phones out, so this is my last chance. The trick will be surviving the Clogged Drain while reading.

I turn the corner and start maneuvering through the crowd. Of course my APUSH class is smack-dab in the middle of this mess, so there isn't an alternative.

I shoulder my way forward, steering around a kissing couple and Gretchen, who tousles her jet-black bob and gives me a little nod. I'm jostled this way and that, but in my mind I'm practically floating my way toward Mr. Cooper's door in a haze of high-test-score-plus-chemistry-camp-interview glory.

Oh my God, I forgot to tell Lily. Even the elbows jamming into my sides don't stop me from tapping out a quick message.

> Can't believe I didn't tell you. I made it into the finalist round at JC. I get an interview!

Someone lunges in front of me. Nate. It's always strange to see him, so familiar with his cowlick and broad shoulders. We've been apart longer than Henry and Mariana, and there isn't drama, but there is plenty of awkward. He offers me a small salute, and I give him a tight smile as I lurch left, bumping into two girls I couldn't name if you paid me. They shove back into me so hard that I wobble to the right, off-balance. My backpack smacks into something, but I manage to stay on my feet, finding my center of gravity.

And then someone screams. It's shrill and shocking and *close*, the kind of sound that conjures images of car accidents or horror movies. I spin around, my skin prickled up in goose bumps at the sudden silence in the hall. Everyone is frozen, but I don't see anything. Gretchen catches my eyes, some long-gone instinct from when we were friends I guess, and for a split second, she looks every bit as confused as I feel. But then her gaze shifts to my right and her face darkens.

I follow her line of sight past the couple with their kiss-swollen lips, past Jackson Collins, who already has a phone out recording, past Nate, who looks truly shocked. Past more faces, all of them pointed at something beside me. Something on the ground.

The first thing I see is blood. And then I see Vera. She's holding her nose, but blood is dripping through her fingers, spotting the hallway floor with crimson drops.

Vera's eyes are welled with tears. She lets out a strangled sob, and that sound or maybe the blood—it drags me back to that terrible night two years ago. The smell of chlorine. The twinkle of fairy lights. The sound of Cadence screaming.

Vera pulls one bloody hand away from her face and points in my direction. It plucks me right out of the memory, dropping me into the present.

"Oh no, I'm so sorry," I say, wincing. My backpack must have walloped her when I got knocked off-kilter. I reach for Vera, but she recoils.

"What is wrong with you?" Vera's voice is nearly a shriek.

"Vera, I didn't—"

"Why did you knock me down?" Her scream cuts me off.

I open my mouth to argue, but the streams of blood are trailing down her lips and chin. I want to tell her it was an accident, but isn't that obvious? Can't everyone see that?

Vera scuttles away and I realize no one cares if this was an accident. Everyone in this hall is happy to put the blame on *me.*

THREE

Vera sits in the nurse's office with an ice pack to her face. I can see her from where I'm waiting outside Principal Chang's door, so I try to plead my case.

"Vera, I swear I didn't shove you," I say.

"I saw your face, Clara. I looked right at you, and then you whirled around with that giant backpack."

"I know my backpack hit you. I'm saying it wasn't intentional."

"I saw your face," she repeats, enunciating each word. Then she drops her eyes and her voice. "And it's not like you don't have a history with things like this."

I recoil from her words and slouch against the back of the chair. So she doesn't believe it's an accident because of what happened two years ago? Wonderful.

I glare at Ms. Chang's door feeling extra sorry for myself. I tell myself it isn't fair. That I've changed. I even consider the possibility that Vera might believe me if I wasn't wearing thrift store jeans and Lily's hand-me-down sweater. What I try to *not* think about is why Vera isn't being completely ridiculous to suspect me.

After all, I swore up and down the last time was an accident too. It *was* an accident. But I was still 100 percent to blame.

There is a soft conversation inside the nurse's office, and then someone closes the door. I'm alone for a few minutes until Officer Grimes strolls in. He's a bald guy with broad shoulders and dimples. He seems far too friendly for a police officer, even one who spends his hours inside a typical high school.

Grimes looks over at me with a frown. "What are you doing in here, Toosey?"

I sigh. "I got bumped into Vera in the hallway, but she thinks I did it on purpose."

"In the Clogged Drain?"

I nod.

"That whole hallway is a disaster waiting to happen."

Officer Grimes is a good dude. He's one of the few people who remembers (and still uses) my junior high nickname. If his friendliness is any indication, he may also be the only adult in this school who doesn't still think of me as a criminal.

Ms. Chang's door swings open, and she appears, looking calm and professional.

"Ms. Cutler?"

I stand up, and Ms. Chang beckons me into her office. She is a slim-shouldered woman who favors old-lady hair buns but twentysomething shoes. Today she's sporting bright purple heels with her gray pantsuit.

Before I'm even fully seated, the words start tumbling out of me.

"Ms. Chang, I swear I did not intentionally shove Vera down. It was super crowded in the hallway, and if we can just talk to her—

"Vera is getting picked up for the day."

"I get it. I'd go home too if I got a bloody nose. I feel awful, but someone shoved into me and apparently my backpack slammed into her face."

Ms. Chang watches me with an even expression. "According to Vera, she made eye contact with you before you collided with her. She felt it was intentional."

"Well, it wasn't. And she definitely didn't make eye contact if she looked at me."

"You're sure about that?"

"I was nose-deep in my phone. Besides, what possible reason would I have to hurt Vera?"

Ms. Chang watches me closely. "You are both in AP Chemistry, correct?"

There's something about the way she asks that makes me uneasy. She already knows what classes I'm in, I'm sure of that.

But why would it matter? Vera and I have never even disagreed in a class discussion that I remember.

"You recently took a big test in that class, didn't you?" Ms. Chang asks.

"Yes, but I did well. There wasn't anything to be upset about."

"Not even that Vera beat you despite how well you did? Not even that she moved into the number-one spot in the ranking? I know your performance in that class is very important to you."

I blink, trying to put it together. I didn't even realize Vera moved into number one. Hiba must have bombed the test. Which is bizarre for Hiba but not impossible. And Vera could have aced it. That's way less impossible. I know we're separated by a pretty thin margin, so it wouldn't take much to shift things around. But that's not the point. The point is, I didn't know the rankings changed. I only looked at myself.

But I could have checked.

The top-five rankings are right there on the class page, a not-so-friendly competition Mr. Philpot thinks is fun, but usually just induces anxiety for everyone involved. And yeah, I like being in number two, but I'm not about to make someone bleed for taking number one.

"I didn't even know. I only checked mine," I say, and my voice sounds flat because it doesn't matter what I say, only how it looks. After all, I am the girl who pushes people—or so the rumors say.

Ms. Chang frowns like she doesn't quite believe me. It's a look

I'm familiar with. Once the police haul you out of a classroom to handcuff you, people question every word that comes out of your mouth. To be fair, they weren't too sure about me before all that happened. I'm one of the Apartment Kids, the lesser third of Tuskegee High School students, the ones who don't live in houses with wraparound porches and West Elm furniture.

A soft knock on the door interrupts us.

"One moment," Ms. Chang says, her eyes never leaving mine. "Clara, you've turned things around remarkably in this last year and a half. You were a Chemagination finalist and won honorable mention in our STEM showcase."

I lean forward, because if she remembers that, then there's a chance she might see more than I'm giving her credit for. "I'm really committed to chemistry. I'm looking into pharmacy degree programs, and there's a summer program at John Carroll."

"You applied?" Her arched brows indicate surprise. I get it; the programs run several thousand dollars, and I'm pretty sure the address on my school file makes it clear we don't have several thousands of dollars lying around.

"I'm a finalist for the full scholarships, so I'll be interviewing for a spot. It's a good opportunity for my college applications, right?"

"It is. It's also important for your resume that your record here at Tuskegee High remains unblemished for the duration of your tenure."

Especially since I blemished the hell out of it at the end of my freshman year. That's what she doesn't say.

"I'd like to see you in college," she says with a little sigh, as if she doesn't quite expect it. Then she stands, apparently done with her wistful thoughts of my future. I stand too, a little uncertain as to what to do. Should I stay? Leave? Start pleading with her for mercy?

"So what happens now?" I venture.

"There will be a formal incident report," she says. "There won't be discipline, because we have reports from two opposing viewpoints, and without any staff witnesses, it's hard to be certain of what happened."

"So I can go?"

She's already looking past me. I escape out into the cool, bright administration office without another word.

Officer Grimes is eating a cookie and watching the fish tank when I emerge. He raises his brows at me.

"Detention?"

"A warning, I think." I hesitate, shaking my head. "Actually, I'm not sure what that was."

Grimes leans back in his chair, watching me with a blank expression. He's never stressed. "You don't look too happy about it."

"Vera thinks I intentionally shoved her because she did better on a test than me. But I didn't. No way would I have done that." I smirk. "But my reputation apparently precedes me."

He nods. "Some people tend to get the benefit of the doubt. And some don't."

He isn't quite telling me he believes me, but it's close, and it helps.

I text Lily that I'm on my way down. She doesn't reply, but she's been in a super non-texting phase these last couple of weeks. Some sort of phone detox book she's been reading.

I'm just leaving the office when I almost run into someone. I stop short, sucking in a tight breath. Perfect, pricky Paxton. Once upon a time, Paxton and I were friends. In elementary school we lived a few duplexes apart and loved to make mazes for the pill bugs in our front yards. Then Paxton's father hit some sort of investment jackpot, and they traded in their rusted Chevy for matching Volvos and their duplex for a four-bedroom house on a cul-de-sac in Lily's neighborhood.

Now, Paxton is the class president and maybe the only student the teachers love even more than Lily. In junior high, he was in Lily's crowd. He used to throw these huge pool parties, but at some point after freshman year, the parties stopped. It wasn't too long before he quit showing up at the cool kid table in the cafeteria. I don't know the details, but I know he keeps his distance.

Except from me, of course. He may ignore the others, but he makes no bones about his dislike for me.

"Paxton." His name comes out of me like a four-letter word.

He, of course, doesn't say my name. He looks at me like he sometimes lies awake at night dreaming of lighting me on fire. Hell, maybe he does, though God knows why. It's hard to believe this preppy little shit with his sideswept blond hair once kneeled in a dirty yard setting up mazes for bugs with me, but it's true.

"I heard about what happened with Vera," Paxton says with a sniff.

"Oh, because you're worried about her? Or is it just a great opportunity to kiss some random staff member's ass?" I ask, my voice chipper.

Paxton narrows his eyes. "You sure have a lot of attitude for someone leaving the principal's office for *another* assault on a student."

My face feels hot. I step left, trying to move around him, but he's standing directly in my path. "Do you mind?"

"Do I mind being in the same room as you?" he asks. "Yeah. Every time it happens."

I have nothing else to say to this tool. Instead of answering, I brush past him, heading for the stairwell. He pulls back like I've punched him.

"Now you're happy to get out of my way?" I ask.

He arches a brow, his expression mean. "No, I just don't trust you around stairs."

I don't say another word as I thunder down the steps. Maybe

he's right not to trust me. There's not much on this planet I'd love to see more than Paxton Bryce taking a fall.

FOUR

I'm vibrating with rage when I push out of the exit doors. It's gotten hotter than I expected since this morning. That's April in Ohio for you. I scan the back section of the lot where Lily always parks her car. But she's not there. And it's looking really gray. As if on cue, a fat drop of rain splatters my arm.

Awesome.

Just then, I spot her car in the parking lot near the art wing doors. Weird. But it's definitely her red Honda Civic with the faded *Geldis Klein Tennis Center* sticker in the rear window.

The back door is open, and Lily is putting something inside, taking her sweet time about it despite the patter of a few more drops. Is she not noticing the rain? Wait, has she even read her texts? Does she know my ass has been stuck in Ms. Chang's office? She closes the back and opens the driver's door.

"Lily!" I call out.

She freezes but doesn't respond. Her shoulders are hunched, and she keeps her back to me. Really? I do not have it in me to walk the mile and a half to my house today, especially since it's about to start pouring.

She opens the driver's door wider and moves like she's getting in. Seriously? She obviously heard me.

"Lily!" I shout her name louder this time, and she freezes again, turning extra, extra slowly.

Her smile looks pinched and uncertain. Is every single thing about this stupid day determined to be bizarre? I keep walking and watch Lily's face. She looks like she's seen a ghost, jaw clenched and eyes wide. I think of taking photos at the haunted forest event every October, the we're-so-scared faces we pull to make it seem like a better time than it ever is. What is up with her? Did something happen?

I close the distance to her. "Lil, you okay?"

"Hey, Clara, what's up?"

"What's up? I just spent the last thirty minutes getting grilled in Ms. Chang's office for knocking Vera down in the Clogged Drain. And then I had a little do-si-do with Paxton the Prick Bryce."

Her face registers shock. "You knocked down Vera Johnson?"

"Obviously not on purpose, but she sure the hell thought so. And Mr. Droesch was all too happy to agree. He hauled me to the office *so* fast."

"What an asshole," she says. The words and tone are right, but her face is off. Her eyes are darting around. Her posture is tense. Lily detests Mr. Droesch and is always ready for a bitch session, but not today.

"Hey, seriously. You okay?" I ask.

"Just another shitty day in Tuskegee High," she says.

"You too?"

She shakes her head like she's not going to talk about it, but something is really eating at her.

"Did you hear back on one of your early admission apps?"

She flinches. Lily is a master of hiding her emotions, but I know that look—that little startle where her brows draw in and her mouth thins.

"Who said no?" I ask softly.

She glares at me for a long moment, like she's not going to respond. Or maybe like she's angry that I figured out what was wrong.

"Clemson. But it's whatever."

Except it's *not* whatever. Practically everyone is desperate to get away from Southwest Ohio, but it's different with Lily. She's obsessed with going to an out-of-state college. It's the only issue I've ever seen cause a real argument with her parents. She's got everything she needs, from the GPA to the extracurriculars, but her parents have zero interest in sending their only child away.

"I'm sorry," I say. "But it's only one application. I'm sure you're going to hear from others."

"I said *It's whatever*," Lily snaps.

I go quiet. She's more upset than I thought. She's still stiff, and she isn't moving out of the way. More rain is spatting down on us.

She lets out a breath that sounds forced, and when she talks again, her voice is closer to normal. "Sorry. I'm in a mood. People here have been assholes all day too."

"Do tell," I say, trying to crack a conspiratorial grin.

"Want to guess?" she asks.

"First let's go home," I say. I head around the front of the Civic to the passenger door and fling my backpack inside, tossing my denim jacket in after. I slide into the seat and fasten my belt, but Lily is *still* standing in that open doorway. She's looking left and right like she's waiting for someone. Or maybe just distracted.

But it's odd. Something's definitely up with her. Is it more than the thing with Clemson? Maybe her parents found out about these applications. I think she hoped to produce a full-ride scholarship that would be hard to argue with, but I never felt too sure that would work.

When she finally gets in the car, I slouch into the seat while she buckles her seat belt and puts the car in reverse. She slowly, slowly begins to back out and I can't help but to turn and stare. Has she been possessed by aliens? Because the Lily I know and love backs out of parking spaces like she's trying to break land-speed records while doing it.

Finally, she rolls forward, and she does that slower than normal too. She comes to a full and complete stop at the school entrance and, as God is my witness, puts on her turn signal before easing into a right-hand turn.

I can't keep my mouth shut another second, "Are you literally reliving your driving test?"

She zips up to normal speed at the end of the school property, apparently snapping out of whatever weird thing possessed her. "Sorry. Just distracted."

She comes to an abrupt—and far more typical—stop at the next light and then twists around to the back seat, grabbing a red folder. "Shit, my backpack is in the trunk. Will you put this in yours so I don't forget it tomorrow."

"Is this your English paper research?" I ask, tucking the red folder into my bag.

"Yeah, but before you even think about asking, put it away, and let's pretend it doesn't exist for a minute. I cannot discuss it right now. I've done nothing but search for source material all week, and I'm so sick of Droesch and his shit."

"To be fair, it's only Tuesday," I say.

"True," Lily says. "But don't you get sick of this place?"

"Sure."

The light turns green, and she stomps on the accelerator. She instantly changes lanes and cranks up the radio, and it's almost like any other day.

At the next light, she turns to look at me. I can't read her expression, but I can feel the intensity rolling off her. Maybe it's Clemson, or maybe it's the English thing, or maybe it's something totally different. Whatever it is, it's clear something is still up with her.

"What's going on with you?" I ask, no more humor this time, just a straight question.

"I don't know. I guess they're getting to me."

"Who, your parents?"

She tenses, but shakes her head. "No. It's school. Just so many assholes."

I nod. "It is an epidemic."

"They get away with everything."

I chuckle and resist the urge to remind her that she gets away with everything too. Something tells me she wouldn't take that joke well. Not today.

"What's on your mind?" I ask.

"I just..." She looks up, eyes bright. "Do you ever think of ways to take them down?"

I pause, surprised. I don't know what to say, but she doesn't wait long before answering her own question. "I think about it. I mean not everyone, but the real assholes. Like Mr. Droesch and Nate Turner and—"

"Paxton the Prick?"

Lily smirks and the light turns green. She hits the gas. "Yeah, what did he do this time?"

"He was heading into the office when I was leaving, and I swear to God, it was like he was waiting for me." I tell her the rest—his snotty little attitude and comments about the stairs. "The dude despises me."

"He is an asshole and a poser," Lily says mildly.

"I will never understand why teachers don't see his shitty attitude. He's like Teflon. Nothing sticks." I shake my head.

Lily's smile turns wicked as she pulls to another red light. "That's exactly what I mean. Paxton is the poster child for why murder is occasionally totally justified."

I laugh, relieved that she seems to be blowing off steam rather than having a full-fledged meltdown. "No doubt."

The light turns green, and Lily takes off with a cat-that-ate-the-canary grin. It's nice to see her ornery again—like whatever weird fog was settled over her earlier is finally lifted.

"There are so many dicks here that deserve it. If some real-life version of the Purge ever happens, I have a whole plan cooked up." She laughs as she says it, sweeping her arm wide like she's showing me just how far-reaching that plan would be.

I snort. "I'd be happy to just take down Paxton. Okay, maybe I'd steal a ticket to Aruba or something."

"The trouble is, murderers are always getting caught," she says, ignoring my Aruba comment. "It's like they've never watched TV. I would be smarter."

"Oh yeah?" I ask. I'm only half listening, because the rain is growing a little steadier, and I really need to figure out if the shit weather is sticking around. Lily's doing tennis before and after school the rest of this week, so I'll be doing a lot of walking. When I tune back in, Lily is still rambling about her grand plan, big dramatic hand gestures and all.

"I mean, don't you think you'd be able to commit a perfect murder if you needed to?"

I look up from my phone and Lily is watching me with that wicked gleam in her eye. She's grinning and relaxed and clearly lost in some rabbit hole of dark humor.

"Maybe I should be giving this some serious thought," I say, hamming it up.

Lily waggles her brows, and I give in with a laugh. For the rest of the drive, we zip down the road with the radio blaring and us both arguing all the best ways to get away with murder.

FIVE

While Lily waxes on about all the people worthy of being offed, I point out the dull stuff like the necessity of wearing gloves and a hairnet. Then I give my detailed and geeky explanation of the role of chemistry in forensics. Lily rolls her eyes as she drives us along Spring Street with its lines of strip malls and chain restaurants. This ribbon of pavement is the dividing line between the haves and have-nots in Pikeville. It strikes me how normal everything looks, how this backdrop is a mundane mismatch to Lily's monologue.

"Okay, you're boring. I'd go full James Bond," she says. "With a heavy dose of John Wick maybe. I would end them all."

"Well, you would look great in a snappy gray suit."

"No, I'm serious. And you said yourself that taking out cars in a parking lot would be easy to get away with because people are distracted in parking lots and no one would even notice us, making it a super easy location for planting explosives."

I laugh. "Oh my God, are you talking about the weekend when we binged all those old Jason Bourne movies last summer?"

"Yeah, maybe. And I think you're right." She nods decisively. "That's how I'd do it."

"Okay, Jason Statham, tell me all your nefarious parking lot plans."

"Like cut the brake lines, or overfill the tires so they'd all blow. It would work."

I shake my head. "It wouldn't work. Don't you remember our hour-long conversation after *Retribution*?"

"Okay, fine, then tell me how you'd do it."

"I wouldn't do it," I say. "I'm not that damn bothered by anyone."

"Oh, come on. Not even Paxton?"

"Paxton is annoying as shit but not worth all that." I say. What I don't say is that Paxton is the one who has a problem with me. I don't have beef with him, other than his attitude toward me. Attitude that's probably somehow related to the same incident with Cadence. One awful hour of my life, yet I'm pretty sure I'll be uncovering the problems that hour caused forever.

You're not allowed to feel sorry for yourself.

The reminder comes swiftly. Cadence is the only one who gets to bitch about what went down because it ruined her life too. Difference is, it was my stupid decision that did the ruining. Not hers.

I turn my focus back to Lily's ridiculous exercise. "I wouldn't pop tires, that's for sure. That's barely more than an inconvenience," I say.

"It's all hypothetical," Lily says, turning onto a wide residential street. We pass between two brick walls, each bearing an ornate glass lamp and dark metal letters that spell out *Fox Chase*. Thick-limbed trees rise up on either side of the road, standing sentry in front of houses. Perfect houses, my mom always says. Not too big and not too small.

"Well, you know what I'm going to say. My hypothetical solution is always *just blow it up*!" I wave vaguely, checking my schedule at work next weekend on my phone. It's incredibly slow for May. Not one shift this weekend, and funds are running low. "You don't have to be anywhere near an explosion. You can set it up and go out to lunch. Or catch a plane to another country. Explosions are the way to go."

Lily chuckles. "Funny, I'm not sure your Chemagination project would have won if you'd included that slogan in your report."

"That would never have been my slogan. My project was a cautionary tale for homeowners everywhere."

The project in question, "Hidden Explosives: Household Items and Why They Combust," won me national attention in high school chemistry. It was part science fair, part exposé on the dangers of things like gas grills, aerosol products, and even plain old flour. It was my golden ticket to a new future. And it all happened because of Lily.

That's the part no one knows. I would have never risked entering if Lily hadn't called me. She's the reason it happened. She is the only reason I'm not still Back-of-the-Class Clara with a bad reputation and zero chance at a real future.

"You are such an adorable nerd," Lily says.

"An adorable nerd with an interview for that summer program."

"Oh, that's right! I saw that text, but I'm not surprised!" Lily glances at me with a grin. "Hey, maybe you should ask them vaguely accusatory questions about their storage policies for cleaners and flour?"

"Mock if you must, but I still say there should be better education or controls."

"So in your big spy-thriller plan, you'd blow things up by what, attempting to light gas grills with the lid closed?"

"That's clearly not practical."

"Isn't that the whole basis of your big award-winning project?"

"One of the pieces of my project outlined all the reasons combustion is likely in that situation, but it isn't something you could weaponize."

"No? What could you do, then?"

I shrug. "For a car? You can get your hands on all kinds of things that would work to at least put a car out of commission, maybe worse. You don't need C-4 or whatever."

"But you could blow up a car, right?" she asks, sounding worried.

I laugh. "In the highly unlikely event we would need this skill, yes, Lily, I absolutely know how to blow up a car. You probably do too if you think about it long enough."

"Not me. You're the chemistry whiz."

"Oh, please. You're like six points behind me. You're great at chemistry. You just don't love it the way I do."

Lily turns into her driveway, and I glance up at her fairy-tale house with its wraparound porch and French doors. I'll never get used to the idea of being friends with someone who lives here. We pull into the garage and Lily parks on the left. We make our way around her Mom's Jaguar to the garage door. Inside the mudroom, Lily throws her sweatshirt on the floor, and I set my backpack carefully on the bench.

"Lily?" Lily's mom's voice floats into the mudroom from somewhere in the house.

"Hey, Mom. Clara's here too."

"Hi, you two!"

Random rustling. A pan on a stovetop. While Lily and I toe off our sneakers, I can already picture Mrs. Dalton—who insists

I call her Jenna—in the enormous kitchen with gleaming white marble counters and appliances hidden by panels that match the cabinets.

I take a vanilla-scented breath and follow Lily through the cavernous living room to the kitchen. Jenna is standing much like I imagined her, in a pair of dove-gray yoga pants and a peach-colored T-shirt that looks both unremarkable and expensive. It's like looking at Lily in twenty-five years—the same pale hair and warm brown eyes. The same slightly upturned nose and dimpled chin.

"How was your day, girls?"

"Okay," I say, forcing brightness.

"Bleh, it was shit," Lily says.

"Well if you need a pick-me-up, you can help me decide on a shortbread recipe. I've tried three, and I need taste testers."

"Oh, I'm not sure," I say gently. For reasons that have never been clear to me, Lily can barely stand her mother. Every day we exchange about twenty seconds of pleasantries—and it's a stretch of the word on most days—before tucking into her room with the door shut and the music on.

Normally, I'm the one dragging my feet, feeling bad to leave someone who's always been so kind to me. But today, Lily isn't bolting. She's thumbing through a pile of mail on the counter and glancing at the baking sheets lined up on the impossibly large stove.

"Sounds delicious," Lily says.

Her tone does not match her words, and her expression matches them even less. I'm not sure if I need to call an exorcist or an alien expert, but the person wearing my best friend's skin today is not Lily Dalton. Still, when she slides onto a stool, I can't see any way around joining her. And I love shortbread, so whatever.

Jenna hides her surprise with a big smile. "Okay, I'll set it all up. I'll get you some iced tea too. Tell me about your day."

My heart squeezes at Mrs. Dalton's eagerness. I glance left at Lily, hoping she won't change her mind, but she seems distracted enough to stay put, her phone already out on her lap.

"Did you learn anything interesting?" Mrs. Dalton asks.

"Let me think on that," I say, because sharing that I learned Vera thinks I'm out to attack her doesn't feel like the thing she's after.

"Why don't you tell us about the recipes first?" Lily says, looking up from her phone to roll her eyes at me like her mom is oh-so-boring. Then she starts tapping out a message.

My phone instantly vibrates with an incoming text.

Lily: Back to the explosions thing.

Me: Yes?

Lily: You said that you know how to blow up a car.

Jenna starts a meandering play-by-play of her adventures du jour, and Lily and I make all the right noises. We even dutifully nibble shortbread—all delicious—from each of the small delicate plates she puts in front of us. But all the while, we are texting back and forth under the counter. A continuation of our conversation from the car.

Me: Sure.

Lily: How serious would it be?

Me: Depends. Some explosives would be small or start a fire. Others would blow the whole thing to pieces. Explosives = options.

Lily: People could get seriously hurt...

Me: Hell yeah they could. Maybe even killed.

Lily: With firecrackers or something?

Me: Lots of things would do it. Things almost everyone can buy.

Lily: That's scary.

Me: Chemistry is scary as hell. That's one of the reasons I love it.

Yeah, cool story, but it's not really true. What's true is that my grandmother died of Alzheimer's. We were close. My grandpap died when I was five, and my dad was never around. So it was just Mom, Grams, and me. Thick as thieves, Grams always said. She said a lot of funny things. She knew French and some Russian, and she read constantly.

And then, when I turned fourteen, she called my mom from a few blocks away, frightened because she didn't know where she was or how to get home. Six months later, she was a shell of her former self, screaming at my mother to get out of her house. Asking who I was and if I'd ever met her granddaughter, Clara.

It went too fast for most medicines to help. But they *could* help. The right chemistry can cure all kinds of diseases, and that's what I want—to research Alzheimer's medications until I can find a cure.

Beside me, Lily pockets her phone looking satisfied. She takes a bite of shortbread sample three, and I can tell she's thinking. Sometimes it feels like I can hear Lily's brain spinning up like a turbine, and that's the noise I'm imagining as she slowly rises to her feet.

"Number two is best," she says. "Thanks, Mom. we've got to study for Statistics."

I stand up too, finishing my last bite. "Thank you so much. I think they're all great, but number two is my favorite also."

"Thanks, Clara. Good luck with Statistics."

I smile and nod and follow Lily out. I may not have much criminal left in me, but I still have plenty of liar. Neither one of us is taking Statistics. I don't know why Lily would choose this moment to lie, but it's clear it doesn't matter. Just like everyone else I know, Jenna believes every word Lily says.

SIX

In her bedroom, Lily closes the door behind me. She doesn't flop on the bed like normal, and she doesn't turn on any music. But she does turn the fan on high, a tactic to make sure her mom can't hear what happens next.

And what is going to happen next? My heart stutters as I watch her lean back against the wall. This stillness is unusual. She's always a touch off at home, but once this door is shut, Lily usually snaps back on like a switch. She'll chat about the daily drama or her plans for the night. Or she'll conjure up some new version of our ever-morphing plans for an after-graduation trip.

But this afternoon she is quiet and watchful. It makes me rethink our funny banter in the car and the texts that followed. Was that more than ordinary venting? What am I missing here?

"What's going on, Lily?"

"Nothing."

"It doesn't seem like nothing."

"Well, it is," she says, a thin layer of attitude frosting her words.

She glances at her desk. Quickly, but long enough that it draws my gaze too. Nothing looks amiss. The same books are on the shelf with a box of tampons strategically placed in the middle. It's not actually tampons though—that's where she hides her stun gun. Next to the books is a vase of dried flowers from her homecoming corsage. Six tennis trophies line the shelf above that. And the desk below is the same too—her laptop right where she always leaves it, on the left, leaving space for my laptop on the right. But I don't get out my laptop.

"Did someone do something to you today?" I ask.

"Why do you ask?"

"Oh, I don't know. You're just randomly talking about how to get away with killing people." I laugh, and I mean to sound nonchalant, but I don't. I sound nervous, because I am. "It's been weird, Lily. You even voluntarily hung out with your mom. Which is fine; she's totally nice."

"My mother's an idiot," Lily says, her face hard.

I frown. I hate it when she's tough on her mom, and she's *always* tough on her mom. I'm ready to snap at her a little for it, but then she touches the edge of the world-flags garland around her desk, and I soften. I love Lily's travel obsession. While half of the girls in our friend group wax on about Hilton Head Island or Palm Beach, Lily dreams of going to Thailand. Denmark. New Zealand.

"Can you tell me what happened?" I ask gently.

"Do you realize that we've been friends for seventeen months now?" she asks, totally ignoring my question.

"I guess so."

I don't know why it matters. It's not an answer to my question, and it's a strange thing to say. But what *isn't* strange with her today?

"Seventeen months is a long damn time," she says softly. She looks weary. "Just don't forget that."

"Okay, I won't," I say with another awkward laugh. Chills roll up my back. She's saying it like there won't be another seventeen months. She's looking at her flags like she's going to slip out in the night and disappear on a transatlantic flight. And I have no idea why.

"Will you please just talk to me?" I ask.

She bites her lip and looks at the fan as it oscillates, back and forth. Back and forth.

"Did something happen in French? Or maybe with...?" I try to think of someone she's been dating recently, but Lily doesn't date seriously. She studies, plays loads of tennis with her dad, and writes and rewrites her college essay. "I know the Clemson thing sucks, but—"

"I don't want to talk about Clemson."

I swallow hard. There is a faraway look in her eyes that scares me. "Are you sure?"

"What is there to talk about, Clara? Haven't we said everything there is to say?"

The front door slams open in the distance. Lily jumps, her hands rolling into fists.

"Lily Bear, Lily Bear! We ready for the net?"

She flinches at the boom of her dad's voice. She's really a mess today. I glance at the clock, which reads only 4:50 p.m. A little early for tennis practice, but I know he's obsessed and likes to get there early. Hell, maybe it'll help knock some of this weirdness out of her. Or maybe she'll talk to him.

She gives me a look as her dad's footsteps thunder closer. He tosses the door open.

"Hello there, ladies!" Jim Dalton is a strapping guy—one of those dads who used to be an athlete and never quite lost the wide shoulders and hand-eye coordination.

"Sorry to interrupt, but I was hoping to grab some pizza on the way there. What do you say, LB?"

Her father gives her a warm sideways hug, but Lily offers nothing more than an indifferent shrug as she grabs her coat. In her strange silence, I ask Jim about his day and he high-fives me about the results of my Chem test.

Lily says nothing. She doesn't even look at us as she pushes her feet into her court sneakers. She grabs a hoodie out of the closet and her tennis bag off the dresser, and then she gives me a long searching look that makes as little sense as everything else.

"We'll drop you home on our way, Clara," Jim says, clamping a heavy hand down on my shoulder. He's already in shorts and a T-shirt, clearly eager to go. But he doesn't rush Lily or gripe. If I made my mom wait like this, I'd hear about it for a week, but she takes her sweet time with every step, collecting her racket and then a water bottle from the wicker table beside her bed.

She moves past me, and my eyes catch something under her nightstand. A huge thick textbook I don't recognize and can't quite read from here. God knows the girl is a high achiever, but now she's reading textbooks for fun?

Jim whistles his way down the hall, and we follow him into the garage. I slide into the back seat, and he tries making small talk with Lily while he pulls out. She is utterly silent, so I feel forced to offer a few feeble chuckles in response to his terrible puns.

When her silence continues, he tugs at her hair playfully. Lily jerks away with irritation in her eyes. So apparently, she's being pissy with everyone today. We weave out of the wide tree-lined streets, down the main drag again. We turn on a side street that winds past small cookie-cutter ranches, and then even smaller duplexes. Mine is no different than the others unless you count the metal frog on our front stoop or the container of treats by the mailbox we leave for other dogs who come to visit.

"Hey, text me later," I say.

She nods but doesn't meet my eyes, and a dreadful feeling pulls low in my middle. Wrong. All of this is wrong.

"Have a great night!" Jim's voice booms out, and I lift my hand in a wave.

Then I look at Lily one more time. "I'll see you later."

She doesn't even look at me. I walk to my door, doing mental gymnastics in hopes of figuring this out. Something is happening with Lily, and whatever it is, she can't or won't talk about it. And she tells me about everything, from bad periods to the misery of class with Mr. Droesch to her secret dreams to escape her parents' wishes and go to school in California or Washington.

So what wouldn't she talk to me about? What would be too horrible to share? An awful possibility lingers in my mind like a shadow. She wouldn't hurt herself, would she?

I think of those suicides sometimes featured on news segments, where no one saw it coming. Could I miss something like that in Lily? I guess anyone could. But Lily doesn't seem sad; she seems angry.

I head up the sidewalk and into my house. Inside, George lets out a low woof and drags all 120 pounds of himself to his feet. He eyes me anxiously and I fumble the back door open with shaky hands. I watch him lumber into the yard to pee. It is a routine we follow every night, but tonight it feels different. It feels like something terrible is coming.

SEVEN

My mind runs in circles all night. At nine, I make a decision to write it all off as a bad day. Everyone is entitled to being completely weird once in a while, especially Lily. She was here for me when this entire high school avoided me. If she's off-kilter for a day, that's fine. I can let this go.

It feels like the most sensible decision, so I do it. I wash my face and check to make sure I have clean socks. Mom gets home from work and we eat slices of cold pizza at the kitchen counter. She tries (God, she really does) to make small talk but her eyes are bleary, and her whole face droops like a wilting plant. I offer to clean up the dishes and Mom kisses the top of my hair before stumbling off to bed.

I'm finishing my Precalc homework when I reconsider. If something did happen to Lily, should I just give up on trying to talk to her? She could need help, but her parents are both so relentlessly positive, I don't know that she'd talk to them about something that has her in a dark place. But she might talk to me.

Of course she never texted after tennis, which... I check my phone to confirm that she should have been home for a while. Now that I'm looking, I notice that before our back-and-forth in the kitchen this afternoon, her last text was four days ago. And the one before that was a week ago. Her few messages are short and unenthused.

I thought it was a no-phone phase, but now I'm not so sure. I check my call logs and realize she hasn't called me either. I've called her. My stomach sinks. Oh my God. Have I been ignoring signs that something's really, truly wrong?

I text her immediately.

10:04 P.M.

Me: Hey, are you back from tennis yet?

I know she's back. The center closes at 9:00, so when twenty minutes goes by, and then thirty, my worry grows stronger.

10:21 P.M.

Me: Seriously do you have a sec?

10:44 P.M.

Me: Ok dude. What's up with the ghosting? Are you trapped under heavy furniture? Lol

11:02 P.M.

Me: Hello?

I call her at 11:04. No answer. The tendril of worry weaving through my mind grows into a heavy, twisting rope. Could her phone be dead?

None of this feels right. Lily compulsively keeps her phone charged, so that doesn't seem likely, and she's nervous about her alarms, so I know for a fact she tests them every night. I used to tease her for it until I started to suspect it was part of a real anxiety struggle. Probably the same struggle that makes her sleep so badly at night.

I call her again, and it rings and rings. The next call goes straight to voicemail. I stand up, feeling squirmy and restless. I just need to think. My feet automatically start pacing laps around my tiny room. Two steps to my dresser, three back to my bed.

Did something happen at home? Maybe they had an accident, and they had to go to the hospital? I open the map where we've shared each other's location. I can see her right there on the map screen. She's at home. Everything's fine. I need to chill out.

And then, a few seconds later, a notification.

Lily Dalton has stopped sharing her location with you.

I freeze midstep. A terrible unease grips me. What the hell is this?

I set my phone down for a second because I need to get this shit locked down. I do not need to be panicking about her not texting me. This is probably a system glitch or a parents-gone-rogue phone confiscation. Or, hell, maybe I pissed her off, which explains all of the snapping earlier. It could be nothing. It's *probably* nothing.

I will see her tomorrow and ask. And then I will have a come-to-Jesus meeting with myself. Because no single person should be so central to my universe that not hearing from them makes me feel vaguely nauseated, but here I am. No matter how forcefully I tell myself this is an overreaction, I can't shake this feeling of dread.

At midnight, I give up on sleep. I grab my phone and scroll through the last month of our messages (no small feat before the last week) and all the socials. Lily's social app of choice is one of the everything-deletes-in-twenty-four-hours varieties, and I'm not as active, so we don't use it much to chat. But she uses it. I check her user ID on my friends list and relax marginally when I see that she was active two hours ago.

Okay, she's alive. Granted, she's being a dickbag leaving me on read, but she's alive.

Or it means she bumped the app open in her phone.

It maybe means something, but not enough to reassure me that she's really okay. Our last month of texts don't reveal any red flags of suicidal thoughts. But still, I scan them like I'm investigating a crime scene. I look for anything particularly snarky or strange. There isn't much. A few bitchy comments about the Jacksons. A couple of cryptic nonanswers that probably mean less than nothing. But my eyes do snag on something from two months back.

Lily: You don't like Mr. Droesch, right?

Me: Does anyone?

Lily: After today, I sincerely doubt it.

Me: What happened?

Lily: I'll tell you later.

Me: Did that asshole do something?

Lily didn't answer then. In fact, I don't think we've talked about Mr. Droesch at all since, but she did say his name in the car. She listed him when she was talking about making people pay. Of course, she mentioned Paxton too, and Nate, but those two are more linked to me than her.

On a whim, I check my other friends. Paxton and I aren't linked because Paxton is the spawn of Satan these days and there is no way in hell. But Nate and me... That's more complicated.

I think of his sandy hair and the freckled bridge of his nose. The little salute he gave me in the hall today and the sweaty press of his palm against mine the first time we held hands freshman year. We were fourteen. Babies just tiptoeing into high school. He was my first kiss, my first date, my first breakup. The breakup happened after Cadence, of course, though he swore it wasn't about that. He offered a list of vague it-isn't-you-it's-me reasons his parents probably helped him drum up, and he did it with a soft voice and red cheeks.

It hurt, but hell, everything hurt that month. And I never really blamed Nate. He was never cruel or dramatic. There was no performative unfriending or obvious avoidance in the halls. He remained cordial, and I took it on the chin. I got a hell of a lot worse from most of the assholes in my school. So no, Nate wasn't my enemy, but Lily seemed to feel differently. She offered him dirty looks and barely bothered to speak to him after we became friends. She called it sisterly solidarity, and I laughed it off, feeling touched that she'd care enough to be angry on my behalf.

But now my eyes are locked onto the 2 hours ago next to Nate's name on my friend's list. Just like the 2 hours ago next to Lily's. It's a stretch. A *big* stretch. The two things could be entirely unrelated. But maybe they're not, and he talked to her?

I consider texting him, but immediately scrap that idea. There is no version of a universe where texting my ex-boyfriend at 1:00 in the morning doesn't look completely unhinged. And to be fair, all of this feels a little unhinged. But it also feels like instinct. Like the marrow of my bones is involved in this warning—this whisper that something bad is coming.

My throat feels suddenly tight as I move past the fear of Lily having some sort of awful depressive episode. I scroll up to our most recent text exchange and let myself go to an even darker place. A place where the something that's coming isn't about sadness—it's about violence.

Me: Sure.

Lily: How serious would it be?

Me: Depends. Some explosives would be small or start a fire. Others would blow the whole thing to pieces. Explosives = options.

Lily: People could get seriously hurt...

Me: Hell yeah they could. Maybe even killed.

Lily: With firecrackers or something?

Me: Lots of things would do it. Things almost everyone can buy.

Lily: That's scary.

Me: Chemistry is scary as hell. That's one of the reasons I love it.

The words on my screen shake, but it isn't the words. It's my hands. I'm shaking all over. I stand up and drop my phone on the bed. My palms are hot and slick with sweat, and that terrible curling feeling in my stomach is turning into a barbed hook.

All the pieces are adding up to something truly horrific. Lily was angry and distracted. She talked about some sort of payback. Then she cut off all contact with me with no warning and no explanation. And the last real thing we talked about?

Ways to get away with murder.

EIGHT

Is Lily planning to kill someone? The idea of it makes my heart beat faster. I feel seasick and stand up, pacing in tight circles. I think of calling her again and dismiss it. I think of driving to her house. Calling her mother. Sending a message to one of our friends.

I think of a lot of things, but I only act on one. At two thirty in the morning, I send one final desperate text.

Me: Whatever you're thinking, Lily, please talk to me first.

Lily never answers.

I doze fitfully, waking on and off until the light in my room shifts. It's morning, and if the clouds outside my window are any indicator, it's going to rain.

I stand up and get dressed automatically. The clock reads 7:10 when I drag my backpack onto my bed. I have no idea what to do or who to talk to about this, but I know I'm running out of time to figure it out. If Lily won't talk to me this morning, I'm going to have to get help.

I open the top flap of my backpack to toss in my umbrella and then I see it. The red folder Lily handed me in the car. Her English paper research.

I open the front cover thinking of the countless times Lily has complained about her subject. Fifteenth-century Scandinavian agriculture. She chose the primary source and the subject, of course, but then moaned daily about how she never should have chosen such an obscure historical period with such limited source material available.

But I don't see the obscure article snippets I expect, or a rough draft of the paper. I see a formula sheet.

I pull it out with a frown, sure I'm misreading it, but I'm not. This is a formula sheet for chemistry. And when I look at the first formula, it's familiar. Hydrogen peroxide and propane and fertilizer components. We aren't working on this in Chem though. I flip behind the formula sheet to find a second paper, typed like the first, but there are diagrams at the bottom. Back-of-the-napkin math jotted in the margins.

This isn't from our class at all. It's familiar though, but my sleep-deprived brain can't connect any of the dots. I flip through another page. Some kind of diagram or floor plan. And then a list that feels even more confusing than the other pages.

Randy Droesch: Green Honda Civic—HXD X215

Paxton Bryce: Black Volvo XC90—BRYCE3

Nate Turner: Red Mustang convertible—NCO 12P5

Gretchen Price: Silver Nissan Sentra—GG7 4JO2

Mary Chang: White Honda CR-V—JJ2 C93N

For a breath or two, I'm not sure what I'm looking at. A list of names, sure, and cars, obviously. And license plates? That's what those have to be. Why would Lily have a list of names and cars?

Something sour and prickly blooms in the back of my mouth. I pull the papers out one by one and turn my attention to the page that looks like a floor plan. I move it to my desk lamp to examine it. It's a map of a parking lot. Not just any parking lot either—it's the Tuskegee High parking lot.

My hands are shaking when I flip to the formula sheet. I am fully awake now, the fuzzy smear of fitful sleep gone. My finger runs beneath the formulas, and my body goes cold.

My best friend's folder contains a map of the school parking lot. A list of cars. And recipe cards for explosive materials.

I lean back against the dresser because my legs feel wobbly. I can't believe I'm looking at this. I take pictures of each sheet, because my first instinct is to send them to Lily with a giant Help, I just found this truly scary thing—what do I do? Obviously, this isn't an option.

So what *do* I do? Is this just a joke? A weird parking lot assignment from her work in the office? It would explain the license plates, maybe, but not the chemistry formulas. And not the fact that she hid it in my backpack swearing it was an English paper. Or that she was talking about this kind of thing—explosives and cars—in a roundabout way.

I think of her in her bedroom, the long strange look she gave me before her dad arrived. Was she weighing whether or not to tell me about this? Because, my God, if this is a real thing, I have to tell someone. But who?

I text Lily one last time, a Hail Mary in digital form.

Me: Lily, we need to talk about the folder you left in my bag. Call me ASAP.

Of course, she does not answer.

Her silence is forcing my hand. I have to tell someone; the question is who. Lily isn't just my best friend; she's my *only* real friend. Everyone else is closer to Lily than me, and even if they would talk to me, I don't trust them not to spread rumors that

Lily has lost it. God knows everyone loves to see a golden girl go down.

So who's left? My mom? She's already headed to her shift at the hospital. I could text her, and she wouldn't panic. After five years working at the hospital emergency clinic, she's pretty unflappable. Still, I can't imagine her reaction wouldn't involve a call to Lily's parents at some point. And Lily's parents? They're tried-and-true panickers, especially her dad. He's always worried about something happening to her.

Okay, could I talk Mom out of calling them? Maybe. Possibly. But this folder is absolutely some kind of threat. Even if Mom doesn't call the Daltons, my guess is she would call the police.

A memory of my own arrest runs through me, every detail painfully sharp in my mind. I feel the bite of the officers' fingers on my arm. The cold weight of the handcuffs. The hungry mix of shock and sometimes delight on the faces that watched from classroom windows.

No. I cannot do that to Lily. I don't trust the police enough to give this to them. They don't know her like I do, and I know this has to be some kind of misunderstanding. This is Lily, the girl who makes a mustache out of her cotton candy at the fair, the girl who still wears teddy bear slippers. This cannot be what it looks like.

Can it?

The doubt spreads through my mind, casting shadows on

everything I felt sure about. Is it possible I don't know her as well as I think? I spread the pages out again and turn them over and over in my head, willing them to look like something other than what they are. But the pieces refuse to add up to any better conclusions.

The only possibility that makes sense is that Lily is planning something awful. Something violent. Something involving explosives and cars of people she doesn't like. People I mostly don't like either, come to think of it.

I desperately want to believe this is a terrible joke, and I almost do. Almost. But what if I'm wrong? It's simple: If I'm wrong, people will die.

I go through my options again. Not my mom. Not her parents. Not a friend. I need to take this to a trustworthy authority. And of course those are growing on trees around here.

Except...One authority figure is coming to mind.

I think of him in Ms. Chang's office, bald and smiling and, most importantly, calm. Officer Grimes is always calm.

I take a bracing breath and look at the clock. I need to move fast.

I leave the house at 7:40 a.m., my backpack heavy on my shoulders. Half a mile later, when I step into the school parking lot, I check the clock above the door. Fifteen minutes until the bell.

I hope it's enough time.

I hope I have the guts to really do this.

I check the last text I sent, willing her to respond. But of course she doesn't. The rules in this new version of the world dictate that Lily will not reply. The Lily in this world is a stranger.

The school doors open. Teachers I vaguely recognize head toward the drop-off line with walkie-talkies. The line of cars driven by eager-to-get-to-work parents crawls toward the front of the school.

I cut through the parking lot and up the walk to the entrance. My heart is pounding, and my palms feel sweaty when I pull open the doors and slip inside. I have to go through the main office, which is open even though school hasn't started. To my surprise, no one is in the front, so I make my way past the dividing wall to the back of the administrative area.

Principal Chang's office is situated against the farthest wall. It's half glass for transparency's sake, but Ms. Chang isn't in her office—she's right here, and she's not alone. I stop short, seeing Principal Chang, Vice Principal Jackson, a guidance counselor I can't name, and two police officers.

"Ms. Cutler," Ms. Chang says.

She looks nervous. Her voice trembles. She swallows hard and looks to one of the officers. Something cold moves through my bones. They are here for a reason.

They know about Lily.

I do not know why I'm sure of this, but with the way they are looking at me, I'm certain it's true. They're here about what Lily is planning. Maybe her parents found something. Or maybe she said something to someone else.

In the end, I realize it doesn't matter. I just need to give them everything I can to help keep everyone safe. For a second, I feel the weight of guilt over what I'm about to do. Because I know better than everyone that it will ruin everything for Lily. But there isn't really another choice here. Not one I can live with.

"I have something that might help," I say. Then I reach around my shoulder for my backpack.

Everyone tenses, and the female officer raises her hand sharply. "I need you to stop what you're doing, Ms. Cutler."

I pause, confused. "No, I think you need to see this folder."

I pull my backpack off one shoulder to give them what they're looking for. Even as my fingers graze the zipper, the second officer unholsters his gun.

"Do not move, Ms. Cutler!" the female officer shouts.

I don't move. And as I stand there, not moving, I realize something. This police officer knows my name.

"Put your hands in the air!"

My mind reels. I don't understand. Is she talking to me? Time slows to a crawl. I am a fly trapped in honey. I try to turn, try to see if there's someone behind me—maybe Lily.

"Hands in the air! Right now!"

I throw my hands up, my backpack thunking to the ground and flopping onto its side. My chest and throat constrict. My heart beats wildly.

The female officer lifts her other hand, that palm facing her partner while the other faces me. Her eyes stay right on mine. "Everybody just stay calm. Clara? Your name is Clara, right?"

I nod, shaking.

"You're doing great, Clara. Keep those hands up where I can see them."

"Okay." My voice is high and frightened—my little-girl voice. I can't look away from the gun the male officer is pointing.

"Put your hands on top of your head nice and slow." She says it slowly, like the serenity of her voice might lull me into compliance, but she doesn't need to lull me into shit. I am terrified and plenty compliant.

The fear shifts me into autopilot. It is another version of a morning from my freshman year. Another room where officers are giving me instructions. Every set of eyes in this room is on me. Every inch of my skin is growing hot with shame. I am burning alive, just like I did then. But two years ago, I knew why they were coming for me. I knew exactly what I'd done.

"What's happening?" I ask. My voice is a croak.

No one answers. Ms. Chang's face is blank, and the guidance counselor's face is a study in disappointment. I can't bear to look at them. So I turn to the female police officer instead. A pointed chin and honest eyes. I swallow hard.

I move my hands slowly to the top of my head. "Can someone tell me what's—"

"Hands on your head!"

I jump at the male officer's shout. My knees are trembling, my teeth chattering. I can barely breathe.

"Her hands are on her head, Stolski," the female officer says as she moves forward, kicking my backpack a little farther away from me. "I'm going to move toward you now, Clara, but you need to keep those hands right where we can see them. Can you do that?"

"Can you just talk to me? Can you tell me—" I hiccup around the question, my voice strangled. I sound like I'm going to cry. And then I feel the wet heat of tears on my cheeks. "Is it about Lily? I don't have anything explosive. She only gave me the folder."

"You can tell us about it at the station, Clara," the female officer says.

The station? I look at the gun the other officer has trained on me. The tight, nervous faces on the staff members. They think *I* did something.

I shake my head frantically. "I'm not working with her. I'm not—wait, what about my mom? Don't you have to call my mom?"

"You best keep your mouth shut," Stolski says. "We're not the ones who don't seem to know the law."

"Officer Stolski." The female officer again. Her sharp tone does not leave an inch for argument. I notice the embroidered yellow letters above her badge. *Fleming*.

"I need to approach you now," Officer Fleming tells me. "You are not to move. Do you understand me?"

I nod, feeling seasick. None of this makes sense. If they think I'm in on this with Lily, then where is she? Someone is moving inside Ms. Chang's office. I can see their shadow through the glass, a glimpse of navy blue movement. A uniform.

Is that Officer Grimes?

Officer Fleming tells me she is going to place me in handcuffs. I nod again, even though her voice is reduced to a garbled smear in my ears. She pulls my right arm downward and nudges me to take a step forward. More of Ms. Chang's office comes into view now, the sleek wooden desk and the chair I sat in not even twenty-four hours ago. Officer Grimes is standing beside the desk, and Lily is seated in the same chair I was in yesterday.

My pulse stutters, the world gone sluggish and strange. Lily's eyes are red and puffy. Her parents stand behind her, wearing worried expressions. Her mother weeps openly, but her father stays stoic, his hand resting on Lily's small shoulder.

It is like being dropped into another universe. I cannot make sense of what's happening. Officer Fleming places my other hand into cuffs and begins to read me my rights. In the office, Officer Grimes drops his gaze to the floor. Mr. and Mrs. Dalton look away. But Lily turns toward me. Officer Fleming tightens the cuffs on my wrists, and Lily looks me dead in the eyes.

It isn't anything like yesterday in the classroom. Today, Lily isn't here to save me. She is here to watch me go down.

NINE

My mind is a jumble in the back of the cruiser. I feel like I'm underwater—everything is hazy and dark. Except for Lily. I recall her face perfectly, with her puffy red eyes and the cold smile that briefly curved her lips. I only half trust the memory. Lily looked devastated, so did I imagine that smile?

I take a breath that smells like metal and coffee and, faintly, vomit. The car bumps over the rough patch at the end of the school driveway, and my stomach churns at every jostle.

"Jesus. Think they could spend some of my tax dollars paving that," Stolski says. He has a bad buzz cut, or maybe hair that's too pale to tolerate even the slightest barber misstep.

"You don't live in this school district," Fleming says. "Not your tax dollars."

He grunts as they pull to the stop sign. Officer Fleming isn't driving, and she wasn't the one who used the radio to report my arrest and imminent arrival, but something in her tone and posture tells me she's in charge. Maybe they even said as much. I can't remember. The entire last hour is disjointed in my brain—the whole thing playing like a badly glitched video.

I stare at the tight knot of dark curls at the nape of her neck and try to focus on her voice. Stolski has already convicted me. I can feel it every time his pale eyes catch mine in the rearview mirror, an expression similar to the ones I received from officers after my last arrest. But Officer Fleming is different. She told me to watch my head getting into the cruiser. Her hand on my arm was firm when she led me out of an emergency exit door in the administrative area. It was a longer route, but it kept me away from the main hallway and the hundreds of greedy eyes waiting outside to see what shit was going down on a random Wednesday morning in the front office. She's the one who knows what's happening, so maybe she can fill in the blank spaces in my mind.

"Excuse me," I say, trying to sound polite. "Can you tell me what I'm under arrest for?"

I expect Stolski to snap back something nasty, but he turns left and doesn't even acknowledge my presence. After a pause, Officer Fleming's voice rings out, calm and low.

"You were arrested for threatening to commit a terrorist act."

"Threat—" My mouth feels strange and cottony. "Terrorist act?"

"Yeah, that's it's called when you create a plan to blow up a bunch of people in the school parking lot," Stolski says.

The formulas and map and license plates from the folder. It absolutely could be interpreted as an explosives plan. My stomach sinks. Stolski isn't wrong about what this looks like, but he's wrong about me.

"I know about the plan, but it's not mine." I say. "I wasn't in on this with her."

"Of course you weren't," Stolski says, using his best not-buying-your-bullshit tone.

I do not take the bait. "The whole reason I'm at school early is because I was trying to talk to Officer Grimes about this. That's literally why I came to the office."

"Sure you were," he says. "That makes more sense than just calling the police."

"Why don't you just wait until we get to the station, Ms. Cutler?" Officer Fleming says. "We'll have plenty of time to talk there."

"I don't know what else there is to say. I didn't even know any of this was happening until I found the folder she shoved in my backpack."

"The folder *who* shoved?" Officer Fleming asks.

"Lily," I say, and I can hear the frustration slipping into my tone. I take a deep breath. "This is Lily's plan. Or something. I don't even know what it is; maybe it's just a stupid joke or a terrible misunderstanding. All I know is it is *not* mine."

"Of course not!" Stolski says. He's mocking me. My throat squeezes. I look at Officer Fleming's neck again, willing her to step in, but she stays quiet and I follow suit.

We pull into the police station parking lot—not the visitors' lot out front, but an area past a secured gate in the back section of the station. Criminals and officers only, I guess.

When we park, it's Officer Stolski who speaks again, twisting around in his seat to look at me through the cage separator. "Tell me, did you decide the folder was fishy before or after you sent Lily the messages about blowing things up?"

"What? I didn't send—"

I cut myself off, realizing what he means. Yesterday while Mrs. Dalton served up shortbread, I *did* text Lily about blowing things up. Because we were joking.

I don't even know how they'd know about those texts already. Unless they saw them.

"I thought that might quiet you down," Stolski says.

Chills roll up my back, but I don't say a word.

Did Lily's parents see those texts? Her dad can sometimes be a little intrusive, but Lily's super guarded with her phone. But maybe they somehow saw them and confronted her. Maybe this whole thing snowballed from a misunderstanding. Except why wouldn't Lily say something? Would she really just stand there and let them all think this was me?

She saved me sophomore year. I was a total pariah. Not a person in that school would talk to the girl who took down Tusky's beloved soccer star. But Lily did. She put me on the chemistry path that opened up my future. When literally no one wanted anything to do with me, Lily invited me to help her study. Then she brought me to her lunch table. To her house. She turned my world around.

No. There is more to this. There has to be, because Lily wouldn't hurt me like this.

"This is a misunderstanding," I say, twisting around to look for another cruiser. Or an unmarked police vehicle. Lily has to be here. She has to clear this up. "Where is Lily?"

"My bet is she's back at home trying to cope with the fact that her best friend is a damn terrorist," Stolski says.

"*Officer Stolski*," Fleming says, and from her tone, it's clearly a reprimand. She turns to look at me then, and her face is unreadable. "Ms. Cutler, I'm going to strongly suggest that you refrain from any further questions until we have the opportunity to call your mom."

They pull me from the car, and I blink in the brightness of the morning sun. When my vision adjusts, I spot the police station entrance in front of me. I shiver, though it is not cold. My knees knock as we walk toward the doors.

A scraggly sparrow hops across the parking lot fence. There are a couple of other cruisers, but otherwise this lot is empty. It is just me making my second walk into the station with my hands cuffed behind my back.

After my mom is called, Officer Fleming sets me in an interview room and removes my handcuffs. She tells me to hang tight and knock on the door if I need anything. I have a long list of things I need in this moment, starting with my backpack and phone, and ending with someone telling what the hell is actually going on.

It feels like hours before the door of the interview room opens. Mom stands in the open doorway, smoothing down her scrubs and apologizing to an officer I can't see about traffic and how long it took to arrive. As she steps into the room, I spot an unfamiliar elderly man behind her with stooped shoulders and thick glasses.

"Hello there. Are you Clara Cutler?" he asks me.

"Yes."

He nods, shuffling closer to the table. "I met your mom in the lobby here."

Mom looks at me briefly, her face tight. "This is the attorney they've assigned."

"Yes, my name is John, John Pruitt."

John starts chattering on about processes and steps, and my brain cannot make sense of a single word he says. Everything is a low, staticky hum. This is the person who's going to defend me? John is wearing a too-thin dress shirt and carrying a brown messenger bag that looks worse for wear. He also appears to be about ninety-five years old, and I'm immediately curious as to why he's here instead of the attorney from my last case.

I try to catch my mom's eye to ask, but she keeps her gaze on anything and everything but me. John gradually opens his battered bag and then slowly removes sheets of paper, one at a time. It's excruciating.

He finally hands us a series of forms to sign, and there's more waiting of course, because the main thing I've learned about being arrested is that it involves an absurd amount of waiting in bleak rooms with uncomfortable chairs.

When Mr. Pruitt leaves again, Mom and I are alone. She turns to me for the first time. There are dark smudges beneath her eyes. I burst into tears, feeling a mix of awful things. Terror at being in here. Hurt that I still have no idea what's happening. And shame for putting my mother back in a police station.

She hugs me, but I can feel the tension in her arms. And when I calm down and pull back, she's frowning.

"What's going on, Clara?"

"Lily was planning something bad. I'm somehow mixed up in it. Where's Tim?"

"Tim?" A crease forms between Mom's brows like she's searching through all the Tims she knows, but I can only think of one. Tim Egan—the smart, kind, teacherly attorney who helped me so much last time.

Mom finally shakes her head, realizing who I mean. "We can't afford Tim again. What kind of bad thing are you saying Lily did?"

"I don't think she did anything, but she wrote up this stupid plan about bombing a parking lot, I think. Obviously I don't think she meant it. It's just a stupid joke."

"*Stupid*? You've used that word twice, but this doesn't feel stupid. It feels scary, Clara."

"It is scary, but I don't think she meant it. She and I were talking yesterday..."

"You were involved in this plan?"

"No! That's what I'm trying to tell you. We were joking around about people we hate at school, and Lily started talking about getting away with murder—"

Mom swears, leaning back in disbelief. I put up my hands.

"Mom, it was a joke! We were exaggerating."

"You were in on this?"

"No, I wasn't in on anything. We were having a hypothetical conversation."

"People don't get arrested for conversations," she snaps.

"I wasn't arrested for a conversation. They found Lily's folder in my backpack, and that folder had the plans inside, so they think they are mine."

Except now that I'm thinking about it, they didn't find that folder. I did not pull it out. They knew about it, but until Officer

Fleming unzipped my backpack while I waited in the cruiser, they couldn't have been sure, could they? Unless someone told them.

Mom lets out a slow, shaky breath. She covers her face with her chapped hands, and guilt sits on my chest like an elephant. My mom works almost seventy hours a week, full-time in the emergency room clinic and part-time at a bar. She does this so I have a safe place to live, and this is how I'm repaying her for that. Again.

Mom uncovers her face, and I can tell she's trying to compose herself. Her voice is calmer when she speaks again. "Why would you take a folder without looking at it?"

"It wasn't like that. We were driving home. Her backpack was in the trunk. She just told me to hold it so she didn't forget it. Then it was in my bag, and I totally forgot about the stupid folder until I found it this morning."

"You found it? Clara, why didn't you talk to me? Why didn't you call me immediately?"

"Because you were at work," I say, and now in the harsh light of an interrogation room, it sounds like the dumbest logic of all time. "I was going to bring it in to Officer Grimes. I thought he could help. But when I got to school, the police were already waiting."

"And have you told them about Lily?"

"They know about Lily. Lily was there this morning with her parents."

"What? Then why isn't she here?"

"Because they think it was me."

I want to say more, but I suddenly feel flattened by the weight of it all. I don't know why Lily threw me under the bus or how it all played out, but it's clear the police had no problem believing her. I guess her word and a few text messages were enough to warrant an arrest. After all, I already have a criminal record, but Lily? She's as pure and perfect as they come.

Protecting her reputation is the only reason I can imagine her letting me take the blame for this. She will come around. I have to believe that.

"The police said this is an explosives plan and there were text messages. Is that true?" Mom asks. She's trying to make sense of it, and she looks so, so tired. Her short dark hair is limp and clinging to her face.

"No. I mean, yes, it's definitely about explosives, and there were messages, but it was a joke. We were joking!"

"You were joking about explosives?" She's nearly shouting now, and I don't know what to say. Everything is coming out wrong.

I start to cry again, and it feels like no other response would make sense, but Mom lets out a strangled laugh.

"I just don't know how I can do this again, Clara."

Her voice is not unkind, but I can hear the fatigue in every word. The reminder that we are right back to the world of accusations and police interviews. The world I worked so hard to leave behind.

TEN

Mom leaves to get a coffee, and I sip on the lukewarm water she brings back with her. Instead of talking, I pace the room, feeling wired and antsy. I feel caught in that endless loop of *why*. Why didn't Lily say something? Why isn't anyone even questioning her? Why did Lily put this plan together at all? The questions bounce around in my head with no answers.

By the time John Pruitt comes back with even more paperwork, it's almost noon, and I'm so hungry I feel like my stomach is turning itself inside out. But food isn't mentioned. Instead, we tuck into a feast of paperwork releasing me to my mother with about a million conditions and dire warnings.

John stacks the signed papers on the table, and I try to avoid staring at his age-spotted hands. "Well, the bad news is, you are going to be charged with a few pretty serious crimes. The good news is, we've got some time for you to think about a plea bargain."

"A plea bargain?"

John nods, sitting down heavily in the chair. His teeth are smoker-yellow, and he looks as uninterested in me as I am in being in this room.

"You'll need to enter a plea of guilty, not guilty, or no contest. One of the judges is on unexpected medical leave, so the docket is behind schedule. We are looking at an arraignment early next week."

"And what happens at the arraignment?" Mom asks.

John looks either confused or annoyed. Maybe a bit of both. "Like I said, she'll be formally charged, and she'll need to enter a plea. Didn't you do all of this before?"

I stare at him. I'm not sure why I'm stunned by his question. Maybe it's the way he glibly delivers it, like I've been arrested oh-so-many times, and don't I have this all down by now?

"I don't remember all of it," Mom says. "It was a rough time. Do you have a recommendation?"

John leans back, the chair (or maybe his bones) creaking. "Well why don't you tell me what you think first, Clara? You pled guilty last time, right?"

"Yes, because I was actually guilty," I say.

John thumbs through the records. "Well, the notes on that case show you initially denied everything then too, even after pleading guilty."

I flush with a mix of rage and shame. He's right and he's wrong. I was a terrified freshman burying my head in the sand. But how do I explain that this is different?

"This is not my plan," I say simply. "It is not my folder."

John blinks at me. "Maybe that's true. But they found it in your backpack containing formulas you created. They have several text messages between you and Ms. Dalton, an email that appears to be pretty incriminating, and that's quite a start before a prosecutor has even gotten involved."

My formulas? Incriminating email? None of this is adding up. I shake my head. "I don't know what you're talking about. What email?"

John stands up, looking impatient. "Maybe you should think on it for a few days. I'll reach out when they provide the intended charges and the arraignment time."

"How do *you* think she should plead?" Mom asks, her voice small.

"Well..." John pulls something out of his tooth with a pinky. My stomach knots in protest. "The evidence doesn't look good from what I've seen. If she's willing to plead guilty, they'll probably lower some of these charges."

"And if I plead not guilty?" I ask.

John zips his ratty bag shut. "It will be an uphill battle."

John leaves, and I push my now empty cup of water into the trash can. My mother and I do not speak again until Officer

Fleming arrives. As we walk through the station, a dispatcher ducks out of a break room to offer Fleming a warm and brief congratulations.

"Oh, did you…get married?" I ask.

She laughs. "I received a promotion. Detective. I'm in between two worlds right now."

She winks and sits me down with a desk sergeant who processes even more paperwork. At 1:05 I am released to my mother without my phone or my backpack. I am told not to travel more than ten miles outside city limits, and to stay away from the high school and Lily's house.

The sergeant says all of this without the remotest bit of inflection, and when she slides the paper across the desk, Mom signs it without any questions.

I walk into the parking lot feeling numb. The sun is warmer now, thawing my cold hands. I close my eyes to soak it up, and Mom's phone rings.

"Hello?" She stops walking. "Yes, Ms. Chang, thanks for calling."

I listen to her side of the conversation feeling helpless and distant.

"Yes, we understand the suspension…" Mom's face shifts from weariness to stark fear. "What do you mean by *expulsion*?"

I freeze, staring at her, hearing the tinny murmur of Ms.

Chang's voice. It's too quiet to make out any words, but my mom goes pale.

"Yes. I understand the zero tolerance policy," she says. "When is the board meeting?"

A short answer on the other end of the line.

"Well, the Board of Education ultimately decides on expulsion, correct? Until then it's just a suspension; is that right?"

Mom listens for a while and then nods. "I understand. May second. We'll be there."

Mom disconnects the phone with a heavy sigh. I don't dare ask what the call was about. I'm smart enough to piece it together, and she's smart enough to know I already did.

We settle into our old Dodge, and I stare out at the road beyond the station parking lot. A school bus trundles past. Bus 79. Six hours ago, I could have ridden that bus. Funny how much can change in six hours.

My brain dredges up an old school memory involving that bus. I rode Bus 79 to school every day in sophomore year, including the day Lily changed my world. She'd contacted me out of the blue on winter break, and we'd hung out a few times, working on a chemistry project. But it all felt separate from the real world. It felt like a bubble, and riding back to school on January 3, I was sure that bubble would pop.

But that day at lunch, Lily found me outside the cafeteria. I nearly jumped with shock when she followed me into line. My memory of that moment unfolds, still crystal clear.

"Want to sit at my table?"

Lily nods toward a hallowed table at the back of the cafeteria, one I wouldn't attempt to walk past, let alone sit at. Not just because of Cadence either. Even back when I was a snot-nosed freshman, I had enough sense to know that I don't wear the right clothes or live at the right address to belong at the beautiful and popular table.

But Lily is still looking at me, waiting for a response.

I chuckle. "No, I'm sure you guys are all full. But I'll catch you later."

But Lily grabs my arm with a surprisingly firm grip.

"Look, I know you don't sit with anyone. You haven't all year. So now you can sit with us, okay?" Her smile looks genuine, and her grip doesn't leave much room for argument.

So I follow her, approaching the table and its row of carefully coordinated lunch boxes with a mix of dread and misery. Paxton slouches with no lunch at all at the farthest end of the table. He looks surprised to see me, and, hell, doesn't that make two of us?

I've still got my backpack on and I don't know how to sit down without bumping someone. In that instant, Henry slides into the seat next to Mariana.

Between his golden eyes and dimples, it's almost impossible to not stare. Henry is clearly the exception to all rules. I know he's an apartment kid like me, and now I spot his lunch tray, same as the one I've set down. But when he sees me, he smiles warmly.

"Hi, Clara." He reaches out a hand for my bag. "Let me take that so you can sit down."

I sit next to Lily. I'm beyond hungry, but no way in hell am I going to risk the red-sauce-laden slab of pasta. I opt for the roll instead.

Lily nudges my arm softly, leaning in to whisper. "See? I told you it would be fine."

Mom's car stutters, tugging me out of my memories. I turn my head to face the passenger window. We blur past freshly budding trees while the same question rolls over and over through my mind. How does someone who saves your life change into someone who watches it blow apart?

Mom hits the brakes when she turns right onto our street. Startled, I search for a kid or a dog, but then I see them. Two police vans lined up at the curb in front of our tiny duplex. They're already here, waiting on us. They're treating my house like a crime scene.

ELEVEN

Two people in police department polos slowly amble out of the van, joined by an officer in uniform. We pull into our driveway and the second I open the door, I hear George barking, offering us low, booming warnings that a stranger is near. Mom accepts the search warrant from the uniformed officer and unlocks the front door. George bounces behind the glass side panel, all fluffy black fur and nervous energy.

We've been told more than once that he looks more like a bear than a dog. Proving that claim, the uniformed officer and the technicians behind him all shrink back from the door.

"You should let us get him put away first," Mom says.

"Is he aggressive, ma'am?"

"No, but you're scaring him," I say. "So just give us a minute."

To their credit, they give us space as we step inside. George's cold nose presses frantically at my palms and legs and down onto my shoes. He pants and paces, a massive furry heap of worry. Mom finds and hands me his leash, and I take him into the backyard. Without the leash he'd just bark and howl at the door, so it's the best option we have.

He walks in anxious circles around me, and I stare into my house through the back sliding door. They rifle through papers in the kitchen. On the fridge. On the counters. The light in my bedroom goes on, and then I can see them in there as well. They collect my laptop and notebooks. I feel sick when I see them at my dresser. A stranger is opening my underwear drawer. His gloved hand is probably in there right now, moving the box with Nate's old homecoming invitation note and a few spare tampons for tossing into my purse.

I walk George to the tree and scratch behind his ears when he whines. When I look back at the house, they have left my room. One of the technicians is in the kitchen again, speaking to my mom. It's the worst feeling watching strangers in your house, touching your things and collecting anything that interests them.

It's probably thirty minutes in total before they pack up to leave. George is bored now, flopped over on his side on my left foot. I watch them all file out of the house. I step back inside when I see Mom return to the kitchen from walking them out.

"Did you ask them when I'd get my backpack?"

"They said they weren't sure. There are things in it they need to hold on to for now."

"What about my phone? How am I supposed to call people?"

"I don't know, Clara; maybe you're not." She runs her hands through her hair, looking frayed. Guilt pinches the space beneath my ribs. Life seems to thrive on inventing ways to wear my mother out, and I hate that today I'm one of those ways.

I hate even more that it isn't the first time.

And after the last time, I can't blame her for not believing me. I did every damn thing wrong. I ran from the scene of the crime. I said nothing that night and nothing the next morning. Just got up and headed off to school like I hadn't sprinted from my injured, wailing friend six hours earlier. And then, because I guess that wasn't enough, I also lied to the officers and to my mom when they took me in. I dodged every question and twisted every answer. As if I could somehow knit the lies into some sort of bullshit story that would make me less guilty.

I stay quiet in an attempt to be helpful. I unload the dishwasher and wipe the counters. I offer her a cup of tea, but she declines and goes to her room without explanation. Since it's 4:15 p.m., I have a whole lot of hours to fill with overthinking, so that should be fun. I refill George's water bowl, and he drinks greedily, pausing to trail a river across the linoleum floor while he checks the door again. Still nervous. Still half expecting strange invaders to descend once again.

"I get it, dude," I tell him, scratching his head before I mop up the dog dribble.

I'm just as nervous and twitchy as the giant dust mop at my feet. And since my phone and laptop are currently in an evidence locker at a police station, I have literally no way to answer any of the questions running through my mind. I have no idea what's happening or what people know. Restlessness pushes me to sweep the floor.

When I'm out of things to do, I head into our living room at the front of the house. We have a sagging gray sectional and a ratty TV stand with water stains, but it's comfortable and clean. I curl up in a corner of the couch trying to figure out what to do.

The answer presents itself when I notice a familiar figure passing by outside. Sleek black hair. Cropped sweatshirt. A hot pink backpack I'd recognize anywhere. My shoulders straighten. It's Ava, making her way home from track practice most likely.

Maybe there is a way to get some answers.

I bolt outside, surprised by the chill in the air. The sun is low in the sky, but there's still an hour or two of daylight left. Early enough that it makes sense for me to be outside, maybe taking a walk. I loop around the back side of my house. Ava and I aren't exactly friends, but she lives around the corner, the wrong edge of the right side of town. I know where she's headed and just which alley to take to cut her off. I dart behind trash cans and shove my hands in my pockets so that I look casual. Or at the very least, not threatening

I stop short a few yards from Ava, forcing a surprised expression. Like I didn't see her coming half a block away and plan this whole encounter out ahead of time.

"Hey, Ava." I keep my voice soft.

Ava's pale green eyes go wide with fear. Ava is beautiful, athletic, and almost as beloved as Lily by teachers. But she keeps me firmly at arm's length. She probably expected me to wind up in trouble again.

"Excuse me," Ava says, her voice cracking as she turns to cross the street, headed in a direction away from her house.

"Ava, you live two blocks that way," I say, with something that isn't quite a chuckle.

There isn't a way to get where she's going without passing me, not unless she adds ten minutes to her walk. And because she's smart enough to know this, Ava looks left and right, as if she's hoping a portal will open to save her from the terror of walking past me.

"Are you that nervous to be on a sidewalk with me?"

She flinches but doesn't deny it, and if I try hard, I can imagine being in her shoes well enough to understand.

I look down at my feet with a sigh. "I guess that's fair. But I wouldn't..."

I hear Ava hitch her backpack. She's hesitating. She definitely doesn't want to get any closer to me, but if she turns around, she's admitting some part of her is afraid, and we both know she doesn't want to do that. What she's hoping is that I'll move, I'm guessing. Which is too bad for her, because now that she's holding still, I'm not going anywhere.

"You don't need to be afraid of me."

"I'm not afraid of you," she says, looking haughty. Haughty or not, she doesn't move a single inch closer to me. "But I'm not talking to you either."

I shake my head. "I know how this looks, but it definitely isn't what you think."

"Nice try, Clara, but Lily already told us. We know you weren't arrested for running a stop sign or whatever. You were targeting people!"

Her words douse me like ice water. *Lily told them.* A breeze kicks up, and I shiver, crossing my arms over my chest. It was one thing to think she panicked and lied to her parents. I could even believe she was still panicked, maybe even more so, when the police got involved. But telling our friends?

"What exactly did Lily tell you?"

"You know what she told us," Ava says. She shoves her hands into her pockets and fidgets. Her eyes are darting down the street. To the windows in the houses around us.

"Well, it's not true," I say. "I don't want to hurt anyone. I've never hurt—"

But I stop myself before I finish, because we both know that isn't true. In my mind, I feel Cadence's arm in my grip. I hear the awful gasp she made before she fell and the sickening *thump*, *thump*, *thump* of her body tumbling down those stairs. The muted snap that I later learned was her tibia breaking. And then her scream, the one that replays in my mind on sleepless nights.

"Just let me go already," Ava says, gesturing at me to move.

So I do. I step backward off the sidewalk to give her space. I suppose it doesn't matter now. I know now that Lily is letting me take the fall for this.

No. She's making me take the fall. Not just with the police—with everyone.

And it hasn't even been a challenge for her. People were ready to believe that I'm in trouble again. This is what they expect of me, and Lily must have known that. Framing me was the easy part. Explaining why Lily would do it feels trickier.

TWELVE

I wake the next morning with a stiff neck and a cottony mouth. I reach automatically for my phone, my palm patting the contents of my end table for a few half-conscious seconds. Then I remember. My phone isn't here. It's sitting in an evidence locker downtown.

This fact daisy-chains to my arrest and Lily's betrayal and the folder with a recipe for parking lot bombs. Queasiness comes over me in a hot wave. I sit up, sweaty and sick. Am I going to throw up?

I take one breath and then several more. The waves of heat and nausea recede. What time is it? Again I reach for my phone, instinct overruling memory for a split second. I look around my room. My desk looks mostly undisturbed, but my backpack is missing from its normal perch on the chair. Also part of the evidence, along with the laptop.

In the kitchen, I hear Mom grabbing her keys. Opening the cabinet with the coffee mugs. So it's morning, but what time? I scour my room for something that will tell me and laugh at the absurdity of such a basic piece of information being so difficult to find. I give up, waiting until I hear my mom leave for work.

Then I slip outside. I walk down the hallway and into the kitchen. The stove helpfully informs me that it's 7:08. A note on the counter tells me she hasn't forgotten yesterday's horrors.

Clara,

I'll be home around 2 p.m. Call me if you need me. Please try to eat something.

Love,
Mom

I shuffle toward the kitchen. George materializes at my feet, but disappears when I fail to produce some snacks to share. No way can I eat something right now. So what do I do? I can't go to school. Can't call anyone or try to figure out what's going on.

I spot the card from Officer Fleming—now Detective Fleming I guess—on the counter. She helpfully jotted the time for my second interview at the police station this afternoon, but until then I guess I just sit here and...what? Knit a scarf? I can't imagine anything distracting me from the whole I've-been-arrested-for-plotting-a-terrorist-attack situation.

I start pacing the house again. A loop of terrifying what-ifs races through my mind. I have to stop this. I need to focus on what I actually know and how it might help.

I can't change those text messages, but that folder was not mine. Can I prove it? Lily told me to hold it, but we were in the car, so no one would have seen. Will there be fingerprints? I don't know. But what feels more frightening is that I don't know why she would have any of this to begin with. Why would Lily want to hurt someone?

I can admit things weren't normal with her. The lack of calls and texts. The quietness. Hell, even where she parked yesterday. The murder conversation stuff wasn't the first clue that something was wrong. It's just the first one I noticed.

"So what the hell is going on with you, Lily?"

My voice is a surprise in the quiet of our small house. The sink drips. The fridge begins to hum. George trundles in from another room, his tags jangling. I stare at my dog's dark eyes, thinking about my question and finding no answers.

And even if I wave off the giant-ass *why* that's looming all over this mess, there's still the *how*. How would she know I'd take the bait of that conversation? She's been my friend long enough to know me pretty damn well, but she couldn't have predicted everything I'd do.

I have to be missing something. I need to look at our

conversations again. I stop short, automatically grabbing for my phone, which of course is not around. I growl, and George tilts his head. Figuring this out is impossible without a phone or laptop. Even my old iPhone with the cracked screen and the two-hour battery life would be a dream right—

Wait.

Do I still have that phone?

I am moving toward my bedroom before the thought is fully formed. We did not turn that phone in when we got my new one last year. I saved for months, and Mom upgraded her phone plan, which offered the same discount as a trade-in.

I remember laughing at her at the time for tucking it away, but she said, *If you break yours, you'll be glad we kept it.*

I check my desk, the boxes under my bed, even my underwear drawer. I search the box of random cords and chargers in the hall closet. Then the junk drawer. Then the tub of random shit underneath the TV stand. Maybe the police took it. They could have taken it, because it doesn't seem to be here.

Except there is one place I haven't checked.

I drag a chair into our galley kitchen. Move the spoon rest so I can prop one foot on the narrow sliver of counter between the stove and the fridge. The cabinet above the fridge is nearly impossible to reach, which is why it's where all things go to die in our house.

Inside, I find the mandoline slicer we've never used, a pair of weird candleholders, and a jar of dead batteries. Then I find a small plastic tub. More cords. Random screws. My fingers brush something cool and hard.

I pull it out and feel a rush of excitement. There it is—a small metal-and-glass rectangle with a cracked screen and a yellowing plastic case. It takes an hour to charge it. It takes another hour for me to figure out how the hell to navigate the Apple help center to restore my phone's data and reactivate this phone. By the time I'm done with all that, the phone is hot to the touch and glitching again. Forgot about this little problem. I power it down and put it back on the charger. And then I wait.

Twenty-five minutes later, I can't stand it anymore. I power it back up. My phone loads, all the familiar icons popping into place behind the cracked glass. And then my messages load. Some part of me expects something more. A deluge of missed calls and text messages, that little red number in the corner creeping up, up, up.

But, no. There are three missed calls from numbers I don't recognize. Spam, most likely. And four text messages.

My upcoming dentist appointment.

A message from Ohio Northern University's College of Pharmacy inviting me to an informational session.

A similar message from Northwestern University.

And one more from Gretchen.

Gretchen. I haven't heard from her since…well, probably since Cadence.

I click on her name and double-check the icon just in case it's some sort of hack or scam. Her profile picture is a green anime-style monster. It looks like something Gretchen would choose. Her face flashes through my mind. She has hard eyes, a sharp chin, and jet-black hair that she always wears in a severe bob. Despite all this, she's a softie, and I would know.

After all, Gretchen didn't break the lock on the gate that night at Cadence's. She didn't get into the hot tub or try to figure out how to get the outdoor stereo loaded up. And when the back deck light came on and Cadence appeared at the top of the stairs, shocked and annoyed to see us, Gretchen apologized. While I bounded up those same stairs with wet feet and a loud laugh, Gretchen pleaded for us to go.

But we didn't go. Not until I destroyed everything.

I tap to open the message beside Gretchen's name. It is the first time she has texted me in close to two years, but her message doesn't bother with any long-time-no-text pleasantries.

Gretchen: Were you really going to do this?

I know she's talking about the plan in the folder. And the fact that Gretchen is talking about it tells me something I didn't know. Lily may have only texted our friend group, but gossip travels fast. Now, everyone knows.

THIRTEEN

I tap out a response. The cracks in the screen make it difficult to get it right.

Me: It's not my plan. I know how it sounds, but I swear. Not me.

Lily's name is on my fingertips. I want to type it in. The flare of anger is so sudden and hungry that I'm sure it will consume me. But in the end, I leave it off. Hit Send and drop my phone on the counter.

Gretchen's response is almost instantaneous.

Gretchen: That's not the word around here. People think it's legit.

Me: What people?

Gretchen: You don't already know?

Me: Maybe. Have my suspicions.

Gretchen: I'm sorry. I shouldn't get involved.

I don't blame her. What happened with Cadence changed all of our lives overnight. Britt and I got probation, but Britt's mom decided she couldn't handle her wild daughter, so Britt wound up in Columbus with her grandparents. Cadence spent the summer at home. Sophomore year she won the exchange program in Switzerland, and it was off to private school after that. But Gretchen was stuck here like me. She wasn't completely ostracized, because she tried to do the right thing that night. But the rumors couldn't have been easy to navigate.

Me: I get it. Thanks for texting.

There is a long moment when I think it's done. It's enough time for me to think of all the car sing-alongs and late-night ice cream runs that made me love hanging with Gretchen. And then another message pops underneath mine.

Gretchen: It's Lily. I know you're friends, but she's saying a lot of shit. Be careful, 2C.

CC. My heart squeezes. Gretchen is the only friend who kept using that nickname which everyone would say as "Toosey," after junior high. And I remember with awful clarity exactly when she used it last.

"Let's go, Toosey!" Gretchen says. She's at the bottom of the stairs, trembling. "Please!"

"Just listen to her!" Cadence hisses, her arms crossed over her chest. "Go!"

"You're both killjoys," I say, my teeth chattering. Water pours off me, pooling onto the stairs around my feet. Everything drips.

I pull Cadence's arm, almost slipping with the effort. "Just get in! Hang out with us!"

"Come on!" Gretchen says again.

In the hot tub, Britt laughs and laughs. Cadence ignores them both, jerking her arm free of my grip. She keeps looking back at her house, and I don't know why, but her Snoopy nightgown makes me giggle. Snoopy! Even now when we are five weeks away from the end of school and us being official sophomores.

"You have to go!" She looks angry.

"No one's awake. Stop being so prissy!" I burp sharp cherries. One hard seltzer, stolen from the fridge at Britt's house. I'd never tried one before, and it went right to my head.

"Stop being a baby, and get down here," Britt says, splashing wildly in the hot tub below.

I reach for Cadence again. "Five minutes, that's all I'm asking!"

"I'm serious, Clara! You can't be here." Cadence twists, looking back at the dark windows on her house. "Just get out!"

"Okay, I will, I will. But first—you're getting in!" I lunge for her, my laugh too loud, my hug too eager, my feet slipping on those wet stairs.

My head spins, and then it isn't my head; it's my body spinning. Tilting. My grip tightens on Cadence, all animal instinct. And then we fall. We tumble backward, a tangle of limbs and thumping and pain. My knee scrapes the lip of the step. Splinters push into my palms. My ankle twists and pain hits like a lightning crack.

Something snaps. I hear it so clearly. And then Cadence screams,

The house lights bloom to life, as blinding bright as the scream is loud.

"Cadence?" An adult voice—still inside the door maybe. Swinging it open?

Crazy sloshing and swearing behind me and the slap of wet feet.

"Shit, we gotta run! Run!" Britt screams.

"I'm not leaving her!" Gretchen says, looking up at me. "We can't leave her like this!"

Hard fingers on my arm drag me back. Britt's fingers. Pulling and panicked and insistent.

"Clara, let's go!"

Britt starts running. I stumble toward her. But Gretchen kneels beside our screaming friend, and reaches for Cadence's hand.

George bumps his wet nose into my arm, startling me out

of my memories. I stroke the top of his head and try to tether myself back to the world. George goes suddenly still, tensing under my hand.

"What is it?" I ask, even as the doorbell rings.

He thunders toward the entry, barking like he's lost every one of his marbles. I chase after him, finally snagging his collar.

"Just a minute," I say, hauling him into my room.

I return to the kitchen, some delusional part of me hoping that it's Ava or, hell, maybe Nate dredging up some old former-boyfriend fondness to check on me. But then I see a telltale sliver of navy blue and a distinctive hat outside the window.

The doorbell rings again, and I jump.

A police officer. There's an officer at my door, and this time there's no one here but me. My heart bangs against my ribs. George lets out a long and desperate howl inside my bedroom.

When the knock comes again, I know I have no choice but to answer.

I twist the knob and pull the door open.

"Afternoon, Clara."

"Officer Grimes," I say, exhaling his name in a rush. My shoulders sag in relief, but then I see he isn't smiling. My heart falls. He holds out a box.

"I'm here to deliver some printed assignments from your classes. We were informed that you don't currently have a laptop at home."

I take the box awkwardly. "Wouldn't it have been easier to give me a school loaner laptop?"

It's his turn to look uncomfortable now. "That wasn't permitted."

"Right," I say. To my horror, my throat feels thick and my eyes are welling with tears. I try to blink them back. "Well, thank you for bringing it by."

"You're welcome." Grimes looks at me then. Officer Grimes met with my probation officer, Ms. Chang, Mom, and me the day before I started back after suspension. There were only a few weeks left in my freshman year.

The meeting was brief and dry and full of words like *expectations* and *behavior* and *compliance*. I barely said a word. After school released for the day, Officer Grimes walked me back to my academic meeting with Mr. Philpot. We crossed the first half of the hall in complete silence, me dreading the idea of all the stares and whispers that would be waiting for me the next morning, And then, Officer Grimes blew out a sigh.

"That may have been the most boring probation officer I've ever met," he said, and I laughed, for real and out loud.

Officer Grimes has made me laugh dozens of times since that day. It hurts to see him watching me like this, with clear hesitation in his eyes.

"Grimes?" He nods and I go on. "I need to tell you something."

His hand comes up immediately to stop me. "I can't talk to you about any of this, Toosey."

Hearing my nickname softens the edges of this awful situation. My shoulders drop, and I feel like I can breathe.

"I know. I just..." I don't honestly know what to say, but there's a vague unease growing in me. Because I know all the ways I'm shitty, and there are plenty, but I didn't make that plan. Lily put that folder together. And she's still in that school.

I take a breath, "Lily put that folder in my backpack. I told the police, but I don't know if anyone told you. And you should know, just in case."

"That's a very serious accusation."

I put up my hands. "I'm not trying to make an accusation. I don't even know what the stuff in that folder means. Hopefully nothing. But it's scary."

He nods. "I'll keep it in mind. We've taken a lot of precautions to keep Tusky High safe. I hope you're taking care of yourself too."

I laugh bitterly. "Yeah. No idea how I'll do that, but thank you."

Grimes pauses then, lips pressed together like he's not sure if he should say what's coming next. But then he speaks all the same. "If this plan isn't yours, try to think about why it might have been left in your bag. If you think of something, tell the investigators. It might help."

"Thanks," I say. "I'll keep it in mind."

He smiles and touches two fingers to the brim of his hat.

I watch him walk back to his car, not a department cruiser, but an older gray Ford Ranger. I wave as he drives away and let George out of my room. I sit at the table with my box of books and papers. A packet of Precalc worksheets sits at the top, and the mere glimpse of an equation inspires me to push the entire box away.

Officer Grimes has a point. I can't just keep sitting here waiting for someone to tell me why this is happening. I have to figure it out. Which is a challenge, because I don't even remember who the hell was on the list to begin with.

I remember Paxton and Mr. Droesch, but what about the others? I wish I remembered more about that formula sheet or the list.

Wait a minute.

I stand up, realizing I took pictures of everything in the folder. I was going to send them to my mom, but I was too afraid of what it might do to Lily. I changed my mind, but I didn't delete those pictures. They're still on my phone.

Of course *that* phone is downtown, but my photos automatically upload online. So can I get them?

I have to update the photos app twice on my old phone, which takes forever. Finally, the updates are done, and the connections are restored. My photos app loads hundreds and hundreds of pictures from the last year.

I watch the succession of thumbnails flash open on my splintered phone screen. Fragments of a life that feels like it belongs to someone else now.

Lily and me with a giant stack of pancakes. Me at the Chemagination Finalists Reception. Holding the ribbon. Hugging my mother. Standing awkwardly next to tall Jackson on our single less-than-zero-chemistry coffee date. In Lily's room two weeks ago with her preschool ballet tutus on our heads. Our faces bright with smiles, open-mouthed and laughing.

The last three images appear blank with a download symbol on them. They're too recent to see, but I can log in online to attempt a download. Which…is impossible with this phone. The website refuses to load. I need a computer, and Mom's old iPad is the closest we've got, and she keeps that in her bag to read at lunch.

Still, the photos exist. There is a chance, and a decent one, that I'll be able to download them or at least view them if I can log in. Maybe there's something on those papers that will make sense of this or maybe prove it wasn't me.

It feels like a long shot. And it also feels like the only shot I have.

FOURTEEN

Mom calls on break to remind me that I have a second round of questioning at the police department and a meeting with my attorney this afternoon. Now that they've had time to go through my backpack, laptop and phone, they have new questions. Or maybe the same old questions, just to see if my story sticks. Whatever the plan, the meeting isn't until 3:00 and since it's 11:15, I've got time.

I fling my mostly empty old backpack over my shoulder and walk the twelve blocks to our nearest library branch. It's been a long time since I've been to the library. Last summer, Lily and I were obsessed with winning one of the summer reading prizes. We doubled up checkouts, putting everything on my card to see if it increased our chances. In the end, I won the same sticker and ice cream combo everyone else did, but with the side effect of reading a fair bit more than I usually do.

By the time I reach the library, I realize that as familiar as this place is, it's the first time I've needed a computer, and I have no idea how to go about requesting one. Is there a fee? Do I have to tell them what I'm looking up?

I scan the lobby area, with its bulletin board crowded with advertisements for tai chi classes and early-literacy programs. An old man in a tweed newsboy cap reads a newspaper in a maroon armchair, and just past him a little girl rushes toward a checkout station, dropping board books behind her as she goes.

I walk a little farther into the main room, where a woman behind the desk looks up with a brief smile before returning to her work. Next to the newspapers and the new-release shelves is a computer area with two open seats. So how does this work? Can I just sit down, or what?

A sign above the nearest computer tells me that the first hour is open access, but if I need longer, I can book an appointment with any librarian. That feels like an invitation for a librarian to ask me questions I don't want to answer, so I'm hoping I can wrap things up before then.

I sit down and quickly open a private window in the browser (probably overkill on a public library computer, but whatever) and log in to my photo account. While I wait for my photos to download, I pull out my phone and double-check the text messages Lily and I exchanged yesterday.

Lily: How serious would it be?

Me: Depends. Some explosives would be small or start a fire. Others would blow the whole thing to pieces. Explosives = options.

Lily: People could get seriously hurt...

Me: Hell yeah they could. Maybe even killed.

Lily: With firecrackers or something?

Me: Lots of things would do it. Things almost everyone can buy.

Lily: That's scary.

Me: Chemistry is scary as hell. That's one of the reasons I love it.

There is something about this exchange. My mind searches for a word that fits the uneasy feeling looking at these words. It doesn't quite sound like Lily. The whole thing feels...

Scripted.

It comes to me like a lightning bolt. I feel sick when I read the texts again, because the word fits. It's as if Lily planned every single part of that exchange to make me look like some kind of supervillain. And it worked like a charm.

On the monitor, the final thumbnail image sharpens, pulling me out of my thoughts. And there they are, one, two, three: the pages from the folder. I click the option to load the photos on my crappy, glitchy phone. After a quick look around to be sure no one is watching, I pull up the first photo. My stomach feels wobbly as it fills the screen. The formulas.

They're familiar, just as I thought the other day. I'm fairly sure at least some of these formulas were from the explosives section of my Chemagination project. So they could theoretically blow things up, the key word being *theoretically*. Being aware of dangerous chemical combinations is one thing; controlling or predicting explosions that could result from those combinations is another entirely.

What if I prove that the plan wouldn't work?

I look at the formulas again. As far as I can tell, they involve natural gas explosions—fireworks and propane tanks stored improperly. These would not be viable in this scenario. Not in the real world. I can prove it, I think. But since I don't have my laptop with my project work, I'll sort of need to reconstruct what I know.

I sit back in my chair and look around. I'm pretty sure I can still use my library card, even if I'm arrested. Or out on bail or whatever this is. I zip back to the chemistry shelves on autopilot and grab three thick volumes that I used during my research and that probably haven't been checked out since.

Back at the self-checkout station, I type in my card number. The computer beeps, a box popping up on the screen.

Unable to check out. Please see a staff member.

Have I landed on a library bad-guy list because of this folder situation? Okay, I need to stop. I know I'm feeling like the whole world is against me, but an all-points bulletin going out to every organization in town seems a little far-fetched.

I double-check my card number at the top of the screen and try scanning the first book again. The same beep.

Unable to check out. Please see a staff member.

I tense and look around. I don't want to see a staff member. I barely want to make fleeting eye contact with people right now.

My eyes drift to the *Exit* sign over the front door. Tempting. But then what happens? My options for research completely suck right now, and Google is not the best place to find this sort of information. I need these damn books, and I know my card should be fine, so this is probably some quick-fix thing that shouldn't come between me and a possible solution to this nightmare.

The woman at the desk is sorting a cart of books and talking to a small child about the very cool ant farm on the second floor. She's maybe a little older than my mom, but she's giving off energy that's more I-make-my-own-granola than libraries-should-be-quiet, which is encouraging. Her name tag says *Jody*, and the button next to it informs me that reading is my superpower. I sort of wish my superpower was convincing the police I'm innocent, but fine.

I wait for Jody to finish up. When it's my turn, she smiles at me like I'm a normal person. Not a beloved teacher's pet or a chemistry whiz or a potential school parking lot bomber. Just a person with a question. I explain and she offers to look up my account.

"I don't have my card, but I have the number memorized," I say, and then I give her my card number.

She pulls it up on the computer and scans the screen with a nod. "Okay, here's the issue. There are three books out on the account that were due a few months ago."

I shake my head. "I don't have anything checked out. I returned everything last summer. Didn't I?"

"I do see that big return you're talking about, but these three books weren't checked out in the summer. They were taken out at the beginning of January."

January? I'm completely confused now. "I don't think that's me. I had mono in January. I haven't been in at all since the summer reading program."

Jody has me verify a couple of my summer titles and then frowns. "This is your account. Is there anyone else who might have used this number? A sibling or a parent?"

Anyone else. My face feels flash fire hot. A memory forms in my mind—Lily at the counter with a stack of picture books. Determined to add them to her total count because a book is a book. She punched in the number without even asking. A million times she did it this summer. I realize Jody is still waiting for a response because I've gone catatonic.

"Is there maybe someone else?" she ventures again, quietly and slowly.

"Yes," I choke out. "It's possible. Can you tell me what books were checked out?"

"*Chemical Impact*, third edition, *The Perkinson Guide to*..."

Jody's voice fades out to the rush of blood behind my ears. My face feels strange and numb, and my vision is going gray at the edges. Jody hands me a slip of paper with the titles she's jotted down, and I take it with a shaking hand. I thank her for the help. And then I fold the paper in half and shove it into my backpack, because it does not matter what books she says I have. I was bedridden for nearly the entire month of January, but Lily? Lily was healthy as a horse. And apparently she was in a library mood again, because she had to be the one that used my card.

Has she been planning this whole thing since January? Are these books part of it? I feel sick as I make my way slowly back through the lobby. Lily was my best friend. She saved my life, and now she's destroying me, and I have no idea how to stop her.

I pause at the door to zip my hoodie, and then I spot something in the corner near the ceiling. Discreet but definitely there. A camera.

I whirl around, searching the other corners in the main room. If Jody notices my sudden stop, she doesn't acknowledge it. She also doesn't notice or interfere with my sudden frantic camera search, the way I gawk at every high shelf and corner of the ceiling. I count four cameras in the main room, and each one of them is pointed at one of the checkout stations.

Whoever checked these books out is on camera.

Hope flares through my chest for the first time since Lily stopped sharing her location two nights ago. It isn't much, but it's something. If Lily is on camera, it might not prove I'm not guilty. But it will sure the hell make her look a little less innocent.

FIFTEEN

The sun is out when I leave the library, and it feels like a good sign. My stomach grumbles as I walk, and I realize I haven't eaten a single thing since this whole mess started.

The Neat-o Burrito food truck is right around the corner. Waiting tables at a buffet hall in Dayton has the worst hours and zero tips, but I'm pretty sure I have enough in my account for two chicken tacos.

I eat them as I walk home, saving the last bite for George. He gobbles it greedily the second I'm in the house, and I down a full glass of water at the kitchen sink while he stares up at me adoringly.

It's 1:04 p.m. Still some time before the police interview and our appointment with John, the ancient attorney. I need to use it wisely.

I hole up in my room, pulling up the photos from the folder

again. I pass the formulas, moving on to the second paper, with names and license plates. It sends a chill up my spine. Why would Lily target these people?

Most of them seem more closely connected to me than her. Maybe because this isn't a real plan, just a list that would work to frame me.

Paxton and Nate make sense, from a distance. There's no love lost between Paxton and me, and Nate is my ex-boyfriend. I could see them inventing a motive for Gretchen, who severed our friendship. It would make sense, but it wouldn't be accurate. Gretchen had every reason to end our friendship. So what about Mr. Droesch and Ms. Chang? I'm not crazy about either of them, but I don't have particular beef with either.

Why these people? I try to think of common threads, but it all feels...flimsy. Would anyone even buy this as a real threat if it was attached to Lily and not me? No way. This is because of my reputation. If I accused Lily with this evidence, they would laugh me out of the police station.

Because Lily is a girl you can trust. And I'm a girl who is bound to wind up in trouble.

My mom gets home at 2:15, and I meet her in the kitchen. I don't know if it's just me, but the lines around her mouth look deeper. The last thing I want to do is to bring up the fact that we're leaving for the police station in fifteen minutes, but talking about anything else feels ridiculous. But I should try, right?

"Hey, how was your day?" I ask.

Her flat eyes are her first answer. I'm surprised when she offers, "Not the best, as I'm sure you're aware. Have you thought any more about what John said to you?"

I haven't. Not specifically, at least, but I nod anyway. "Yes, and I need to talk to you before we get to the attorney. About all of this."

Mom tries for a neutral expression. It's hard though. It's always just been the two of us, so I know her inside out. If something flits across her face, I know what that something is before she completely hides it. This time it's a mix of hesitation and annoyance.

"I went to the library today. I was just trying to figure out... I don't know. I guess I was trying to make some sense of this. It barely feels real."

"It feels pretty real to me." She leans back against the counter. Today there are flowers on her scrubs.

"I know this is serious. And I absolutely know how it must feel to you after everything that happened before. But please try to believe me when I tell you I did not do this."

"I want to believe you, but it's hard. You have a history of lying to me about these sorts of issues."

"You're right. I lied at first with the Cadence situation."

Mom shakes her head. "No, not just at first. You lied for *days*, Clara. You swore you did nothing until the lawyer finally teased the truth out of you. Do you remember how many interviews that took?"

My cheeks burn, and my throat feels sticky when I try to swallow. She's right. She's absolutely right. I want to say it was just because I was scared. And I was *so* damn scared. Barely fifteen years old with my first hard seltzer still burning the back of my throat. I don't know what the hell I was thinking lying to everyone. It was fear, yes, but it was more than that.

The small terrible secret of it all is this: I was lost in it. I was hungry for something more than my shitty two-bedroom duplex and hand-me-down school clothes. Something in me was raging against all the girls with hot tubs in their backyards and moms who had time to go shopping and send cookies to school.

That wild, restless part of me burned bright and fast my freshman year. I wanted to feel grown-up and badass, and I did. Stealing eyeliner from the CVS and skipping class just because I could. It all came to a head that night, sneaking through backyards with Gretchen and Britt, drinking a single stolen White Claw from Britt's fridge.

My stomach was empty, and my head was spinning when we busted that latch on Cadence's gate. When we giggled our way across the yard and wrenched the hot tub lid open. Cadence was supposed to be at national travel soccer league tryouts. She wasn't supposed to be there, and she sure the hell wasn't supposed to slip down eight stairs, snapping her tibia, dislocating her kneecap, and tearing a bunch of ligaments to boot.

None of that was supposed to happen. None of it was intended.

Except I didn't accidentally break into her yard. I didn't accidentally open that hot tub or plead with her to come down, pulling her on those wet, slippery stairs. Every single one of those things was a choice I made that caused Cadence to fall.

I can see that now. I should have told the truth the minute it happened and faced the consequences of my actions, but I ran then and lied later. As if I could run fast enough or lie hard enough to change the truth into something I could live with.

"I did lie to you," I say, my voice rough. "I was young and stupid, and I was horrified by what I'd done. But I'm not lying now."

Mom sighs, and I can see the uncertainty in her eyes.

"Mom, planning something like this *isn't* me. What happened to Cadence was my shittiest mistake, but it *was* a mistake. I didn't plan it. I lost control, and then I panicked."

Mom meets my eyes then. She is looking at me, not around me. And she is finally, truly listening.

"Planning a school parking lot bombing? Could you see me doing that?" I ask.

Mom watches me for a long beat. And then her expression softens. "No. I can't."

My ribs unclench. Not enough to make everything better but enough that my next breath comes easier. "Okay."

She shakes her head. "It's not okay. No matter what I think, they found this folder and these plans in *your* backpack. How did this stuff get there?"

"Lily," I say. "I told you, Lily gave me the folder."

"Lily is a good kid. It doesn't sound like her."

"Can we not pretend that you suddenly love Lily and believe she's wonderful?"

Mom has never loved Lily. She's never said it out loud, and I've never specifically asked, but there was always the tiniest edge of tension when Lily was nearby.

"She wasn't my favorite, but that doesn't mean I think she's evil," Mom says. "What possible reason would she have for setting you up?"

"I still don't know," I say, heaving a sigh. "But I can tell you what happened that day."

Mom nods, urging me to continue. So I do. This time she listens when I talk about the weird conversation in the car, the long night at home, how I texted and called, and how Lily ignored me and stopped sharing her location. How she literally severed our connection without a single word. And then I tell her about the checked-out books and the cameras I spotted in the library.

"We need to tell the police," she says. "You have to talk to them."

"I will, but I'm worried that we don't have a lawyer who is really going to help. Is there any way we can call Tim?"

"We can't afford Tim." Mom lets that hang there for a few long seconds before she goes on. "I'm still paying for your last case with him."

"Okay, then we talk to the police. And we hope to God they believe me."

Mom's blank face tells me everything I don't want to know. She doesn't think they'll believe me. The police are like everyone else. They already think I'm guilty.

SIXTEEN

John Pruitt meets us in the lobby of the police station. His thin white hair is sticking up in a different place today, and he smells like coffee and the hand lotion my grandma used.

"Good afternoon, Claire. Mrs. Cutler."

Mom and I exchange a look.

"It's Clara," I say.

"And it's *Ms.* Cutler," Mom says.

Before John can say anything in reply, a tall, broad-shouldered man with a bit of a gut arrives. Detective Jones introduces himself. He has the hard, pinched look of someone with a temper, and he walks heavily, leading us to the interview room.

"Have a seat," he says, taking off his blazer. He rolls up the cuffs on his shirt, and I can't help but to think he looks like a drill sergeant dressed up as a history teacher. We all take seats around the table.

I hear footsteps in the doorway, and then, to my surprise, Officer Fleming steps in. Her mouth turns up just a little at the corners, like she's at the edge of a smile, and I can't tell if it's friendliness or just the shape of her face, but it makes me feel better.

"Hello," I say automatically.

Officer Fleming smiles. "Hey, Clara. Can I get you both some water?"

"I'd like to talk about the prosecutor's plans for charges," John says, but Detective Jones waves that off.

"You know that's not why we're here, John. We have some additional questions." He sits down in the chair across from us. Now that we're closer, I can see that he has very white teeth and sweat stains under the arms of his light blue button-down.

"Can I tell you something before we get started?" I ask.

Fleming starts to nod, but Jones cuts her off. "No."

"The folder in my daughter's backpack wasn't hers," Mom says, not bothering to ask. "She came to the school to talk to Officer Grimes."

"Who put the folder in your bag?" Officer Fleming asks.

"Lily Dalton. My best friend."

"Why—"

Detective Jones clears his throat to cut off Officer Fleming. Then he lifts his hand to make sure she gets his point.

"I'll ask the questions for now," Jones says, "and we've noted your claim that the folder belongs to Lily."

Officer Fleming takes a seat in a chair at the side of the room, where she begins to take notes.

Detective Jones pushes a piece of paper across the table toward me. I recognize the list of cars and license plates and corresponding owners. "Tell me about the people on this list."

"Like my mom said, this isn't my list."

"But you know these people?"

I nod. "Mr. Droesch is a teacher and Ms. Chang is our principal. The other people on the list are students."

The smile Detective Jones offers is patronizing as hell. "How about you give me a little more? Tell me how you feel about these people. What's your relationship with them?"

I freeze for a moment, looking at my mom. And then John. But since neither says anything, I try again.

"Okay. Mr. Droesch teaches English. He's not my favorite, but he's no one's favorite. Ms. Chang is fine. I've never had any problems with her."

"Never? Not even when she initially excluded you from the Chemagination team?"

I open my mouth and close it. It feels like ancient history, and yeah, I hated when she called me in for a meeting to lay out expectations. But I understood.

"No, not even then," I say honestly, though my cheeks feel hot from remembering it.

"Uh-huh." Jones leans back. "And what about Paxton?"

I shrug. "We don't get along."

"And why is that?"

"We've just never clicked." It's a lie. I think of pill bug races and sharing Capri-Suns on my porch stoop. Maybe that isn't enough to call us friends. But we were friendly.

Until sophomore year. When I got back from winter break, Lily and I were suddenly friends, and that was enough for most people to relax. But not Paxton. Even though he was on his way out of the popular crowd for whatever reason, his distance from me seemed to morph into hatred.

"Are you telling me that you and Paxton simply don't get along?"

This feels like a trap, but there's no way to elaborate on this because I honestly don't know what his deal is with me. I nod in response but he waits for me to say more.

"This feels irrelevant to the charges being brought against my client," John says.

Jones just raises his hands, all innocence. "I'm just trying to understand Ms. Cutler's relationship to the people on this list. That feels relevant."

John sighs and looks at me. "You can answer the question."

I definitely don't want to answer the question, especially since it's clear everyone in this room already knows all the answers I'm going to give.

"I honestly don't know. He's just been really weird with me ever since…"

Jones leans forward. "Ever since the first time you were arrested for hurting a fellow student? Were you friends back then?"

"I thought you were here to ask questions about the current situation," Mom says. There is the thinnest edge to her tone that tells me she doesn't like this man.

Detective Jones holds my gaze for a beat longer, then taps the list. "What about the others? Let's go on to Gretchen and Nate."

"Gretchen and I were friends, and I'm sure you know why we aren't now since you also know about what happened two years ago. Nate and I dated for a while, and then we broke up."

"After you were arrested," Jones clarifies.

"Yes, after I was arrested, but we haven't had any issues since. I don't have problems with any of these people but Paxton, and that's more about Paxton's issues with me. I'm telling you, this list is not mine, so I can't make sense of it, but if you would give me a chance, I do have something that might help."

My panic is coming through in my volume. I try to steady my breath. Mom takes my hand, but my fingers still shake.

"All right, Clara. Tell us your side of things," Detective Jones says. He crosses his arms like he's ready for a great joke.

I sigh. "Two nights ago, my best friend brought up a bizarre thing in the car. It seemed like she was venting, going off about people who should get taken down. It felt like a joke."

"What do you mean by *joke*?" Officer Fleming asks.

Detective Jones whirls to look at her, the chair squeaking. It's crystal clear he doesn't like her asking, but I'm a big fan of Officer Fleming and her question. It's the first one that doesn't sound like someone's just trying to wrap up the details of a confession I never gave.

"I mean the way you vent after a horrible day," I say. "Just dumb exaggerations and threats. The way some people say they'd light their house on fire if they found a nest of spiders. It's not true, but it's funny."

"You think it's funny to talk about bombing cars?" Jones asks.

"No!" I stop myself. Take a breath and look at my mom apologetically. When I start again, my voice is very quiet, but I walk them through the weird interactions and conversation in the car. And then I talk about the folder. "Just before we started driving, she handed me this folder to hold because her backpack was in the trunk, and I totally forgot about it until the next morning. When I found it, I tried to take it to Officer Grimes at the school."

"It seems convenient that you didn't give it back or take a peek."

"I completely forgot. She was acting really weird. I was worried about her."

"First you say it was all a joke, but now you're saying it was weird," Detective Jones says. "It's not adding up here, Clara. How close are you and Lily?"

"It *was* a joke, and then she kind of wouldn't let it go. That's when it started getting strange. And we're super close. She's literally my best friend."

"Your best friend." Jones leans forward, looking surprised by that. "Your best friend, who gave you a folder to hold that you totally forgot about. Your very best friend, who you were getting along with just fine over the last couple of weeks."

My breath catches. There's something I don't know here. This detective has something he hasn't shared. I look at John and my mom helplessly, but they look as baffled as me.

"I want you to take a look at something," Jones says. He pulls a laptop out of his briefcase and sets it on the table between us. A video. Security footage of what looks like of an empty parking lot. Or not quite empty.

He presses Play at the moment when I realize it's the school parking lot and Lily's car is almost center screen. There's Lily, grainy on the recording but clearly her, with her long pale hair. She's putting stuff in the back seat of the car.

"This was taken two days ago. Look familiar?" Jones asks.

The question doesn't really need an answer. We all know I

rode home with Lily. But why are we showing that? I see Lily's body suddenly tense. Even the fuzzy video quality and the distance don't hide the obvious stiffness in her body language. It's over-the-top.

And then I see myself walking into the frame.

A chill runs through me, seeing this moment replayed. Knowing this whole scene was captured perfectly by the parking lot cameras, because Lily wasn't parked where she usually parks. Lily was right smack-dab in the middle of the camera's gaze. And it feels...convenient.

Scripted.

The word comes back to me as video-Lily hesitates, and I remember it. I was annoyed when she ignored me calling her name. I thought she was distracted, and I can see that irritation in my body language too as video-me walks around her to get into the car. Lily stays by the driver's door. She looks left and right. Like she doesn't want to get in the car.

Back then it was an unremarkable moment of annoyance. Looking at it now in this cold metal chair in this horrible room, it's different. Lily looks she doesn't want me in her car.

"Does this look like best friends who can't wait to hang out?" Jones asks. "Is that what you see, Clara? Or does this look like Lily is uncomfortable and looking for a way out?"

On the screen Lily looks left and right again, her hand briefly touching her throat. She hesitates before opening the driver's side door. She could win an Oscar for the silent performance she's giving in this video, and that's exactly what this is. She's putting on a show.

Video Lily gets into the car. You can't see us inside, but I remember the conversation. And when the car begins to slowly roll forward, I remember that too. I noticed how strangely she was driving, and now I know why. She knew this was being recorded.

"This video is only one of the things that makes me question your story, Ms. Cutler."

I can't speak. I know I'm being judged for my silence, because they think I feel guilty, but all I actually feel is rage. From the folder to the library books to the spot she picked in the parking lot. How damn far has Lily gone to destroy me?

SEVENTEEN

Detective Jones leaves before I can even mention the library, and John takes Mom and me to a coffee shop near the station to debrief. My mom doesn't touch her Americano. She stares in stone-faced silence as I try to explain that Lily was performing in that parking lot and that it's just one more part of a big setup. John tries to listen, but I can tell he doesn't believe me. Who could blame them? I sound like I'm laying out a wild conspiracy theory.

I'm briefly saved when a waitress stops to drop off an egg sandwich for John.

I take a deep breath, trying to calm my voice. "Look, I know this all sounds bonkers, but there is one piece of it I can prove. I think Lily checked books out on my library card."

John puts down his sandwich to consult a paper in his case. He pushes it toward me, and the words *three or four books about chemistry* are highlighted in a long stretch of handwritten text. "Three or four books, correct?"

I go cold. "How do you know about those?"

"Because it was part of the initial report. Lily said she was with you when you checked them out, and she noticed it because the content felt odd because you didn't have any large projects or unusual tests coming up in Chemistry."

The chill that's come over me intensifies. How deep does this shit go with Lily? How carefully did she weave this story?

"They were checked out in January, but I had mono. I think it was Lily. And there are cameras in the library."

"You didn't leave the house at all?"

"She had mono," Mom says. "She didn't go anywhere."

"But Lily has my card number. I'm sure it was her."

John's face does not change. It's 100 percent clear he does not believe me.

My mom pushes her Americano away. Just an inch or two. "Clara said the library has cameras. Can we have them check the footage?"

John shrugs. "We can try, but most places only keep footage for thirty to sixty days unless there's an incident. Video takes up a tremendous amount of storage space."

"And what if there was an incident?" I ask, even though I know this is a thin chance. "Maybe they kept that day for some other reason?"

"I can call," John says, but he doesn't look very intrigued. He doesn't really look like a guy who wants to defend me or prove my innocence. He looks like a guy who wants me to take a decent plea bargain and call it a day. "You both realize that accepting a plea deal will mean lower charges. You might have probation and community service."

"What I'll have is a criminal record," I say, my voice thick. I think of the John Carroll program and the interview I'm supposed to be scheduling in the next couple of weeks.

Getting into programs like that, let alone college, is hard enough, and that's with an expunged record. Applying with an active probation? Fat chance.

"I've worked so hard to get into college. I want to be a pharmacist. I already have a list of schools, and a criminal record isn't going to help me get into any of them."

"Well, even if you were to have to wait on college for a year, maybe two, these things often work out better than you think in the long run."

I let out an exasperated breath. Clearly, when John was in law school fifty years ago or whatever, things were different. I have scholarships to think about. Loans. Letters of recommendation. There is a window of opportunity in high school to make all the right moves at all the right times. If *anything* goes wrong, that window slams shut forever.

Mom clears her throat. "Other than the folder that anyone

could have put in Clara's backpack, it feels like this entire case would rest on Lily's word against Clara's. This is hugely impactful to her life. What real evidence is there?"

I'm surprised by this. My mother didn't say much in the station. Even after admitting she didn't quite buy the idea of me being a terrorist, she's been quiet and guarded.

John finishes another bite of his sandwich, looking between us mildly. His blue eyes are watery, and the age spots on his hands flex as he puts it down. "I sympathize with your situation, but I'll be frank. The folder doesn't look good. The police have also uncovered that video footage and the library books and the project research for her"—he pauses, consulting the paper again—"household explosives science fair project."

"That was to raise awareness!" I say.

John ignores that. "You also have a recent disciplinary issue at the school—"

"What?" Mom's face shifts in an instant, shock and betrayal clouding her eyes. "What issue? What are you talking about?"

"It wasn't an issue! A girl at school said I pushed her down in the hallway, but I didn't."

I'm not even finished speaking before Mom looks away from us.

"There are also text messages between you and Lily, and—"

"Those messages were staged!" My voice sharpens into a shout. "Lily did this! Why isn't anyone listening to me?"

Mom looks around, and even John pauses, his egg sandwich forgotten, a single crumb of it left on some of the gray stubble on his chin.

The whole cafe has gone quiet. I look around, face burning at the curious eyes watching me. I sound like I'm losing it. I am every unstable person in every movie, and I am mortified.

I lower my gaze and hear the bells over the cafe door behind me. I don't bother to look to see who's come in. I just want to go. John tells us again that he will call us as soon as they set the time for the arraignment. Before that hearing, I'll have to decide how to plead. If I plead not guilty, it will make things harder. If I plead guilty, I will be lying. And I don't want to think about no contest because it feels like me saying I won't even bother to fight it.

When John is finally done, he stands and brushes 40 percent of the egg sandwich crumbs off his shirt. Mom stands next, and I follow last, squeezing my way out of the booth.

Soft whispers erupt behind me. A prickly feeling crawls up the back of my neck—a certainty that I am being watched. That I've *been* watched for a while. John shakes my mother's hand and then mine. He's saying something, but I'm trying to make words out of the whispers I hear behind me. A big table. Lots of people.

Mom puts a tip on the table, and I tense, my neck and face positively crawling. She touches my shoulder briefly and tells me she'll see me after work. I try to follow her, but I stop at the door, because the whispering table has gone quiet now. That silence is its own message, an alert that someone is still watching me.

I turn, just enough to see the large circular booth in the corner and the colorful heap of backpacks piled next to the booth. One of them is a familiar hot pink. Heat blazes up my neck and into my face as I turn fully to take in the familiar faces seated around the table in the back booth.

The Jacksons short and tall. Mariana. Drishti. Ava, of course—who else would have that putrid backpack? And Henry. There are only two people missing from this scene. Lily and me.

I try to turn away, but Ava catches my eye. I expect her to look away, embarrassed by being caught staring. But she lifts her chin and holds my gaze.

"You should probably go before Lily gets here," Jackson Collins says.

Someone else at the table whispers. A hissed "*Don't, Jackson*" that I'm sure comes from Drishti given her flushed cheeks and downcast eyes.

"You've done enough to make things hard for her," Ava says.

Her words sting, but a cough of a laugh comes out of me. Ava doesn't flinch. I shake my head and look at every face around this table.

The Jacksons, enjoying the drama. Mariana, looking faintly sick at the scene. Drishti, who won't look up. And Henry, who is glaring, but not at me. The full force of his expression is aimed at the back of Ava's head.

The hardness of his eyes is the last thing I see before I turn. Ava's laughter trails behind me as I leave.

EIGHTEEN

I walk home from the cafe, wishing I wasn't wearing the loafers that pinch, because all these try-hard clothes didn't make a bit of difference. Everyone sees what they want to see. The detective and John and all those people who called themselves my friends seventy-two hours ago—one slick lie from Lily's perfect lips is all it took for everyone to condemn me.

I could kill her.

The thought slips through me, lighting fast and undeniable. I don't know that it's true. But I know I thought it. I know there's a pulsing, hungry anger trapped behind my ribs, and if I let that anger out, I don't know where it stops. Maybe they're right to believe I'm bad.

I stop at a crosswalk and take a slow breath. I don't have time for navel-gazing or pity parties, I need to do something. And since I'm out of ideas, I think I need help.

I slip inside my house, stripping off my respectable-person outfit, leaving it in a crumpled heap at the foot of my bed. George positions himself directly between the dresser and me, and it's like wrestling with a moose to get around him to grab a pair of yoga pants and my mom's ancient Nine Inch Nails hoodie.

I let George out and pull out my phone, trying to think of who to talk to. Drishti maybe? She's always kind, and she looked pretty uncomfortable with Ava's scene in the diner. We're not exactly close, but who else is there?

Henry.

His face from the cafe is locked in my mind, jaw set and eyes dark. He was pissed for sure, but I have no idea why. If he didn't like her being rude, then he might help me. But if he's angry that she deigned to speak to me at all? I don't know if I can handle Henry Toussaint unleashing cold fury in my direction.

If I were Henry, what would I think about me?

I know I'm far from perfect, but would he think I'm capable of this? It all sounds so ridiculously Machiavellian. Henry knows about what I did to Cadence, but he's also seen me at community litter pickups and working the concessions for all of Lily's tennis competitions. Who knows where his opinion would land.

So, should I talk to him? He's never shown much interest in

Lily, though he's never been outright rude. And of course there's the awful truth that as a Haitian immigrant living in southwest Ohio, Henry probably knows more than I could possibly imagine about being judged unfairly. He might be willing to hear me out. Especially since I've never seen him be anything but kind.

I pull out my phone and try to find him. I don't want to risk anything on socials. Of course, for all I know, the cops are still looking at every text message I send. But no one said I couldn't text. Trouble is, I don't think I have his number. I finally find him on a group chat from a full year ago. Am I really about to text this guy for the first time to help me get out of a criminal charge?

Apparently so.

I settle onto our living room couch, the one that still has wax stains from my third-grade obsession with making my own crayons in the oven, and tap out a text.

Me: Hi, Henry. It's Clara. Do you have a minute?

I instantly feel a twinge of regret and toss my phone on the table. This is stupid. Henry and I aren't *friends*. We've floated around each other's orbits for the entirety of high school, friendly but distant. And now I'm texting him out of the blue asking if I can call him not forty-eight hours after being arrested.

I need to stop thinking of who can help me and get back to figuring out how to get out of this mess. I pick up the phone to text him never mind. But my phone lights up and vibrates in my hand. It's Henry's number.

My heart thumps faster when I press the button to accept the call. "Hello?"

"Hey. It's Henry."

His voice is warm. Gentle.

"Hi," I say stupidly, my voice a bizarre chirp. "How's it going?"

"Clara," he says, his tone telling me he's not buying my fake cheer.

I exhale and close my eyes, feeling calmer. When I speak, it's my real voice. Lower pitched and a little worse for wear. "Hi."

"I wondered if I'd hear from you."

My eyes fly open. "You did? Why?"

Henry's phone shifts. I can hear the distant murmur of traffic, the slightest uptick of his breathing. He's outside somewhere, I think. I imagine him walking. "Maybe you should just tell me why you texted."

"I guess I need to talk to someone about what's happening. Have you heard why I was arrested?"

"Lily texted everyone about the plan to bomb the school parking lot," he says flatly.

I feel myself sag. "Right. Of course."

"So do you want to tell me the truth about what's going on?"

My heart skips three beats. I can't read his tone, and I don't know if I can trust him. But I do know I don't have anyone else lining up to take my calls.

"I'm nervous to talk about this," I say, and I hate the way my voice wobbles.

"How about I go first then?" Henry says. I lean back into my kitchen chair and let him speak. "Lily texted everyone the same day it happened on a separate group chat without you on it. Everyone replied, rushing to comfort her, of course."

He doesn't sound happy about it. "Everyone?" I ask.

"Well, not me and not Drishti. Everyone else."

"Well, Drishti is too pure for this world. And you're..." I honestly don't know why he didn't say anything, so I let the sentence trail off into nothing.

"I'm not convinced that plan is yours," Henry says.

"Why not?" It's a ridiculous question. I should say *thank you* or *no, it's definitely not.*

"Because Lily is a liar," he says simply.

I stand up, feeling like my blood is rushing too fast. Like my whole body is buzzing and jumping. "Well, she is lying about this. This isn't my plan, and I know we don't talk all the time, so I feel sort of stupid dragging you into this, but the truth is, I don't know who else to talk to."

"Very flattering," he says, but he's laughing, a low velvety sound that makes me smile in spite of everything. "Meet me in an hour?"

"Where?"

"At Bon Gou. I'll be in the back."

He hangs up, and I gape at my kitchen wall. I don't know why Henry is helping, but I'm in no position to argue. I need all the help I can get.

NINETEEN

Google helpfully informs me that Bon Gou is a Creole restaurant three miles from my house. The weather is threatening rain, but without a car it's either a bike ride or a long walk, so I risk the former. Fifteen minutes later I find myself in the parking lot of a strip mall. There's a vape and smoke store, a nail salon, and a laundromat. At the far end, I spot *Bon Gou* written on the glass beneath a blue and red flag with a crest in the center.

There isn't a bike rack or a street sign in sight. Terrific. I hop off and start threading my lock through the tire.

Bells jangle nearby, and I look up to see Henry smirking in the half-open door. "What's your plan there?" He's wearing a pale gray T-shirt that's tight enough on his arms to remind me of all my freshman-year feelings.

"Uh...maybe just lock my front tire to the frame and hope for the best?"

His smirk widens to a grin. "Bring it around the back."

I walk my bike around a couple of dumpsters, locking it to a sign about illegal dumping. I hear Henry rapidly chatting with someone inside the open back door. I can't make out what they're saying, but I don't want to interrupt, so I linger by my bike. Something pale flickers beside the dumpster. A curving tail and a notched ear. A cat?

I shift to view it better. The cat, because that much is clear now, presses himself to the side of the dumpster, sizing me up. Between the notch in his ear and the bare patches where his fur has been rubbed raw, he looks as rough as I feel.

There is a broken glass bottle near the dumpster, on the far side of the restaurant's staff entrance, but directly between the cat and me. He inches forward, clearly interested in checking me out, and of course, he's heading right for the glass. I move right and then left, trying to give the cat a different path, but in the end, he is sauntering directly toward certain slicing and dicing, so I rush forward before he can get there. I stand over the pile of glass, using one outstretched hand to scratch the cat's ears and keep him away, while my other scrabbles around for a piece of cardboard. I pile the biggest pieces of glass onto the cardboard without letting up on the petting.

A shadow appears in the open doorway. I expect Henry, but

instead a tall bald man emerges. He has thick arms and hard eyes, and I cannot even fathom what he must be thinking, looking at me in this bizarre wide-armed crouch.

I cringe and bend so he can see the cardboard. "Sorry, I was picking up this glass. I'm waiting for Henry."

He doesn't move for a minute, just watches me with a smile that tells me he knows exactly what I'm doing and it has nothing to do with this cat. Oh, hell. Do I look like a girl who's trying too hard? Because despite every reason not to, I put on a V-neck purple shirt and a coat or two of mascara without letting myself think too hard about why.

The *why* appears in the doorway then, giving me an easy, lopsided smile. "Did Antoine put you on cleanup duty?"

The large man—who I assume is Antoine—grunts and turns, muttering something like *getting a broom.*

"Sorry, there's a cat," I say. But I didn't need to say it, because the cat is doing figure eights around my hand. I gently nudge him away from the glass, stroking his head before I stand up.

"That's Tuna," Henry says. "He stays in the laundromat next door, but Sammy sometimes feeds him." As if on cue, Tuna saunters away from me, and I spot a small blue dish of kibble against the wall. He tips his head toward the open doorway. "Come on. He's getting a broom, and you already handled the worst of it."

I throw the glass away and hesitate. "Are you working?"

His grin appears again. "Any time I can't convince my aunt I'm studying. But it's slow. They don't need anything."

"Henry? Where are you?" A woman's heavily accented voice floats out.

Henry laughs. "Coming, Tati."

He beckons me inside, and I enter to the smell of peppers and onions simmering. My mouth waters instantly. Henry meanders through a long corridor with stainless steel shelves and counters on either side. On the right, I spot the cooking area. There's a TV on in the corner, and a small woman with a bright head wrap is chopping up an enormous pile of small orange and yellow peppers. The TV is turned up so loud, it's hard to hear, or maybe that's because the grill to her right is sizzling wildly.

"What can I do for you?" Henry asks.

The woman chopping peppers looks back at him and briefly at me.

"Hello, there," she says to me, smiling.

"This is Clara," Henry says. "Clara, this is my aunt, Beatrice."

"Good to meet you," she says, but then she quickly shifts her attention to Henry and rattles off something in another language, or at least with a much thicker accent. I can't make it out over the sound of the grill, but Henry stops to reach something on a top shelf, walking his fingers up a tidy stack of matching tubs.

A sliver of brown skin shows above the waistband of his pants, and I feel embarrassed for noticing the jut of his hip bone.

I turn away as he hands over the stack. There is so much happening. Sizzling and steaming and dishes clattering and my cheeks going hot from being this close to a guy I would still be into if I wasn't days away from a felony charge.

Henry offers her a tub full of yellow onions and then starts moving again.

I pause, waving awkwardly. "It's nice to meet you."

Henry leads me through to the front without introducing me to anyone else. Outside the kitchen, the restaurant is quiet and serene. A few booths line the walls, and a scattering of colorful tables fill the space between them. Henry guides me to a booth with green vinyl seats and a small colorful landscape painting above the napkin dispenser. After checking on the only customer in the place, a gentleman dining alone, he steps back over.

"Sammy will cover for me," he says, nodding to a girl seated at a back booth scrolling on her phone. She shares Henry's sharp cheekbones and golden eyes, but she has a narrow mouth and a dimple in her chin. Relative, maybe? I don't ask.

"You want something to drink?" Henry asks.

"I'm fine," I say, feeling nervous. I've never been alone with Henry. And being with him here is a totally different universe than school, one where Lily is not the sun, and there are no other planets whirling by. It's just me and Henry, a boy I barely know who is watching me with a look I can't decipher. I feel like he's searching me, trying to figure out all my secrets.

I squirm in the booth, the vinyl protesting with a groan.

"Are you nervous?" Henry asks.

"Yeah, I am. I honestly don't know what to say."

"Let's just talk," Henry says. "We don't need a plan."

I take a breath and try to relax. "Okay, you said that Lily is a liar. Why do you say that?"

"Wow, no beating around the bush for you," Henry says, but he's smiling, and it draws my eyes to his mouth, which is probably a danger zone. I need to focus.

"She does lie," I say, thinking of other times Lily hasn't told the truth. *Oh, I barely studied*, and *I'm so bummed to miss it, but I've got tennis*, and *Jackson, you know you're my favorite*. "Usually about small stuff, but yeah, she sometimes lies when it suits her."

"I think it suits her quite often. She has a selfish streak," he says.

My neck prickles with heat. Even now, even with everything, I feel like I'm betraying her. But he's right. "Yes." My voice is rough. "But not everybody knows that."

"Well I guess I'm not everybody." Henry says. He shrugs. "So since we're cutting through all of the small talk, I'd like to ask a question."

"Shoot."

"Did you plan to blow up cars in the school parking lot?"

My throat tightens. "No."

"Okay."

I wish it was okay, but it feels weird. I don't understand why he's so quick to believe me. Some small paranoid part of me is wondering what reason he has. "You believe me when I tell you I didn't do this?"

"Yes."

I lean back, relieved and grateful. And skeptical. I tilt my head. "You believe me. Just like that."

"Just like that."

"Why?"

Henry sits forward, ducking his head over the table so that he's a little closer. When he speaks again, his voice is lower. Meant only for me. "Because you are not the only person Lily has framed."

TWENTY

Sammy stops at our table before I can dive into all the questions I have. She has a gorgeous smile, and she scooches in next to Henry in the booth, plopping her elbows on the table.

"Okay, so Tati is not going to stop until you feed this girl something, so you need to order for her." Sammy says, flicking her eyes meaningfully toward the kitchen. Then she looks at me, extending a hand. "Hi, I'm Sammy."

I shake her hand. "I'm Clara."

"Clara Cutler," she says. "Girl, I know who you are. Everyone's talking about you."

"Oh, that's… Well, to be honest, it sucks."

"Fair," she says, and then she looks back at Henry. "Bannann peze?"

He waves, looking a little impatient. "That's fine."

"I'll bring you that and some lemonade."

As soon as she's gone, I lean forward. "Do I need to be worried about her texting people at Tusky?"

"My cousin?" Henry shakes his head. "Sammy graduated two years back. People still tell her all kinds of things, but she's not about drama."

I relax a bit. "Okay. Then let's go back to me not being the only one Lily framed."

"She did something similar to Mariana last year."

I arch a brow at him. "Really? I must have missed the day that Mariana was arrested for a terrorist plot."

He chuckles. "Point taken. But let's just say Lily showed her true colors."

"Let's say more than that. Please."

"It was right before spring break last year. There was a group project in French I."

I remember the one. Lily pitched a fit about how little Mariana had done and how she'd had to beg and plead with the teacher to give them more time so she could finish the project for both of them. "I think I remember her saying something about it."

Henry tips his head. "Did she say that she didn't do the work and made Mariana take the fall?"

My silence must be all the answer he needs, because he

shakes his head. "Yeah, I thought not. So here's how it went. Mariana wasn't great at French. So when Lily invited her to join her group for the project, Mar was really excited. She worked superhard to do her part well, and I'd know, because she forced me to check her work on every single slide."

I nod for him to keep going. He splays his big hands wide on the table. "When it came time to turn the project in, Lily called in a total meltdown. Crying that she'd had a terrible fight with her dad and that Mariana owed her for Lily agreeing to partner with her on the French thing to begin with. She said she was going to ask for an extension and Mariana needed to go along with everything she said."

"That's…not how Lily described it." Understatement. Lily described Mariana as a total flake who screwed around and dropped all the work in her lap. Which begs the question: "Why would Mariana go along with it?"

Henry blows out a hard breath. It's clear he doesn't like the reason now and probably liked it less then. "The social scene is really important to Mariana. She wants to be popular in a way that makes absolutely no sense to me. She thought she did owe Lily something."

"Why?"

"Because Lily is a role model for girls like Mariana. Smart, popular, the girl everybody loves. That's who Mar wants to be."

"So what happened?"

"Lily talked to the teacher. Asked for an extension, but her story was very different than that night on the phone with Mariana. Lily went on and on about how Mar didn't put in the time and didn't understand group projects. And the whole time she was throwing Mariana under the bus, Lily was playing the angel student, begging the teacher to give Mariana a chance. To let her try to help her friend."

"Didn't Mariana deny it?"

"She didn't hear it directly. Lily talked to Ms. Jennings before class started. I only heard because my locker is right outside her door."

"So you told Mariana."

"Of course I did. At first she didn't even believe me, but eventually she saw the light. She said she'd handle it with Lily, and they had this big conversation about it."

"And what happened?"

He shrugs. "After they talked, Mariana completely shut down. Said it was over and I needed to let it go."

"Wait a minute, *you* needed to let it go? Why was she okay with it?"

Henry shakes his head. "No idea. When I pushed back on her about it, she said I didn't get it. Went on and on about how Lily had things harder than I realized and I didn't understand the situation. It was ridiculous. She bought Lily's boo-hoo act completely."

"What happened with the project?"

"They got an A, and Lily took all the credit. She acted like she did it *for* Mariana."

"Did that mess with you two as a couple?" I feel my face getting hot. This is stupid and has nothing to do with what we're talking about and everything to do with my petty-ass curiosity.

"Mariana and me, we were never going to work in the long run. But Lily didn't have a thing to do with that."

I push at the sugar packets in the little holder on the table. "Look, I don't mean this to sound bad, but are you sure Mariana wasn't just putting a spin on it so she wouldn't look like a slacker or whatever? Are you sure she didn't skimp on anything?"

"Remember, I saw her do the work," Henry says. "But even more importantly, I heard Lily. I've never seen anything like it. She didn't flinch with that teacher. Her expression was so locked in, she damn near had *me* believing her."

"But you knew better," I say with a sigh.

"What worries me is that if I hadn't known the whole story, I would have believed Lily. She was that convincing." Sammy delivers a basket of what looks like potato chips. Henry points. "Plantain chips. The sauce is great. Eat one, and then tell me what really happened between you and Lily two days ago."

I take one to give myself a minute to think. It's delicious, and the sauce is some sort of citrus garlic magic, so I eat a couple more before starting. "The weirdest part of this is that nothing bizarre happened. I swear to God, until I found that folder in my bag, I had no idea anything more than a bad joke was happening. But in hindsight, there were definitely signs."

"Tell me," he says gently.

It's like déjà vu telling this story again, revisiting all the things I brushed off, things that should have sent the hairs on the back of my neck standing up. I feel stupid now, admitting that I ignored her parking in the wrong place, driving extra slow, even talking about murder. And then I tell him about the notification that she stopped sharing her location with me.

"I think that's when I knew something was wrong," I say.

"Did you think she was up to something?" Henry asks.

"Honestly? I was worried about her. I thought maybe I upset her or that something had happened to her. Some part of me is still worried."

"About what?"

"About what drove her to all of this. She's my best friend, Henry. What the hell happened to her to make her willing to do this to me?"

He leans back in the booth, his expression neutral. "That's what worries you?"

I'm not sure what to think of the question, but I don't want to fire off an answer without thinking. What Lily did is infuriating and heartbreaking. Even thinking about her face in that office sends fire zipping through my insides. The way she set all this up? The folder and the parking lot—it's intense. But what drove her to all of this in the first place? It doesn't add up.

"Yeah," I answer finally. "I mean, I'm pissed. More than pissed. And I'm scared of what happens next for me, but yeah, I'm worried about her too."

"I'm not worried about Lily." Henry's voice is low, and his mouth shapes her pretty name into something hard and ugly. But then he looks at me, and his whole face softens. "I'm worried about you."

It makes me nervous the way he holds my gaze. He doesn't look all over the place. He doesn't check his phone or crack his knuckles or fidget. He is still and steady, and he does not look away. He believes me. He's the first person who has really believed me.

To my shock and horror, I feel the sudden heat of tears behind my eyes. "I don't know what to do."

My voice is raw and cracked, like admitting this has taken something vital from me.

Henry reaches across the table, his knuckles just grazing the side of my wrist. "Then let's figure it out together."

TWENTY-ONE

Henry hops up to help a young family with twin girls who are talking a mile a minute. He clearly knows them and they make easy conversation while the tired-looking fathers help the girls into red plastic booster chairs. Sammy, who is apparently psychic, comes in with a tray of those delicious plantain chips and coloring books for the girls. She takes over, waving Henry away. He grabs us extra sauce on his way back to the booth.

"Sorry. They're regulars." He takes a chip before nodding at me. "Have you thought of anything that might prove Lily's lying?"

"The first thing that came to my mind is this sheet of formulas that was in the plan. I did that whole project on explosives—"

"I know. You kicked my ass in qualifying."

I almost forgot about that. To be fair, I forgot about everyone else that month last year. My grandmother had just died, and suddenly my interest in chemistry shifted into high gear. I had gone along with Lily's big plans for Chemagination before, but losing my grandmother changed the stakes. If I could do well in this contest, maybe I could do more. Maybe I could get a scholarship. A degree. Maybe I could work in pharmaceuticals that would have given Grams time or even cured her. I knew that project could change things, so I gave it everything I had and more.

"Anyway, some of the formulas from the sheet were mine, which is why I know the plan isn't logical."

"Not logical?"

I pull out my phone to access the photo of the formula sheet. "The explosives from my project aren't easy to control. I can't look back over my notes, so I don't know exactly what all of this is, but these formulas look familiar, so I think they're mine."

I've opened up my photos to stare at the picture of the page from the red folder.

"Can I see it?" He leans in, and I smell something clean and lemony. I hand it over and he frowns. "It's frozen."

"I know. It does that. Sorry, it's my old phone." I reboot it and hand it over.

He enlarges the photo and frowns at the formulas. "I don't know exactly what these are."

"I think they're household cleaners that could be dangerous, but none of them would be easy to weaponize. That doesn't mean there aren't more controllable explosive options too. There are—I ran across them during research."

"Right," Henry says. "But you're saying this plan isn't viable?"

"I don't think so. But I don't know if it matters to anyone whether or not this plan would work. According to the police, the contents of the folder constitute a terrorist threat. They seem pretty determined to throw the book at me without a lot of questions."

"Do you have anything at all to prove that this isn't your plan?"

I nod, and then I tell him about the library books, the ones I couldn't have checked out. Before I can even tell him that Lily used my card, he leans back.

"Let me guess, Lily knew your library card number?"

"How did you know that?"

He frowns. "Mariana again. Lily used her lunch code anytime she ran out of money because she knew Mariana's dad was on auto reload and wouldn't notice."

"But...why? Lily has plenty of money."

Henry shrugs. "She thinks she's owed things. That's one of the reasons I don't like her."

"I have some reasons now too," I say with a sigh.

"Do you know the books Lily checked out?"

"I don't have the list on me—the one the librarian wrote down. I know the first title was *Chemical Impact.* I can't remember the others, but they all sounded like textbooks from the titles. I think I saw one in Lily's room last time I was there—I didn't see the title but it was a big book and I wondered why she had it. Definitely not light reading."

"Okay, then I think the next step is obvious."

"It is?"

Henry nods and stands up. "We need to find out if Lily has those books."

~

I hate Henry's plan. The gist of it is this: He will visit Lily tomorrow morning under the pretense of wanting to get back together with Mariana. Lily loves a little juicy drama, so I can't deny that his plan is solid, but I can hate the shit out of it all the same.

I also can't argue, because I have a plan of my own, one that I'm not admitting to Henry. One I'm not sure I'm fully admitting to myself even though I'm riding my bike in exactly the wrong direction to get to my house and exactly the right direction to get to the tennis center.

The center looks a little worse for wear. The one-story building is wide and squat—a warehouse with potted plants at the entrance and an iron railing leading up to the doors. A fancy logo, the intricate interlocking letters *GKTC*, is on the glass doors, but I can see the paint is chipped, and one of the rungs in the iron railing is missing.

My hands shake when I lock my bike onto the rack at the back of the lot. I've gone over and over it in my head. The police were very clear. Do not go to school. Do not go to Lily's house. What the police did not say was to not go to the Geldis Klein Tennis Center.

I'm not so stupid that I actually think this is smart. But even if I admit this a terrible idea, it wouldn't be enough to stop me. Lily has been my best friend—my only friend, really—for a long time, and she has never, ever done anything like this. I know exactly how it feels to be judged for your absolute worst actions. If there's really some rational explanation for this—if there's some way we can make this right, I have to try.

And if this is just a setup? Well, I guess I have to look Lily in the eyes and make her tell me why. But however stupid it is, I can't completely give up on her. Not yet.

Her father's car is parked toward the back of the lot, but he'll be inside. They both take lessons every day except Sunday and Monday.

I walk through the parking lot, feeling a breeze lift my hair away from my face. I'm chilled and shaking. Or maybe the shaking is just nerves, because I've got plenty of those. But it's fine. I'm not doing anything illegal. Stupid, yes. Wrong, maybe. But it isn't technically illegal.

The center doors aren't locked, but there is a security guard at a small desk in the lobby. I remember this from being here a couple of times with Lily back when she was sure she could teach me how to play tennis. I was surprised we didn't need to show him a pass, but she just shrugged. *They don't care. Now that pickleball is a town obsession, they're happy anyone wanders in. You only need the pass to unlock the doors to the courts. It's a swipe card.*

It's been a few months, but apparently that hasn't changed, because the door pulls open easily. My palms are sweaty, and my heart is hammering when I step inside. The security guard is too large for the tiny desk in front of him. His phone is propped up on a box of chicken nuggets, and a large drink in a fast-food cup is sweating a wet ring onto the blond wood.

Keep walking.

He takes a drink, and I raise my hand briefly. Fear surges into my chest when he looks up. I force myself to keep moving, but panic is tightening fingers around my neck. He's going to get up. He's going to ask me for my name. He's going to call the police because Lily warned him I might show up.

But he doesn't do any of those things. He takes another drink, the straw squeak-shrieking against the plastic lid, and then his attention is back on his phone. I keep moving.

My knees knock all the way down the hall. There are court doors—each with those swipe locks Lily told me about—and the muted *thwack squeak squeak thwack* sounds of a match. I do not dare peek through the narrow windows on the court doors. I keep moving, my attention fixed on the left side of the hall. Vending machines. A weight room. The women's locker room.

I duck inside, exhaling hard in relief as the door shuts behind me. I am left in a haze of sweat and deodorant and the too-damp air of recent hot showers. But the room is empty.

I check my busted phone. Two minutes until eight.

It shouldn't be long now. I sit on the bench across from the locker I think I remember her using. I could be wrong, but it's close enough to the door that she'll see me.

What if someone else comes in?

I think about that. Try to assess the possibility of another woman entering the locker room. What if someone knows about what happened or recognizes me? What if Lily sees me and screams for help? I run through one terrifying episode after the next, and none of it is enough to force me off this bench and out of the building. I need to look at her, and I need her to look at me. Whatever happens from there I'll handle.

I wait until the locker room door opens. Until I hear her easy steps. Until the length of her shadow falls on the floor in front of me. And then she's there. Golden hair and warm brown eyes. Lily.

She has a towel slung around her neck, and she stops short when she sees me, her eyes bright with shock. Maybe even fear. Lily lifts her chin and in an instant I realize how badly this could end. There is no good reason for me to be in this building, and there are no cameras in a locker room. If she alerts someone, they'll come running. If she tells the cops I was waiting in this locker room to ambush her, she won't even be completely lying. I have given her everything she needs to bury me alive.

I hold my breath and wait for her to scream. But she doesn't scream. Instead she does the thing I least expect; she smiles.

TWENTY-TWO

"Clara," she says. It's not quite a greeting, but since I'm not sure what else it is, I respond.

"Hi, Lily."

Her eyes flick to the door, then the lockers to her left. She's thinking about what to do. If she screams or runs, there isn't another exit, and maybe I didn't break a law, but this won't look good, and she's smart enough to know it. But she doesn't call for help or pull out her phone. She opens her locker and grabs a washcloth. She starts swiping her face and neck like I'm not her concern at all.

"What a surprise to see you here in the locker room," Lily says. "At a tennis club. That you don't belong to. Come to think of it, do you even own a tennis racket?"

"I must have misplaced it in the folder that isn't mine. You remember the one?"

"I can't believe you're joking about something like that," she says.

Her tone would tell me this is the most expected thing in the world. Like she's not surprised at all. But I know her, and I saw the way she stopped short. I saw her lips purse in a way that only happens when she doesn't quite know what to do.

"I'm not here about tennis," I say. "Which you know."

"Do I? I think the last few days have proven I don't know you well at all." Lily closes her locker door. She's checking me over. Looking for something.

"I'm not armed for God's sake."

Her expression does not change. She is still searching me. What the hell is she worried about? I'm wearing a thin long-sleeved shirt and leggings. There's nowhere to hide a weapon. So something else. And then it hits me. She's looking for my phone. For a camera.

I sigh. "I'm not recording you. I'm not here for that."

"Then why are you here? I really don't think we should be talking." She doesn't believe me about the recording. I can tell because it's clear she's still on stage. Her tone is off. Every word is being chosen like she's sure she's being watched.

"Can we please not do this, Lily? I'm here because I want to know what this is about. I want to know if something happened to you. Something bad."

Her eyes go wide. A calculation, not a reflex. "Finding

out something like this about my best friend was pretty bad, Clara."

"There was nothing to find out! You gave me that folder. And you are the one who started that entire conversation about taking people down."

Her smile widens in a way that sends goose bumps up on my arms and legs.

"That's not what happened," she says, her voice low with fake worry despite her bright eyes. "I told you that night, I don't want to see anyone get hurt."

"Just knock it off! That's not my plan, and I didn't want to hurt anyone, and even if I did, that so-called parking lot plan would never have worked. Those things are explosive, yes, but you can't control reactions like that."

Her hands come up, all shock and horror. "I don't want to control a reaction."

"Neither do I! Not once in my life have I ever seriously considered blowing anything up, least of all my damn school parking lot."

"We can't talk about your plans," she says, doggedly. "I told you that night. Those plans are crazy. People will get hurt."

A callback to that text conversation at her house. I feel like the world is swaying back and forth beneath my feet. So this is it. There aren't going to be any answers. There is no reconciliation here.

I shake my head, feeling spent. "Nothing about this *plan* is real, and you know it."

Her face actually brightens then, her smile genuine and eyes sparkling. Her look says, *I've got you*, and I don't know why.

"Are you saying you have something else planned, Clara? Something that is real?"

"What? What the hell is wrong with you?"

Lily does not answer. She is all in on her little performance, shaking her head, her hands up and pleading. "You can't keep doing this. You have to talk to someone—

"Stop it, Lily! Stop acting like this—"

"—about this before you do something you can never take back. Don't you remember what happened to Cadence?"

Lily's phone dings. She looks so smug and pleased when she checks it. When she glances back at me, she is the picture of worry. "I have to go. Dad is in the parking lot. Please think about what I said, Clara. Don't do something that will ruin your life. And please, please just stay away from me."

A sickening mix of shock and rage and sorrow is knotting my chest. I don't say another word before she goes. And I don't look at her either. I slump back against the lockers. Tears rise in my eyes, sliding hot and fast down my cheeks. They drip from my chin, and I hate myself for that. Hate myself for being so stupid as to come here. Hate myself the most for not seeing this monstrous version of my so-called friend.

I do not rush out of the tennis center. I don't know that Lily won't tell someone about me, but at the moment I don't care if she does. When I step outside, there are no security guards waiting and no cops in the parking lot. Lily and her dad are long gone.

I walk to my bike in the darkness, any stars smudged out by a thick layer of low-hanging clouds. My chest feels tight as I ride, my tears starting and stopping. I pause now and then to blow my nose on rough old napkin. When I finally pull my bike up to my shed, my eyes ache and my nose feels raw. I am tired to the core of my being.

Mom is waiting in the living room, so no shift at the bar tonight. She has her phone in her hand, and she looks stunned in the worst possible way. For one obtuse moment, I wonder if something happened at work. Then she shakes her head, and I remember where I've been and what she obviously knows.

"You went to the tennis place?" Her voice is high and shrieky. "Knowing Lily would be there?"

"I know. It was stupid, but I—"

"But you what? You thought you'd convince her to lie for you? You thought you'd get her to admit it wasn't what it looks like? What exactly *were* you thinking?"

"I guess I thought if we just talked, that she'd change her mind."

"Do you have any idea how risky this was? We're lucky Lily's parents didn't call the police." Mom's voice is shrill and desperate. I am exhausting her.

"I'm sorry, Mom. I don't know the right way to be wrongfully accused."

She shakes her head, a broken laugh sputtering out.

"Why are you acting like I'm lying?" I ask. "I know what happened, but you said yourself—this is not like me. Because it's *not* me!"

"I want to believe you." Her voice is suddenly soft. Tired. "I do. But Clara, the truth is this. When something looks too good to be true and sounds too good to be true, it's probably not true. No matter how much I wish it was."

She disappears into her room, closing the door behind her. I press my cold fingertips to my eyelids. My eyes are on fire, and when I open them again, they feel gritty and raw. I blink at my mom's closed door for another minute, hearing nothing. And what else is there to do?

I shower quickly, plaiting my hair into a single thick braid on my way back to my bedroom. George is waiting at the foot of my bed when I return, and my phone is glowing on my nightstand. Vibrating right next to Detective Fleming's card.

Henry: Give me a call if you want to talk.

I feel more relief than I probably should at Henry's text. I call him, and he picks up on the first ring.

"Hey," he says by greeting.

"Hi," I say, and I didn't realize it until this moment, but it's very clear by my voice that I've been crying. And his pause tells me he noticed.

"Okay there, Clara?"

It's what he said to me outside the classroom after that awful handcuffing ordeal. I sit on the side of my bed, scratching George's ears and feeling like I might cry again.

"I did a dumb thing," I say. My voice cracks.

"Not as dumb as me, I bet," he says with a chuckle. "Who should go first?"

Even my laugh sounds teary, but I feel lighter as I crawl into bed, pushing my feet into the pocket of sheets and blankets. "I went to see Lily."

I wait for his voice to change into a semblance of my mother's face in the living room earlier. I wait for his scorn or disappointment or just...something. But when he speaks again, his voice is exactly as it's always been. Low. Kind. Attractive, if I'm brutally honest.

"Were you hoping she might come to her senses?"

"Maybe? I don't know." I sigh. "She didn't. I mean she didn't scream or call the cops, but she did tell her parents, who in turn called my mom. So that's been wonderful."

He makes a noise of understanding. "Does your mom believe that you didn't do it?"

"I think she wants to. It's complicated. Can we talk about the dumb thing you did instead?"

Another laugh, soft and breathy. He's so calm. Listening to Henry makes me think of reading on a rainy day. Or sitting by a crackling fireplace. Like the whole world is a bit slower and gentler. Or maybe I'm making all that shit up because Henry is the one part of my life that isn't upside down. He talks to me and looks at me exactly like he always has, and goddamn do I need that right now.

"I went to Lily's house," he says. "I didn't know about tennis, so I thought I might get lucky and run into her."

"Well, that wasn't that stupid," I say. "You told me you were doing that."

"Yes, but I didn't tell you I'd go full-out spy mode on her bedroom."

"Eek."

"And break into her car."

I sit back up with a lurch. "You broke into Lily's car?"

"*Breaking into* isn't quite right, I guess. I opened Lily's car door to check for books, which I'm sure breaks a law. But I had a reason."

"What reason?"

"I thought I spotted those books through the back window."

"Were they in there?"

"Yes. Mostly shoved under a stack of dirty gym clothes and a pair of athletic slides."

Lily keeps her car clean, so did she bring all that shit just to hide the books? I think back to the day in the parking lot. Before I was arrested, but after Lily planned all this. She was messing around with something in the back seat. Was it these books that day? But no, there wasn't anything back there. I would have seen it when I flung my jacket and bag into the back. Since the police have my bag and I forgot my jacket, it's possible I'll never see either again, but the point remains. There weren't clothes back there, and there definitely weren't giant textbooks.

I shake my head. "I'm not sure why she'd have them in there. And I don't think they were in there last week. Her car is usually spotless."

"I think they're in there because she wants them out of her house now that you've been arrested."

"Wouldn't she be worried about someone catching her with those books? They're about chemistry, *and* they're checked out on my card."

"I have a thought about that," he says. "They put a new lock on your locker."

My mouth goes sour and watery, like I'm ready to be sick. "Who?"

"Officer Grimes. He wasn't going through it. He was just replacing the lock they'd cut when they took the bomb dog through."

His words make me dizzy. "They took the bomb dog through?"

"I'm sorry. If it helps, I don't think many people know. They did it while everyone was in the morning pep rally. It was the same day you were..." Henry trails off, then starts again, awkwardly. "It definitely looked like an abundance-of-caution decision."

"Okay. But how does that explain the library books suddenly showing up in Lily's car?"

"It doesn't. Not directly. But I saw Lily near your locker yesterday. She turned the corner and sort of stared in shock at Officer Grimes while he replaced the lock. Up until I saw those books, I thought she was playing up feeling upset, but now I think it was something else."

"You think she was feeling guilty?"

"No, I think she was feeling terrified. Lily probably didn't realize they removed your lock. Like I said, no one really knew about the dog. I think that until she saw Grimes at your locker—"

"She thought she could get into my locker and plant the books," I say, feeling breathless.

"That's my theory. Does she have your combination?"

My heart speeds up. "Yeah, because her locker is on the second floor. She keeps a brush and some other stuff in mine."

"But she wouldn't have the new combination, so she had to hide those books quick."

"So now the library books are in her car," I say. "Did you get a photo?"

He sighs heavily. "I didn't. I heard the front door open so I booked it. Her mom was getting the mail and I have no idea how she didn't see me. Hey, did you look up the books she checked out?"

"Not really. I know they're chemistry textbooks."

Henry pauses. "The books weren't about general chemistry; they were about toxicology."

Toxicology. The word rolls through my mind like a dark cloud, the definition trailing in its wake. Toxicology is the study of poisons.

TWENTY-THREE

I wake on Friday morning with a mission to figure out what in God's name Lily was doing with those toxicology books. I spend the whole morning double-checking each formula from the folder to make sure they are household explosives and not poisons. Not an easy feat since I can only look at the formula sheet on my crappy cracked phone screen. Which would be bad enough on a phone that didn't glitch and freeze every three minutes. It takes me two hours to go through them.

After a bagel, I wander the backyard with George. While he sniffs the same six landmarks he sniffs every morning, I try to decide whether or not Lily would poison someone. Maybe it was just her original plan for framing me. She could have realized the explosives might be easier to link to me given my project last year and changed course.

Or maybe she wanted to frame me for bombs and someone else for poison? Or maybe she had a completely uninteresting, legitimate reason, like her first-semester AP Chem project. Was there a research-heavy thing due then? I'm going through my old classroom emails trying to figure it out when the front door clicks open and Mom walks in.

My phone informs me that it's 3:42 p.m., and my mom's face informs me that she left work early specifically to talk to me. I know it isn't going to be good news before she even opens her mouth.

"John called," she says. "Come sit with me."

I head into the living room, and Mom and George follow. We all take our traditional spots—George in his bed, Mom on the ratty recliner, and me in the left corner of the couch—and Mom offers a tense smile.

"The plea deal is in," she says without preamble.

"Okay." I tuck my feet underneath me.

Mom takes her time, dragging it out like she's opening a present, but this doesn't feel like a present. "I think we should take a look at what they're offering."

"Just to clarify, a plea deal means pleading guilty, correct?" I ask.

"Yes. But they are willing to drop the initial terrorism charge. They're looking at something like aggravated menacing."

"Wow, menacing? That sounds really tempting," I deadpan.

"It sounds a hell of a lot better than plotting to commit a terrorist act."

George watches us from his bed.

"Look, I hear where you are coming from. But how am I supposed to feel good about potentially pleading guilty to something I did not do?"

Mom's face shutters, and something about her expression prickles at my insides. It feels like a warning. Like there's something she's not telling me.

"John didn't just talk about the plea deal, did he?"

Mom looks down at her mug of coffee. After a long pause, she sighs. "Someone submitted a letter to him. It's signed by a dozen or so parents from the school."

"What parents? And why?"

"Because one of the people on the list of targets isn't comfortable with you returning to the school."

"Let me guess. Paxton." I say it with acid in my voice.

"Yes, but he was not the first to mention it." Mom sets her mug down and scoots forward on the edge of our ancient recliner. "Six other kids have come forward about other concerning incidents. Jokes in study hall. Comments at a birthday party about choking one of the teachers on your list. Concerns about how much time you spend in the chemistry lab."

"Because I'm trying to stay on top of my Chem grade. Because I want to be a pharmacist. Do you remember that, Mom?"

"I do, Clara. But there are now seven students who aren't Lily who are claiming concerns about your mental state and about your history of violence in this school. Ms. Chang filled me in on the recent situation with Vera."

"Mom! That was a complete accident! This is ludicrous. They're all acting like I'm a sociopath bent on violence!"

"It's a lot of different people and a lot of different stories," Mom says. "It doesn't look good."

A fresh wave of nausea hits. I feel sideswiped. The birthday party is a blatant lie. We were all talking about Mr. Droesch and how much we hate him. I said I wish he'd retire. It was Ava who said sometimes she thought about choking him. The chemistry lab is true. Because I'm there whenever Mr. Philpot allows it, cleaning beakers and burners because I'm desperate to get a solid recommendation from him. It's bullshit. All of it is.

Except.

Except the study hall.

That's not a lie. I remember it perfectly, and it's the one that has my mouth zipped shut. October of this year. The Jacksons, Mariana, and I were playing Serial Killer Hangman. It was a dumb Halloween thing, and the entire point was to guess murderers. Jackson used Jack the Ripper. Mariana went with Jeffrey Dahmer. I can't remember what Jackson Collins did, but I remember mine. I chose the Unabomber because, in truth, I didn't know that many serial killers and definitely couldn't be sure on last-name spellings.

We laughed and moved on to horror movie villains, and I entirely gave up there because I don't watch horror movies at all. But I laughed along with Mariana and the Jacksons, and never thought of it again. How could I have possibly known a random hangman game during study hall would be one more piece of evidence to add to this fire?

"I'll take it from your silence you can see why I'm struggling. Part of me believes you, and part of me doesn't. And I'm your mom, Clara."

I know what she's getting at. If my mother has reasonable cause to not believe me, where would a jury land? I close my eyes and let out a shaky breath. I don't have enough alibis in the world to make up for all the shit piling up in front of me.

I shake my head, feeling numb. "What would it mean if I took it?"

"You'd agree to pleading guilty to aggravated menacing and a couple of more minor misdemeanors. There'd be ninety days of community service and thirty days of jail time, but the jail time would be suspended as long as you check in with a parole officer and do your community service."

"And school?" My voice sounds like it belongs to someone else. My life feels like it belongs to someone else, so maybe that makes sense.

Mom's lips thin. "Expulsion is the most likely outcome according to Ms. Chang."

"So I'm just a high school dropout?"

"You would have the option, again on good behavior, to open enroll in another school in the county. Or there are some charter schools. You could still graduate."

Graduate, yes. But with no recommendation letters and maybe an active probation. How would that work? The answer feels pretty cut-and-dried. It wouldn't.

I feel the threat of tears clogging my throat. "I know what you think I should do. That's obvious, but I also know that I'll be lying if I say I'm guilty."

"It's up to you," Mom says. "But I don't see a better way out of this right now. And I don't see you denying half of the things they're accusing you of."

"I don't understand why any of this is happening." Tears slide down my cheeks, and my voice is hollow when I speak again. "There isn't a way out. I didn't do this, but it doesn't matter. All that seems to matter is what everyone believes."

Mom's face is a reflection of my pain. "Clara..."

"Just tell me what you want me to do."

"Let's just think about it. We have the weekend."

Mom heads back to work at 4:30. She'll be at the bar right after, which leaves me alone with my thoughts. Pretty much the last place I want to be.

I stand in the kitchen long after she's gone, but I don't think about it. Instead, I hold the edge of the dining table and stare at the stack of college mailers by the napkin holder. Bryn Mawr and Ohio State and Purdue. Dozens of others. Colleges with great chemistry programs. The paperwork poured in after I won that competition. Every day another thick envelope, filled with brochures of smiling kids near a variety of iconic brick buildings. The brochures and invitations made me laugh.

And they gave me hope.

And now it's for nothing.

I hold my phone out and consider what to do or who to call, but I'm out of ideas. And every idea I've tried has been met with a new piece of so-called evidence of my villainy. How the hell do I fight something like this?

When the panic starts to rise like bubbles in my chest, I pad quietly to my bedroom. I drop my phone on the dresser and shut my curtains against the brightness of the sun. George curls into a ball at the foot of my bed, and I burrow into my own ball near the pillow, shutting out the world completely.

TWENTY-FOUR

I wake with a gasp, my body jerking from sleep into a nightmare. Banging. Footsteps. Barking. I lurch upright in my bed, trying to sort the noise into things I understand. Mom is rushing down the hallway. George is barking. It's not his normal squirrel-in-the-yard woof. This is real. A warning.

Bang-bang-bang! Someone at the front door, knocking loud.

I can't see anything. I fumble at my nightstand, searching for my phone or the light. My hand knocks into my plastic cup of water. It spills, drenching my arm and the side of my bed. I stand up, wet and shivering. Downstairs, the chaos continues.

"I'm coming, I'm coming," Mom says.

I hear the door swing wide, and George's barking only intensifies. I hear Mom moving him to the kitchen. Toenails on the linoleum. Heavy footsteps in the living room.

"Hello?"

Indistinct voices are inside now. I find my phone and turn on my bedside lamp. It's 5:21 a.m. Notifications fill my home screen—two missed calls and four texts. All of them are from Henry. It is 5:21 a.m., and people are in my house, talking to my mother. It has to be the police.

I scan Henry's texts on my phone.

Henry: Are you awake?

Henry: Did you hear what happened?

Henry: Mr. Droesch is dead. It was on the eleven o'clock news. They found him tonight.

The voices come closer.

"Is your daughter home right now, Ms. Cutler?"

"Yes, she's sleeping." Mom's voice now. She sounds sleepy and irritated. George is still barking. Someone must pet him because I hear his woof go soft. His tags jangle, and I picture him shaking his massive head in confusion at this early-morning invasion.

"Can you go wake her up? We have questions for her."

"What's going on?" Mom's voice is thin and nervous. "You said I was fine to keep her at home as long as she's not in trouble."

I pull on a giraffe bathrobe I haven't worn since eighth grade and drop my phone into one of the pockets. The sleeves are too short, but I'm not wearing a bra, and my shirt is wet. I don't want to walk into a room full of strangers. But I push the feeling aside. I tie my ridiculous robe and open the door.

I find three uniformed officers in my living room. They are all strangers. "Are you Clara?"

"Yes, what's going on?"

"Where were you earlier tonight? At approximately 8:30 p.m.?"

"I was here. I was here all day." My voice is rough with sleep and my eyes are still bleary.

"Can anyone account for your whereabouts last night at 8:30 p.m.?"

George howls and barks in the kitchen, pushing at the gate that holds him back. I look at Mom, who is pale and trembling, her own bathrobe tied haphazardly, her socks drooping. "She was here. At home."

"You were here with her?" the officer asks. "At 8:30 p.m.?"

"Not right then. I got off at ten. But she was dead asleep when I got home. She didn't go anywhere all day."

The officers shift on their feet. They are enormous in our tiny living room. It isn't so much their size, but their presence, with endless strange items clipped and buckled all over them, handcuffs, flashlights, canisters that I suspect are filled with pepper spray.

George pushes his way through the baby gate in the kitchen.

His barks settle into low rumbles when he sees us. He is less worried now, but these men do not belong here, and his body language shows it. He weaves through a sea of black-clad legs to sit on my left foot. I feel his face nudge my hand, his breath hot and nervous.

One of the officer's radios blips to life, a disembodied voice reading out codes. The officer behind me unclips the radio long enough to say, "Copy," before returning it to his belt.

"Are you listening to me, Clara?" another officer says. I can't make out much about him. Mustache. Mean eyes.

I shake myself, trying to answer a question I wasn't listening to. "Yes. I was asleep."

"Do you normally go to sleep at 8:30 p.m.?"

"No, but I'm not doing well with the whole situation I'm in," I say, feeling and sounding a little breathless. "I have an arraignment Monday."

"And that's the only situation you're in?"

He's getting at something, and I'm pretty sure it's something that will make my world a whole lot worse.

"Can you please tell me what's going on?" Mom asks.

"Ma'am, are you aware of any grudge your daughter might have against Randy Droesch? He's a teacher at the school, and he was on the list of targets your daughter was found with earlier this week."

"I know him, but no. She's already shared that the list isn't hers."

"Randy Droesch was found dead in his apartment this evening."

"Oh my God." Mom's hands are at her mouth. Her eyes are wide. "What happened?"

"We have reason to believe he has been murdered. Poisoned."

Poisoned.

My insides turn to hot liquid. I feel like I might be sick. I instantly think of the books in Lily's car. *Toxicology.* Those books were checked out on my card, and I don't know if there are tapes proving it wasn't me who checked them out.

Mr. Droesch was poisoned. This is not a folder. Not a plot. This is a murder.

"Do you have any access to opioid medications?" an officer asks.

Mom squints in confusion, then shakes her head. "What? No. Definitely not. There is nothing in this house."

"But you work in a hospital, correct? And Clara, you want to be a pharmacist?"

"I do, but Mom is right. We do not have any sort of opioids. We wouldn't. My grandmother..."

I trail off. Mom removed every imaginable medication from the house when Grams got bad. She had a habit of wandering at night, taking what she surely thought were daily meds. Once it was harmless—several melatonin tablets. But one night she found her prescription painkillers. Thank God Mom found her before she took any, but there were other bottles missing. After that, Mom got rid of everything from sinus medicine to Pepto Bismol. The few items we have now sure as hell don't include opioids.

"Do you mind if we take a look?"

"You go right ahead," Mom says, looking annoyed now. "We keep our medicine in the linen closet. There's a childproof case."

Two of the men head deeper into the house. They don't stop at the linen closet. They check our bathroom. Mom's room. Our purses. I watch them in my room, pulling at the drawers in my nightstand.

I flush, spotting dirty underwear peeking out of my hamper. Seeing a stranger's hands moving my rumpled covers and sheets for the second time in forty-eight hours is awful. I feel exposed. But Mom is feeling something else. Her jaw is clenched, and her arms are crossed tightly over her chest.

"Are you satisfied?" Mom asks.

"We'd like Clara to come with us to the station. To answer some questions."

"Is she under arrest?" Mom's voice comes out with a bite. My skin prickles with alarm. The officers slow their lazy perusal, their focus shifting to this middle-aged woman with mascara smeared beneath her eyes and the promise of hell to pay in her expression.

"No," the tallest officer says. "She is not under arrest, but it would be *helpful* if we could ask her some questions. Just to be sure we have all of our facts."

"We do not have narcotics. She did not leave this house. Those are the facts. Is she required to go with you?"

There is a long pause. George leans into my side. The officers in the living room exchange looks.

"We would appreciate and be sure to note her cooperation."

"But she doesn't have to go," Mom says. It is not a question now. She steps in front of me, and I think I should argue. I think I should say something. But then her hand is behind me, pushing me farther back. "The answer is no. You are not permitted to bring my daughter downtown at five-thirty in the morning to talk to you. She was here all day. I have the goddamn dishes in the sink to prove it. And if we go downtown, we're doing it with our attorney."

"Ma'am—"

"Please do not *ma'am* me. If you feel convinced that my daughter was involved in this homicide, then arrest her."

I flinch, because I don't know what they're convinced of, but I don't love her calling their bluff. But whether or not I love it, it clearly works. Two of the officers take a step backward.

The tall one tries again. "Her lack of cooperation does not help us to believe she's not involved."

"You haven't presented me with a single piece of evidence or rationale behind my daughter being responsible for this crime. We are half dressed and half asleep, and frankly, I need to talk to my lawyer before I agree to this."

George is on edge again. He gives a low woof and pushes his way in front of me, in front of both of us.

"Your daughter has already been accused of some serious crimes."

"My daughter has not even been formally charged at this point, and I'll give you that I'm no lawyer, but I'm pretty sure there's a little something about innocent until proven guilty in this country." Mom keeps going. "And she's not the one who's not cooperating. I am. She is seventeen years old, and she is staying right where she is unless you are arresting her."

"Well." The tall officer steps forward, and I like him the least. Something about that single word feels like a mockery. He's poking at my mother, who is trembling and pale, and I hate him for it. He narrows his eyes. "I guess we'll see you in a little bit, because when we come back, we'll have a list of evidence. And you'll be coming with us in cuffs."

When they leave, Mom turns to me. George paces nervously between us, eyeing the window where the officers are making their way back to two cruisers parked on the curb.

Mom grabs my shoulders. There's a clarity to her now. An alertness that tells me she is seeing me and this whole situation with different eyes.

"Look at me," she says. "And keep looking at me when I ask you this. Is there anything else I need to know about what's going on with you?"

"No. The formula sheet is mine, from that big project I did. And I did talk to Lily in the car, but I swear to you, Mom, it was a joke. I have no idea about the map or the car information. I never saw that. I never even discussed anything like it."

"What about that discipline thing?"

I throw my hands up. "We were in this crazy crowded hallway—everyone bumps everyone. I got pushed and wound up bumping into Vera. By the time she was in the office, it looked like she wasn't sure it was intentional, which it definitely wasn't."

"And there's no one else you've...hurt?"

"Mom, I am far from a perfect person. But after what happened to Cadence and the way it has utterly destroyed my life, do you honestly think I would ever hurt anyone again?"

"You wouldn't hurt someone," she says, and it's like the fog is lifting, like she is discovering something she had not realized until this moment. She releases my shoulders slowly, giving me a reassuring squeeze as she swallows hard.

"I'm going to call about a different lawyer," she says.

"But you said we don't have the money."

"I have a little bit of retirement. It's—I don't want you to worry about it. I can always make money. There's always more work to be found. We need a better lawyer."

Worry flickers through me. "Mom, you can't do that. You need that retirement."

"You need a better lawyer."

I shake my head. Mom already works two jobs. I know she took a huge loan out of her retirement when Grams was sick. If she dips into that again, she will have nothing to fall back on. She'll be in an even worse position, and it will be on me. I stand up.

"No. Please don't take out any money. I can figure it out. I can work with John."

"Clara, this isn't a discussion. I'm going to get you a new lawyer. I don't care what it costs me."

Because she will do anything to protect me. For all our issues, and for all I've put her through, my mother still loves me like this. She also loves me enough to force me to eat an egg and some toast because there's no chance of either of us getting back to sleep.

After we tidy from breakfast, I shower and pretend to be busy in my room when Mom starts making calls to any attorney who happens to have weekend hours. I'm not busy, of course. I'm mostly standing with my ear pressed against my bedroom door, listening to one-sided phone conversations.

"Well, I don't have the cash now, but—a credit card? I'm not...I'm not so sure I have that kind of available credit right now." The pause is long enough to give me hope until my mother sighs. "No, I understand. Thank you. Yes, we do have a public defender on the case."

The next phone call is just Mom leaving a message.

The third is a message too.

The fourth is a lot like the first, and then there are calls to the retirement account office. Long holds. My mom's soft swearing in the kitchen.

I feel the knots in my stomach arranging themselves into something else. Something that feels like determination. I have already ruined everything for her, and right now, she's giving me even more—she's going to take the fall financially to protect me from suffering.

The unfairness of it squeezes the center of my chest hard.

What if I could end this before she gets that money? If I find solid enough proof that Lily set me up, then maybe we won't need a better lawyer. Maybe if I get some sort of evidence, then I can take it to the police and get the charges dropped.

I slide on my jeans and shoes and reach for my phone charger and backpack. I know what I have to do, and I know already how much Mom will hate it. I just hope she'll find a way to forgive me, because if I let her suffer for me again, I'm not sure I'll ever forgive myself.

TWENTY-FIVE

I grab my old backpack and the two twenties I got from Gram for my sixteenth birthday and couldn't bear to spend after she got sick. Then I wait for Mom to hop in the shower. When the water turns on, I slip out of my room. George is immediately in front of me, dark eyes gazing at me expectantly, waiting for a walk or a treat. I offer him ear scratches and then leave a quick note on the table.

Mom,

I'm going to try to find something that might help my case. I promise I will be careful and safe. And I promise I will be back tonight. Please don't hire a new lawyer until I get back. Please, Mom. Let me try.

I love you,
Clara

I pause to look at the note, wondering if I should add anything. It tells her enough. And it tells her nothing. So I put it in the center of the table and hope I find what I need fast.

I slip outside and walk toward the street. It's nine thirty now. Saturday morning, so no rush hour, but there's still plenty of traffic. I stop at the corner, waiting for a couple of minivans and a gray sedan to pass. I cross after the traffic clears, following a long curving street into town.

While I walk, I try to come up with a plan. If I can't prove I'm not involved, can I prove Lily is? There has to be something. I stop, noticing a gray sedan about a block behind me. Chills run up my back. Is that the same one from earlier?

I keep walking, feeling the throb of my pulse at the base of my throat. I'm being completely stupid. There are lots of gray cars. No one is watching me.

I don't think.

I speed up without really meaning to, weaving past the rows of similar brick houses until I am at the crosswalk at the big divided four-lane road, the one that separates my neighborhood from Lily's.

I twist and see car after car. More than one gray sedan, and my heart is pounding. Is it that Ford? Or the Toyota over there? Am I actually being followed?

It feels absurd. But I am living in an absurd alternate reality where my best friend has set me up for a potential school bombing and maybe a murder too. I remind myself that it doesn't matter if I'm being followed. I'm not guilty of anything. Not this time.

I ignore my nerves and make my way past the chain restaurants and strip mall offerings until I am at the road that leads to the library. I wait at the corner for one long beat after another. Waiting for the gray sedan. Or a police car. Something. But nothing here is abnormal. It's an ordinary day in Ohio, and hysteria isn't going to help me. I push my anxiety back and make my way up the sidewalk to the library entrance.

It's cool and quiet inside. Faint music drifts from the children's area. A story time maybe? Other than that and the soft, muted beeping of books being scanned in another room, the library is silent.

A staff member who isn't Jody sits at the desk at the center of the main room. I find the same short-use computer I used before and pull up a private browser, immediately navigating to the local news.

Mr. Droesch is a top story. His house is on the muted video, a sagging beige two-story in a neighborhood that looks like mine. A cracked stoop and empty flower boxes peek out behind the yellow police tape around the house. I feel a wave of nausea imagining some kinder, gentler side of Mr. Droesch, a man who would plant seeds and watch those flower boxes, waiting for them to bloom.

I scroll past the video feed and click on the news story.

TUSKEGEE HIGH TEACHER FOUND DEAD, POLICE INVESTIGATING

PUBLISHED APRIL 11—1:05 A.M.

High school teacher Randall Droesch (32) was found dead in his home at approximately 9:35 p.m. last night. Droesch called 911 complaining of severe dizziness and nausea. Paramedics were unable to immediately enter the residence. Droesch's prone body was found blocking the front door, where he is presumed to have collapsed and died before paramedics arrived. Police were on the scene collecting evidence. While comment was not provided on the investigation, Detective Jones did confirm that narcotics and foul play have not been ruled out.

I close the story and check another. And then a third. All of them add up to essentially the same story. Mr. Droesch called 911 just before 9:30 p.m. complaining of dizziness and nausea. He denied taking anything unusual, just his regular supplements. When paramedics arrived, his body was blocking the door. One source reported the police department's narcotics canine was brought in to sweep the house.

Narcotics. The police asked us about narcotics this morning.

After the third article, a stony disbelief sinks in. Mr. Droesch openly discussed having a heart defect, which would probably put him at much higher risk for overdose or death from opioids. And he would know. He's a heart health advocate who generally avoids traditional medicines.

Mr. Droesch drank herbal tea and putrid-looking green juices. And he took a million supplements. Had one of those giant morning, afternoon, and evening pill containers on his desk, and he was very clear about the benefits of things like turmeric and echinacea, but it was all herbal stuff. He refused to take ibuprofen for a headache, for God's sake. I do not buy this man taking vitamins without careful research, let alone doing narcotics on the side.

Especially since he called for paramedics.

So whatever caused this wasn't something Mr. Droesch intentionally ingested. Which means he *was* probably poisoned. The only question is—did Lily do the poisoning?

Would Lily really kill someone? If you asked me a week ago, I would have instantly answered. I knew her inside out. Or I thought I did. Now, I have no idea what she's capable of. So I need to find someone who does.

I pull the keyboard a little closer and navigate to a texting app I haven't used in two years. It was hugely popular when we were all freshmen, thinking we were cool and important and should keep our communications incognito lest a teacher stumble onto our top-secret texts about after-school hangouts.

But as we got older, most of us just auto-forwarded messages from the app directly to our phones. Eventually we cut out the middleman and texted each other like normal people. I deleted the app ages ago, but my login still works. So if the premise is still the same, the messages should pop up on their phones without creating a text trail on my phone. I'm hoping for that, because I don't want to power on my phone and risk my mom tracking my location. Plus, I still don't know what the police can see, but I don't want them seeing the questions I'm about to ask.

I start with Gretchen.

Me: Did you hear what happened to Mr. Droesch?

It's ten minutes before Gretchen responds.

Gretchen: Yes. Why are you using this? I could barely remember my password.

Me: Long story. Not a good one.

Gretchen: L is making it seem like you're involved in what happened.

Me: I'm not. I swear.

Gretchen: I believe you, but I'm on that target list.

The police called Mom and Dad. They're freaked out.

Me: I'm so sorry. I don't mean to keep bothering you, but do you know anyone who might know more about Lily? Like if she might have some reason to do this to me?

Gretchen: I don't know.

Me: I'm in trouble, Gretch. Last time I deserved what I got. But I didn't do this, and I am going to go down for it.

The screen stays blank a long, long time. I lean back in the plastic library chair, which squeaks in protest. I am just about to close the window when a reply appears.

Gretchen: Maybe Cadence.

Cadence? I double-check the screen, but I did not misread it. There are no other Cadences. No way. But that makes it twice as confusing. Cadence didn't even know Lily. I mean, she knew *of her*, but from a distance. A healthy I-am-a-well-liked-athlete-but-I'm-still-not-cool-enough-for-that-social-zip-code distance.

Cadence was in *our* group. Gretchen, Britt, Cadence, and me—we were the core. Sometimes Zach would show up, when he was dating Gretchen, and sometimes Chloe would hang around when she was dating Cadence. Even thinking of the names dredges up ancient memories. Trips to Dairy Queen and movie all-nighters in Cadence's basement. Cheering on Cadence and Gretchen when the rest of us didn't make the varsity soccer team. They were good memories. It was a good group.

But it never included Lily.

New text pops up in the window, startling me back to the present.

Gretchen: I have to go, but good luck.

Me: Thank you. So much.

I hover after the last words. I want to tell her that I miss her, and that I hate this and wish more than anything that I could make things the way they were before. I miss her insatiable late-night hunger and the fact that she sings along to bad commercials. I want to tell that I always thought she looked so badass with her angular hair and winged eyeliner, which was even cooler because she was secretly a gentle soul.

I want to somehow capture all of that and put it into the text, but I know it's too late for that with Gretchen. I left my friendship with her behind when I ran away from Cadence that night.

Cadence.

Dread settles over me as I pull up her name in my email contact list. I immediately push myself away from the keyboard. I can't email her or text her. After what I did, I at least owe her the decency of leaving her alone.

I need someone else who can verify there is a connection between Lily and Cadence. Someone who was in Lily's group back in freshman year. Someone who's still speaking to me, that is. And of course, there's only one person who fits that bill.

Even as I gather my things and pretend this research is my reason, I know it's a half-truth at best. The whole truth is that yes, Henry was in Lily's group freshman year. I'd know because I stared at him endlessly freshman year. And yes, he is a logical choice, but I don't want to talk to him just because it's logical. I want to talk to him because being around him makes me feel normal and calm. And I'm short on both of those feelings right now.

"Excuse me."

I jolt in my chair, my heart instantly in my throat as I look up at the librarian who's staring down at me. She looks as surprised at my reaction as I was at her voice.

"Sorry," I say.

"It's fine. But your session has expired. Do you have a library card with us?"

Cold creeps up my neck, and my voice comes out small and unsure. "Yes."

"If you give me your name, I can look it up, and we can extend your time with that."

I practically leap out of the chair, knocking over the backpack. "No. No, I'm fine. I'm done."

"Are you sure?"

She looks nervous. I'm making her nervous. I pick up my bag and notice the woman at the computer across from me. She's watching me, that same uncertain look on her face too.

Is everyone in here watching me? Do they know I'm in trouble? Has my face been on TV or something? My heart is pounding, but I try to smile and pretend everything is normal, and I am just a girl leaving a library. But the minute I'm outside, I run.

TWENTY-SIX

I'm tired and half-starved by the time I get to Bon Gou, but one look at the red awning has me second-guessing myself. I don't even know that Henry is here. I could call, but I'm so paranoid about my phone now. I powered it off after leaving the house, and if I turn it on, my location will be trackable again, definitely by my mom and possibly by the police, who I'm sure have access to my cell phone service now that they have my regular phone.

So I slip inside, the bells jingling overhead as I walk into the dim restaurant. I scan the room for Henry without success. There is a table with six women on the right side of the dining area and a family with three loud kids on the left. There are a couple of occupied booths too far back to see much, but the only server in the room is Sammy.

She drops something steaming on a table and nods at me. "He's not working today."

"Oh, okay." I turn toward the door, feeling unsure of what to do now.

"Hold on," Sammy says with a grin.

I hesitate while she takes orders, patting my pocket and shifting back and forth on my feet. Sammy zips into the kitchen, speaking quickly in a language I don't recognize. Some form of Creole maybe? I'm terrible with languages, but it sounds playful and vaguely Caribbean in nature. She places two more steaming plates in front of a couple without looking at me. Did I misunderstand that *Hold on*? Was it meant for someone else?

When she finally glances at me, I give an awkward wave. "It was good seeing you," I say, feeling a little dumb and desperate for walking all this way.

She laughs, and it feels a little like she's laughing at me, but her eyes are kind when she waves me toward a table. "Go on and sit down there. I'll get you something."

Five minutes later she sets down a plate of something she calls tasso, which is spicy and smoky and completely delicious. I'm halfway through when I freeze. I have no idea how much this costs; if my math is right, I probably have about twenty-seven dollars to my name.

I startle when a figure slides into the booth across from me. Henry.

A smile blooms to my lips, but I gesture quickly at my plate. "So can you tell me how much this is? Because it is delicious and hopefully not terribly expensive, because my bank account is laughable at present. Wait! Never mind, I have a little cash!"

I pull out the twenties I forgot, and Henry touches my fingers, pushing them, and the cash, gently back to my side of the table. "You're not paying. Sammy fed you; you didn't order. So what's happening?"

"Lots," I say, and I mean it as a joke, but my eyes well up instantly. "I'm in trouble, Henry. I think they think I killed—"

I cut myself off so I don't really start crying. Henry reaches forward again, stroking the side of my wrist with his thumb.

"Have you heard anything?" I ask. "I mean other than the eleven o'clock news. Do they have Wanted posters up with my face on them?"

"No, nothing like that." Henry's golden eyes narrow. "But Lily is spewing plenty of nonsense in the group texts. Are you sure you're really a suspect?"

I fill him in on the cops and my mom's calls to the lawyers. Some anxious part of me wonders if I should tell him so much, but in the end, I give him a play-by-play of the entire day, from my paranoid walk to the library to my perusal of the various news stories on Mr. Droesch, with their comment-feed speculations that range from crafty murder to sad tale of a teacher with a hidden addiction.

Henry shakes his head. "I don't buy him as an addict. Do you know he ran a workshop on vitamin supplements and which ones can be dangerous?"

"Really?"

"Yeah, he offered it to athletes or really anyone applying to use the weight room. I guess those are the guys more likely to take weird shit."

"But that's exactly why I don't get it. How would someone poison him if he was so careful with what he took?"

"I have no idea," Henry says.

"Me either. And the only thing that I have a harder time understanding is whether Lily could have done this and why she'd want to. Gretchen told me I should check with Cadence."

"Cadence?" he asks.

"Yep, Cadence," I say. "But when she and I were friends, I didn't think she knew Lily. Do you know something I don't?"

Henry shakes his head. "They weren't friends as far as I knew. But Cadence dated Delaney for a while, right?"

"Yeah, Delaney Tenor."

Henry nods. "That's the connection. Delaney ran with our group in junior high. She and Lily were pretty tight."

"But not in high school?"

He shakes his head. "Delaney and Lily were friends in eighth grade. I was in half of their classes, and they were always together. They both worked at the school store."

"Like that counter where you could buy pens and pencils and stuff?"

Henry nods. "One day fifty dollars in cash went missing from the store cash box. Lily swore it was Delaney, and Delaney resigned from working the school store. It was a whole big scandal for a week, but it got quiet really quick. Delaney sat at a different table afterward though, which says something."

"Did Delaney take the money?"

He gives a bitter laugh. "Thing is, I never thought about whether she did or not. I didn't have a reason to question Lily back then. I should have remembered about Delaney after what happened to Mariana."

Mariana. Talking to her feels like an easier leap than Delaney, who I barely know. Delaney probably remembers me best as the girl who broke her ex-girlfriend's leg, effectively destroying her future in soccer. I cringe considering it.

"Do you think Mariana would talk to me?"

"I don't know." Henry says with a sigh. "She's mad loyal to Lily."

"Well, Cadence and I don't talk for pretty obvious reasons. I doubt Delaney would be chomping at the bit to have a chat either, but I feel like we should try."

Henry shrugs. "We could try. She moved to Forest Ridge, but I still have her number."

"Do you think she'd talk to you?"

Henry is already texting. When he finishes, he looks up at me with a furrowed brow. "Am I a guy girls don't want to talk to?"

"I don't mean it like that."

He smirks. "Sounds like you might."

I laugh. "Okay, sure. Most girls would trip over themselves to talk to you, but we can play this game."

"Trip over themselves," he repeats. I can't read his expression, but my guess is that he isn't sure if I'm making fun or being serious.

I cock my head. "Please don't tell me you're one of those guys who has no idea that he's hot."

"I don't think I'm a dog, but I don't see girls tripping, that's for sure."

I roll my eyes. "Well, I guess it must have just been me."

No way around it—the smile he offers up is flirty as hell. "Do go on."

"Oh, I've said plenty," I say, folding my napkin. "I should get the check."

He waves that off again and grabs the spoon I hadn't used from the table. He takes a few bites and then scoots out of the booth, grabbing the empty dish and beckoning me to follow.

We wind through the kitchen and place my plate near the dishwasher. The restaurant is quieter today, just a couple of guys near the grill. We're on the washing side, separated by big metal racks of pots and pans and various supplies.

Henry urges me past a stainless-steel sink and into a narrow hallway. I have no experience with commercial kitchens, but he is clearly at home. He closes drawers and moves a stack of prep bowls to a higher shelf. I'm too aware of his body in these small, ordinary motions. The flex of his arm. The line of his neck when he assesses the number of lemons in a basket.

My body clearly doesn't know this isn't the time for these kinds of observations. My eyes linger on his hands and I don't lean away when his elbow grazes my side. It feels ridiculous to react like this when my world is unraveling, but at the moment, it also feels like the most normal thing in my universe.

"I should have said something," he says abruptly. "About Lily."

It's as effective as a bucket of ice water at bringing me back to the terrible here and now. "What do you mean?"

We are by a check-in station, in a tiny alcove near a walk-in pantry. There is a narrow dented table under a stack of handwritten time cards, and a row of hooks for employee coats.

"I should have said something to you about Lily before this happened." He turns until I can see a muscle jumping in his jaw. He swallows hard before going on. "I knew what she could be like and I thought it was weird that she was so close to you."

I stiffen. "Why?"

"Because I didn't see anything she could gain from you. Most of her friends—the close ones anyway—offer her something, you know?"

I shake my head, because no, I don't know. Henry picks up on my confusion, his expression shifting. He rolls his shoulders, letting out a heavy breath. "Mariana has money. So there's that. Ava's mom is on the school board, so she has some leverage. Drishti takes exceptional notes in every single class and she lets Lily copy them. Even the Jacksons have their uses."

"And what about you?"

He offers a bitter laugh. "I'm Lily adjacent. We've never been friends. I dated Mariana. I was friends with Jackson Towns earlier on."

"Not now?"

"I tolerate Jackson now. I think the entire world is in a state of tolerating Jackson."

I chuckle and then remember the point. I am not like the rest of them. And I am not Lily adjacent either. "Your point is that I have nothing to offer."

Henry's fingers are under my chin, warm and calloused, but very gentle. "You have a hell of a lot to offer, Clara. But Lily is too shit to see any of that."

He pulls his fingers free, and it makes me aware of the heat in my cheeks—a heat that tells me I'm blushing. If Henry notices, he has the grace to not mention it.

"I had a feeling there was something devious behind her befriending you, and I should have said something," he says.

"I'm just glad you're talking to me now. No one else is."

"Well, I—"

The door on the far side of the kitchen flies open and footsteps sound out. "Henry?"

"Yeah, Sammy, we—

Sammy talks fast, cutting him off. "There is a police officer here. He'd like to talk to you?"

My heart leaps into my throat. Henry locks eyes with me. His face is a reflection of my terror. Are they here to arrest me for murdering Mr. Droesch? Even if they aren't, will being here tangle Henry and Sammy into this mess?

"Sure, I'm coming," he says.

Panicked, I step forward, a deer moving into oncoming traffic. Henry lifts a finger to my lips, silencing me. He gently pushes me sideways behind an open door—the pantry. I am concealed here if they don't move past the prep tables. Which means I'll be concealed if they aren't actually looking for me.

"He's back here somewhere," Sammy says, presumedly to the police. The strain in her cheery voice is clear and I hear Henry moving, trying to get to the front of the restaurant.

I shove myself sideways, wedging my body as far into the corner as possible. Footsteps approach and they sound like too many to be Henry's alone.

"You Henry?"

"I am."

My heart beats in triple time. I recognize that voice. It's

Detective Jones. And I hear the crackle of a radio that tells me another officer is here too. There's no way they didn't see me. No possible way.

Detective Jones introduces himself and asks if Henry has time for a few questions.

"Sure."

"Are you alone back here?" he asks.

"Yeah, other than my uncle and cousin over there."

Shock freezes me in place. Henry just lied to the police. Henry lied and if they find me, it will ruin us both. Behind the heavy door I clench my fists. There is nowhere I can run and nothing I can do. I close my eyes and wait to be found.

TWENTY-SEVEN

My teeth begin to chatter and my knees wobble. I bite my lip hard to keep myself together. I cannot make a sound. I cannot be found right now.

"I appreciate you talking to me," Jones says.

"Sure, of course."

"It's about a friend of yours. Clara Cutler? You are friends with Clara, yes?"

"Yeah, we're friends."

"Then I'm sure you know she's been in some trouble."

"I've heard that rumor."

"Rumor?" Jones drags out the word. "You say that like you're not sure you believe it."

"I'm not sure. Clara has never seemed hostile. She seems smart and polite."

"Even polite people can hide a nasty side, Henry."

My chest is swelling and aching, a throb right in the center that grows stronger with every heartbeat. I have to stop this. I think about stepping out from behind this door, but what would happen then? What happens to Henry if the police find me here and know he was lying to them about me? I will take us both down if I get caught.

"When did you last see Clara?"

"Couple of days ago. She came in."

Henry's voice is even, but his words send my fear into overdrive. Why is he doing this? Why doesn't he just tell them?

"She came into the restaurant here?"

"Why are you asking? Is she hurt?"

Henry is playing it cool. He sounds genuinely confused.

"Not that I'm aware of, but we need to determine her whereabouts over the past twenty-four hours."

"Did you ask her?" Henry asks.

"Let's get back to our questions," Jones says. There's the slightest edge to his voice now. Henry is flirting with being uncooperative, and Jones clearly doesn't like it. "You saw Clara two days ago? Was that here in the restaurant?"

The way he asks that question pings a radar in my mind. He already knows I've been here. My mom once told me some people only ask questions when they already know the answers, and my gut tells me that's what this is.

"Yes, she was. I think it was—

"Thursday."

My eyes fly open. That voice doesn't belong to Henry; it belongs to Sammy. I didn't even hear her reenter the kitchen, but she's here now. And she's lying too. She saw me today. She served me a meal, for God's sake, and called Henry to tell him I was here. What is she doing? What are both of them doing?

"You're talking about that girl, right?" she asks, sounding amused. "The white skinny one with the braid making moon eyes at my cousin?"

"I guess it was Thursday," Henry says.

"What did she talk to you about?" Jones asks.

"I'll bet she got his number. Or tried at least."

Sammy is even better at this than Henry. I open my eyes, my gaze fixed on a chip in the painted door in front of me. My breath shivers in and out. In and out. I don't know what I expect him to say.

"She wasn't here for my number. She was upset. She's being framed for something terrible."

My breathing stops for a second. I don't know what I expected Henry to say, but if you gave me all the guesses in the world, this wouldn't have come to mind.

"Framed?" Detective Jones sounds amused.

"What do you mean by *framed*?" This is not Detective Jones, but I recognize her soothing voice from the station. From the cruiser before that. This is Officer Fleming. Maybe Detective Fleming now. Whatever her title, she is the single bright spot in that department for me.

Hope blooms in my chest.

"Thank you, Detective Fleming," Jones says, his tone biting. "But I should warn you before you answer, Henry. Framing is quite an accusation. You might want to be careful believing your friend's side of this so easily."

"I didn't say I believed her, but I have difficulty imagining Clara hurting someone."

"She hurt someone before, though, didn't she?"

"I know what happened freshman year, if that's what you mean. And since then she's worked hard to rebuild her reputation. It's one of the reasons I don't buy that plan being hers."

"Give me another reason," Jones says.

"Because she's too brilliant."

My lips part in surprise. Until this week I wasn't sure Henry ever thought of me at all. If he did, I would have never believed *brilliant* was a word he'd use to describe me.

"Brilliant, how?" Officer Fleming asks.

"Chemistry brilliant. She's really gifted. Which means she's smart enough to know how propane explosions work and how difficult they would be to control in a situation like that."

"How do you know all these details, Henry?" There is a layer of suspicion under Detective Jones's words now, and it terrifies me.

Henry needs to stop. Right now. First I ruined Cadence's life, then my mom's. If Henry is dragged into a police investigation because of my stupid actions, I'm not sure I'll be able to live with that.

"I know because Lily Dalton sent photographs of the plan to the entire group chat. Half of the kids in the high school have probably seen that plan at this point. I just happen to be decent enough at chemistry to be able to decipher it a bit."

Another shifting of feet. For once, I think Jones might be at a loss for words, and his silence makes me wonder—did he not know Lily sent around those photos? Because I sure the hell didn't. Until this moment, I didn't know she had taken photographs of the plans, and I'm wondering if anyone should be asking themselves how she got them.

"We'll keep that in mind," Fleming says.

At the same moment, Jones interrupts. "You should be careful to steer clear of Ms. Cutler. You seem like a smart kid, and it would be a shame to get mixed up."

"I'll keep that in mind," Henry says, and I don't think he's using the same words by accident.

"You do that. And if she comes around, you or your sister need to call me."

"Got it," Sammy says. She doesn't bother to correct him that Henry is her cousin not her brother. And she doesn't bother to tell the truth. They are both out there, necks on the line for me. I have no idea why they'd take this risk.

My mind is reeling as I listen to the detectives leave. I wait for long minutes, feeling adrenaline coursing like fire through my veins. I do not know how long I wait. Ten minutes. Ten hours. It feels like years before the door is suddenly yanked forward, cool air rushing at my face. Henry is there, looking me over with tender, worried eyes.

Sammy is right behind him. "Get her out the back. They are pulling onto the street."

One of the chefs is just behind them, a tall man with a backward baseball cap. I remember him from the cat situation out back. Antoine. He is turned facing the kitchen door, his shoulders wide.

"He is gone," Antoine says. "They headed east."

"Not a word," Sammy says, thrusting a finger at the big man. Antoine holds his hands up in surrender, but his eyes move past Sammy. He looks right at me.

"Get her to Tati's house," Sammy says to Henry.

"Gotta take your car," Henry says, pulling me away from the wall. I am barely on my feet, my lips cold and numb. Tears stream down my face. I don't know when I started crying. I don't know why they're doing any of this. Henry's arm is around my back, and Sammy is digging keys out of a purse.

"Why are you helping me?" I mean the question for all of them, but my gaze falls on Antoine of all people.

"Because Henry knows you," he says.

"Oh please," Sammy says, "you're helping because you saw her keep Tuna out of that broken glass. You're a softie."

Antoine doesn't argue, and Henry doesn't add anything else to the conversation. He pushes open the back door and rushes me past the dumpster. An old cobalt blue Ford Fiesta is parked badly near the back door. Henry moves toward the passenger door, and finally, finally my bodily control kicks back in. I wrench open the door and buckle myself in. It smells like cinnamon gum and vinyl seats, and there is a stack of hair ties around the gear shift.

Henry gets in beside me, looking far too tall for this tiny car, and starts the engine. He reverses smoothly and pulls out of the back alley, weaving us instantly into the twisting residential streets behind the restaurant.

"Where are we going?" I ask, still feeling winded and a little sick.

"To my aunt's house. Just to think. Do you have anything on you that they could track? Like your phone?"

"My old phone," I say, my mouth desert dry. "It's powered down. Do you think they can still find it?"

"Maybe? I'm not sure," he says.

I feel like I'm coming back to myself, the world returning to focus. If they can track my phone, they'll find me with Henry. They'll find Sammy. They'll find Antoine. They could come after the restaurant or maybe his aunt. Everyone could be in trouble because of me.

I raise my hands, suddenly sick with dread. "Stop! Oh my God, you need to stop."

He does, instantly pulling to the side of the road, his face the picture of worry. "What's wrong? Are you sick?"

I unbuckle my seat belt. "I can't do this. You can't be caught up in this, Henry. You have got to get away from me."

I am pulling at the door handle when Henry stops me, his long fingers gentle on my arm.

"Clara."

I turn to look at him. His eyes are mesmerizing, even now. It's like I can see the whir of his thoughts, even without him saying a word. I shake my head, pushing back.

"No. This is dangerous. Do you have any idea what could happen to you and Sammy?"

"I have a bit of an idea, yeah."

I feel myself stumble for something to say. "Henry, I'm serious."

"No, you're trying to be noble, but you need help, and I'm trying to be that help. Do you not want me here?"

I open my mouth to refuse—to tell him to go and be safe and all the rest of it. But in the end, nothing comes out. Because the truth is—I do need his help.

"Since you don't seem to be refusing, I think we should keep moving. So buckle your seat belt, please."

I relent, buckling back up even though worry is twisting

my insides. Henry takes off again, weaving though more streets. Turning left and then right and then left again.

We are climbing a hill, and I don't recognize the houses around me. Duplexes mostly. Small, but kept up. I spot flowerpots on porches and old-school painted metal chairs.

Henry pulls into one of the driveways, zipping up the narrow parking area like he's done it a hundred times.

He turns to look at me. "Tati isn't home right now."

"Do you live with her?"

"Around the corner. But just in case the police get the idea to check out my house..."

"We won't be there."

"Exactly." He smiles. "Big families have their upsides."

"I don't understand why you're doing this."

Henry's face clouds over. "It's been a couple of years back now, I think, but there was this day that Antoine found a box of puppies ditched in a dumpster behind his apartment. They were skinny. Weak. In bad shape. Antoine looks tough, but Sammy was right. He's a softie. He doesn't have a car, so he was carrying this box of puppies to the humane society. This giant guy trying to save these puppies. A car pulled up alongside him while he was walking..."

Henry goes very quiet then. His fingers tighten so hard on the steering wheel that his knuckles go pale. And a part of me aches at what he might say when he speaks. I know exactly what he's referring to, and it makes my face burn. What did I do when all those rumors about the Haitian community were flying around two years ago?

I don't even know how it started, but I remember the memes about pets disappearing and the graffiti that sprung up near neighborhoods with Haitian families. I knew it was awful, but even knowing that, I wrote it off as stupid anti-immigrant crap. And even though I was completely caught up in a crazy crush on Henry, I didn't think about the fact that he's from an immigrant family. I never considered what it had to have been like for them to see this shit on the news and internet. Did I ever think about what Henry might have been going through?

Sometimes I hate the girl I was before Cadence.

Henry lets out a low, bitter laugh. "Let's just say my family knows what it's like to be accused of things you have not done."

"I'm so sorry that happened to Antoine. To all of you. But this isn't like that," I say. "You really did nothing to deserve any of that. But I did, Henry. I have a real record because of what I did to Cadence. No one set me up."

"It was an accident."

"It doesn't matter. I was there. It was what they said. I broke into her backyard. Took a swim in her hot tub and then argued with her on the stairs behind her house. She fell because of me. And if she hadn't fallen, the police might not be so quick to believe all this. They are accusing me because they know what I'm capable of. And so should you."

He reaches for me quickly, slipping his hand behind my neck and into my hair. And then he is beyond slow, one rough thumb dragging along my jaw, just beneath my ear. Fire follows the path of his thumb, and I take a deep, steadying breath.

"I know about Cadence," he says. "And I know that's not all you're capable of. I have watched you for a long, long time."

"How long?"

"Since they walked you out of the school in handcuffs."

My face feels like it will ignite. I drop my eyes, but his thumb strokes my jaw again. "They walked you out, and I thought we'd never see you again. You'd transfer schools or something."

"We're too broke to move," I say, my voice cracking. "But I wanted to. Desperately."

"Whatever the reason, you came back. You took everything they threw at you, and you kept getting up."

"Fine, I'm resilient. You are more than that! You're a top-ten student, Henry! Your reputation is impeccable. Hell, you're probably already accepted into five schools, and you're not even a senior."

"Eight schools actually," he says, sliding his hand free of my hair. And then he smiles. "Which means I'm smart enough to decide for myself what's worth getting in trouble for."

TWENTY-EIGHT

Henry's aunt in Columbus with a friend for a concert, so her duplex is empty. Henry's house is around the corner, and Sammy and her mom are half a block south. Antoine and a couple of the other guys live in an apartment complex that backs the duplexes. There are three house keys on Henry's key ring and photos cluttered on every inch of the walls in the duplex. It is the absolute opposite of my universe.

Henry pours me a glass of water and sits me on the couch in the front room. My gaze drifts over pictures of his family, including photos of little-kid Henry with a gap-toothed smile and a skinny arm wrapped around a young Sammy's shoulders. A huge group shot. A picture of an old couple on a beach at sunset, palm trees nestled into the side of the picture.

"You warm enough?" Henry asks.

"I'm fine. A little shaky, I guess."

He pulls out his phone and responds to a text. Then puts it face down on the table and sits next to me. His arm brushes mine when he turns toward me.

"I know this is blunt, but do you have an alibi for last night?"

I shake my head. "I was at home all night and asleep, but there isn't good proof."

"Lily put Mr. Droesch on this list. Do you think she had a reason to hurt him?"

"She didn't like him, and it was a pretty intense dislike. She texted me about it once, but she never really filled me in. Still, killing him feels extreme, doesn't it?"

"Yeah. Are there other people on the list she might have the same feeling about?"

I shrug. "I don't know. I guess there's no love lost between her and Paxton these days..."

Henry rolls his eyes. "Lily and everyone else. It's ridiculous."

"You don't dislike Paxton?"

"No. And I think he's going through some things."

"Well, he hates me for reasons unknown. But that's not the point. The point is that I can't tell you whether Lily has it in for the people on this list."

Henry takes his phone off the table and sends another quick text. He scratches the back of his neck. "Okay, go back to Mr. Droesch. What's her deal with him?"

"I've never really understood it—Lily did fine in his class freshman year, from what I remember. We were both in it, even though we weren't friends then. But I don't know why she'd concoct all of this if she just wanted to hurt him. Doesn't that feel convoluted?"

"It feels more calculated. Like maybe she wanted to hurt Mr. Droesch, but you're the one she wants to hurt most."

I shake my head and put my water cup down on the glass coffee table. "I have no idea what I did to her. My guess is that it has to be about Cadence."

"Cadence? Why?"

"It's the only time I ever lost my way completely. I did terrible things that night, and my gut tells me this is more fallout from my screwup."

He checks his phone. "Well, maybe there's a chance to figure it out. Want to take a little road trip?"

He holds out the screen for me to view the texts.

Henry: It's been a minute. How are things?

Delaney: Wow, Henry T. Blast from the past. Things are good. What's up?

Henry: This is a little out there, but do you have time for a call?

Delaney: lol. Weird request. I'm at work. But why?

Henry: I feel like Lily's maybe up to something. Would rather talk.

Delaney: Stop by the Fairborn Y. I'm working the front.

"The Y?"

"YMCA," Henry says. "I worked as a lifeguard there one summer for a couple of weeks. It's maybe twenty minutes away. You want to come with?"

My tension must show, because Henry smiles. "Look, what if you keep me company on the drive? I'll talk to Delaney first to feel things out."

"I don't know what there is to feel out. I ruined her ex-girlfriend's life."

"Ruined might be overkill. Cadence spent four months in Switzerland, and I've heard she's in Model UN this year. Plus, for whatever the socials are worth, she seems happy at her new school."

"Maybe, but she can't play soccer, and she was amazing. She was practically guaranteed a full ride to the college of her choosing. If it wasn't for me."

"And if she didn't blow out the same knee in a game," Henry points out. "Or an ankle or shoulder for that matter. There are no guarantees."

I roll my eyes, and he lifts his hands in surrender. "I'm not saying you didn't hurt her. I'm not saying it wasn't bad. I'm only saying it's okay to move past a bad choice you made that unintentionally caused a terrible thing to happen."

"Okay." And then maybe because I just don't want him to keep going with all of this, I stand up. "I'll come along."

Henry plays the Rolling Stones softly the entire way to the YMCA. Not a classic rock mix or a greatest hits album either. I don't even realize we're listening to the Stones until "Gimme Shelter" starts. He sings along a little, soft snippets here and there, and he points out hawks he sees on the side of the road. And in the middle of everything else, or maybe because of it, I fall right back under the spell I don't think he means to cast.

"Do you ever think about the future?" I ask.

"Like about college? Or other things?"

"All of the above."

He shrugs. "College is the goal, but I think more about where I might go after. What I might want to see. What about you?"

"Lately, thinking about the future is a scary move for me."

He hums sympathetically and takes the exit ramp off the freeway. "You said you wanted to be a pharmacist."

"I do."

"Why's that?"

An awful vision flashes to life in my mind. My grandmother in the kitchen, smoke alarm blaring, a plastic cereal bowl melting and smoking on the burner. She just stood there, her hands over her ears, crying. And even now I can practically taste that acrid, chemical tang of burning plastic in the air.

"My grandmother had Alzheimer's. It was bad. We knew

something was wrong neurologically, but after she was diagnosed, it just went really fast. We were strangers to her. And the only glimmers of the person we knew before happened because of medication. There are medicines that help, but we aren't there yet. I believe there is chemistry out there that can cure Alzheimer's."

Henry pulls into a parking space and turns off his ignition. "You might be the only junior who has a real reason for their planned college major."

I laugh. "I doubt that. Hiba wants to be a doctor."

Henry cocks his head with a smirk. "Hiba and I are good friends. Her parents and older brothers are all doctors. Sometimes we just end up on a path, without thinking about it much."

I think about Lily, who has a patented answer for why she wants to go into international relations. It's all about global collaboration and harmony and blah, blah, blah. But she doesn't really give a shit about that. She always tells me that it's the degree most likely to get her out of Ohio forever. And I sort of get it. For a family with plenty of money, I'm surprised how little they travel.

Henry unbuckles his seat belt and then freezes, his gaze fixed on the windshield. Outside, a tall familiar blond is standing at the bottom of the steps talking to someone with dark curly hair. The sight of him sends my heart into my throat, and I suddenly can't seem to breathe.

"Is that Paxton Bryce?" I ask, my voice a squeak.

"Yeah, it's Paxton. And he's talking to Mariana."

"What the hell are they doing here?" I ask, my voice a harsh whisper.

"I have no idea, but I can pull out if you want."

Before I can answer, Paxton looks up. Any hope I have of him looking past the car or not seeing me shatters in an instant because Paxton's eyes lock onto mine. His face goes pale with what I can only guess is fear.

Then Mariana turns too, her lips parted in shock.

Every cell of my being wants to run, but it's too late to hide. We've already been seen.

TWENTY-NINE

Henry gets out of the car, and I follow but then freeze.

"I shouldn't be near Paxton," I say. And then I raise my hands, palms out, speaking a little louder so Paxton can hear. "I swear I had no idea you were here."

He says nothing, and his face is utterly unreadable, his dark eyes flashing even though his expression is blank.

Mariana steps in front of him, looking between Henry and me.

"Are you following me?" she asks him.

"Mar, are you serious?" Henry asks. "What are you even doing here?"

"I'm…looking for a job."

Henry does not laugh, but he clearly does not believe her. And why would he? Mariana's father owns the hospital where my mom works. *Loaded* doesn't begin to cover her financial state.

"And Paxton is going to give you a job?" I ask, unable to hold the question in. I mean, Paxton is almost as loaded as Mariana. Why are either of them here? Why would either of them be working?

"I'm researching potential jobs when I'm in college," Mariana says. "But I can't talk to you about this, or about anything else."

"I'm sorry," I say, again raising my hands. "I'm not trying to make anyone uncomfortable. I'll go."

"Does Lily know you're talking to her?" Mariana asks.

She's not talking to me. She's asking Henry. There is a strange silence that falls around us. Henry and Mariana are locked in a strange staring match. And Paxton is turning away, just walking down the sidewalk in his—well, what do you know—YMCA staff T-shirt. Maybe it really is a resume builder.

But I don't have the chance to ask, because he's walking to the edge of the parking lot without a single word to anybody. I don't see the Mustang I swear I remember him getting at the beginning of sophomore year. Probably doesn't want to park that close to the poor folks using the Y.

Henry is muttering quietly to Mariana, but she is frantic. Her hands are shaking. Is she angry that we're hanging out?

"No!" she finally says, answering something Henry said that I couldn't decipher. Mariana shakes her head over and over, looking between us. And then her face falls, and it looks like she might cry. "I'm sorry, I can't. And you shouldn't either. It's dangerous."

Mariana turns away from both of us then, walking across the lot to her Mercedes, so apparently Paxton hasn't taught her the ropes of being a rich kid working in a poor neighborhood. She starts the engine without another look in our direction.

Henry returns to me, his face clouded with confusion and concern.

"Do you think she's going to call the police, or is she jealous that I'm here with you?"

Henry takes a long while before answering. He shakes his head. "Neither. I think she's freaked out. She won't talk to me, but she kept looking in Paxton's direction. Do you think he said something to scare her?"

"Paxton despises me, and I'm the talk of the town. It wouldn't be a stretch to imagine him talking about how evil I am."

"True," Henry says, but he's staring at Mariana's taillights as they disappear out of the parking lot. "I don't know. She flipped out. Swore I was in danger."

"In danger because of me?"

"Maybe."

"Yep. That sounds like Paxton." I heave a sigh, and Henry approaches, touching my upper arms lightly.

"You aren't dangerous," he says.

"Maybe not, but being around me isn't great for your reputation."

"I don't care about my reputation."

"Clearly."

He chuckles. "You ready to go in?"

I shrug. "Why not? I've already had a little chitchat with Paxton. How much worse can Delaney be?"

The YMCA is an inviting brick building. Two women walk out carrying yoga mats, and three teenagers with a basketball pass them on the way in. Henry touches my arm briefly and then slides his fingers down the inside of my wrist to take my hand.

He doesn't release my hand when we step inside, and I'm grateful for the contact. Still, the second Delaney appears at the front desk, I pull free.

She's still beautiful. She has dark red hair and a smattering of freckles across the bridge of her nose. Her eyes are light blue and almost too big for her face. Barbie doll eyes. I used to tease Cadence all the time that Delaney was out of her league, and it never failed to make her laugh.

Shock passes over Delaney's face when she catches sight of me. But she nods and calls over another staff member in a red shirt. "I need to take a break. Can you cover the desk?"

I tense, glancing at the door. Should I go? Should I run?

But Henry speaks first, reaching out to give Delaney a loose hug. "Good to see you."

"You too." Delaney's eyes cut to me. "I...I honestly don't know what to say."

"You probably want to know why we're here," Henry says.

Delaney nods, but she's still looking right at me. So I answer. "On Monday, I'm going to be charged with threatening to commit a terrorist act. I didn't do it. Not even close. I also think I'm a murder suspect, and as ridiculous as it sounds, I think Lily might be framing me for both."

Delaney watches me for a long minute. Finally she exhales softly. "It doesn't sound ridiculous."

"It doesn't?" I ask, because it sounds pretty ridiculous to me.

But Delaney smirks. "No, it doesn't. Because I'm the founding member of the Framed by Lily club."

THIRTY

Delaney takes us to a lounge on the second floor. There are vending machines whirring in the corner and red padded seats with rips in the vinyl. Delaney and Henry plop into two of the chairs with wide arms, but I find a hard plastic chair at one of the tables.

"You're talking about that school store mess, aren't you?" Henry asks.

Delaney nods, glancing at me. "I got suspended for three days for robbing the school store in the eighth grade. Which is really cute, since I did not rob it."

"What happened?" I ask.

Delaney shrugs. "We were close to the end of the year, and the administration team was choosing who to recommend for the high school. The high school store team only had one opening, and it sounded like I was going to get the job."

"So she just took the money?" I ask.

Delaney laughs. "Oh no. She didn't just take the money. She swore that she *saw* me taking it. Cried about how she hated to tell on me and it was tearing her apart."

"Why?"

"She wanted the job. And she got it, by the way. Which is no skin off my back because it's actually a bit of a bitch. You have to go into school an hour early and stay late three times a week. It's not a paying gig either."

"So she threw you under the bus for a crappy job," Henry says.

Delaney nods. "A job she thought should have been hers. See, when Lily thinks she's owed, she won't stop until she gets what she wants."

It doesn't make sense in my brain. "But she wasn't owed that job. Did you tell anyone that she was lying?"

"No." Delaney gives a sad little huff. "Lily threatened to tell Sadie I'd made a pass at her while we were working. Sadie was my first girlfriend. I was thirteen, and I really liked her, you know. Totally smitten. But Sadie and Lily were pretty close back then, and I thought maybe Sadie would believe her. I mean, everyone believes perfect little Lily, right?"

"Yeah, I'm familiar with that," I say drily.

"Anyway, I was worried about her making even more shit up,

so I kept my mouth shut. Then we moved, and Cadence and me were together and I just didn't think about it much."

"Do you ever talk to Lily?" I ask.

She laughs. "Hell no. I wouldn't piss on that bitch if she burst into flames in front of me."

Henry leans forward. "Gretchen told Clara that she thought Cadence would know why Lily was doing this."

Delaney frowns. "I'm not sure why she would, unless Gretchen meant the connection with me. Lily and Cadence never hung out to my knowledge. And no offense, Clara, but wouldn't you be the best person to figure out why she's framing you?"

"I've tried, but it just doesn't make sense for her to do this to me. We weren't fighting. I didn't date a guy she liked or steal from her or whatever else."

Delaney shakes her head. "This isn't about what makes sense. It's about what Lily wants. You took something that she wanted. I'd bet my money that's what this is about."

"What about that chemistry competition?" Henry asks. "That's why you became friends."

"Maybe," I say, "but she won an honorable mention too. I didn't take anything from her that I know of."

I think about it for a minute, honestly lost. "There just isn't anything. Lily's the one who's popular. She has a stronger GPA and two devoted parents, the beautiful house; she has everything. She's the one who scooped me up to save me."

"To save you from what?" Delaney asks.

My face feels hot. "After everything with Cadence, when I came back. I was a pariah."

"You don't think you deserved that?" Delaney's voice has taken a cold edge.

"No, I did deserve it. I still do. I'm just saying, I don't have anything she'd want. It's my own fault, but it's the truth."

"It's a bitch, you know." Delaney watches me with a strange expression. Maybe it's anger or pity, or a strange mix of the two. "I know you didn't intend for that shit to go down how it did. I don't believe you wanted to hurt Cadence."

"Does it matter what I wanted?"

"Intent always matters," she says. "And it also doesn't matter at all."

Quiet passes between us then while I process the dichotomy of her words. The dichotomy of my life, really.

"If I were you, I'd be thinking back to the beginning," Delaney says.

"To the beginning?"

"To the beginning of you and Lily. As far as I remember, you were not friends before."

"No. Not until winter break of sophomore year."

"Why did you start talking? Why did you become friends to begin with?"

Henry turns to her as if the question didn't occur to him

before either. But now that Delaney has put voice to the words, he wants to know too.

Which of course makes me remember. Because how could I forget?

It's the first day of winter break , and there's so much snow. School-is-closed levels of snow, and isn't that a bitch, because we're off for two weeks anyway.

Whatever. After the hell that was the first half of my sophomore year, I'm just happy to be at home. And then my phone buzzes with an incoming text.

Lily: *Hi Clara, it's Lily Dalton. I know you don't really know me, but are you in chemistry club?*

I check the message twice, sure it's a joke. Because yeah, I'm in the chemistry club, and everyone else quit after the first meeting. I guess even an ultra-nerdy academic club loses appeal when there's a criminal on the roster.

I weigh replying for long minutes, before finally tapping out a response..

Me: *Not much of a club. Just Mr. Philpot and me.*

Lily: *Gotcha. Do you have any time over break? There's a chemistry competition.*

Me: *Okay?*

Lily: *I have an idea. Would you have time to chat?*

"Clara?" Henry asks gently, and I shake myself back to the present, remembering Delaney asked me a question. When did we become friends?

"She texted me during winter break. She asked about chemistry club."

Delaney frowns. "I don't remember her being into chemistry before. Do you, Henry?"

He shakes his head. "Not that I know of."

A group of kids squeal from the nearby game room, and Delaney sighs. She looks healthy and happy, despite the current annoyance on her face. "Look, I've got to get back to it."

"Thanks for talking to us. It is good to see you," Henry says.

"Yes, thank you," I say, and then because I can't hold it in, I keep going. "And I'm sorry, Delaney. I know I didn't do it directly to you, but I know you cared about her even if you weren't together anymore."

"Yeah, we were a good thing," she says, a faraway look coming over her. "Just not a forever thing." She points at me. "And you've got to find a way to move past this. You can't live in the shadow of your worst mistake. It's going to break you, Clara."

I don't say anything on our way back out of the rec center. And Henry doesn't push me. He opens the door like we're on a date. Drives steady and calm with Sam Cooke playing softly in the background.

Everything about Henry is a contradiction to the chaos in my mind. My thoughts swirl around Delaney's words and my own memories.

"You zoned out over there?"

"A little maybe," I admit. "I've just been thinking about what she said. It's hard not to look at the last year and a half and see some of this."

"See some of what?" Henry asks.

"That Lily might have befriended me for a reason. I was so in awe of her reaching out to me. It felt like the kindest thing anyone had ever done. And it was because of meeting her that I entered the contest and won. She unlocked this whole chemistry world for me."

"But you were in chemistry club first."

I bite my lip. "True. But she's the one who brought up that competition. Mr. Philpot didn't mention it to me, so I wouldn't have done it."

Is it possible that the chemistry competition was the start of all of this? Visions of our friendship flash through my mind. Going over study slides in Lily's bedroom. Shopping for her prom dress. Holding hands at my grandmother's funeral. For the past seventeen and a half months, I felt uniquely connected to Lily—like we had a special bond.

But of course, Lily does that, doesn't she? She makes you feel completely and totally seen. Ava, who shadows Lily like it's her full-time job, might see me as the pity case. And despite being a senior, Mariana practically leaps at any opportunity to be with Lily. They might each believe they're the true best friend. And it doesn't stop with Ava and Mariana. Every teacher believes themselves to be her favorite. Every Jackson thinks they have a shot at being Lily's true love. Why was I stupid enough to believe I was special?

"You're still in another world," Henry says softly, bringing me back to the here and now.

"Oh, you know. Just thinking about how I've maybe spent the last year and a half living a lie."

"I'm sorry this is happening to you. What would help?"

"I just wish I knew what to do. I don't even know where to start."

He nods. "It's like chemistry, right? You need to find the catalyst. Something caused her to do this, so if you find that thing, then you might be able to stop all of these reactions."

"Sure sounds good in theory." My smile feels a little forced.

"Are you really ready to go home?"

"Yeah. Mom's going to be worried. I'm going to talk to her about what Lily did to Mariana and to Delaney. Maybe she'll have some insight on when Lily and I became friends."

I direct Henry into my neighborhood, and we wind our way

through the streets to my house. He pulls up to the curb out front and turns off the engine. And before I get out, he grabs my wrist. It is the easiest thing, letting him pull me closer until my face is in the crook of his neck and his arms are around me. Even crammed against the center console and the parking brake, being close to him makes my whole body go still. The world fades into the background, and there is nothing but the warmth of his body and the smell of him, clean and soapy.

"Please call me if you need anything."

His words are muffled by my hair, and I know I should say okay. I should also let him go, but I don't. I breathe deep and close my eyes, memorizing the feel of his palms against my back. The rhythm of his breath near my neck. I feel his fingers feather over the tips of my hair, and then finally, we pull apart.

He watches me until I have my front door unlocked. My house is dark. Mom doesn't get home on Saturdays until close to midnight, so I've got a couple of hours to pull myself together. I toss my keys on the counter and plug in my phone. I flip on the light in the kitchen and realize something is wrong.

It's quiet.

Too quiet.

"George?"

I spin in a slow circle, searching under the table, and in the section of the living room I can see. Why isn't he barking? He should absolutely be barking. Is he in Mom's room? I pad down the hallway, a prickling feeling of dread crawling up the back of my neck. Because he should be here.

He should hear me. Even if he didn't hear me before, he should now. He should be lumbering down the hallway, tags jangling and toenails scraping the linoleum. I inch toward the hall light, my heart speeding up. I flick the switch. The hallway lights up, empty. Silent. I feel sick with worry.

"George?" My voice trembles.

And then I hear something in the kitchen. Not dog tags or toenails. It is the scrape of something moving across the counter. I whirl, my body gone cold. And then I see a flash of movement coming toward me.

THIRTY-ONE

My brain cannot wrap itself around Lily being in my house, but here she is. In my kitchen, holding something dark and metallic. For a short terrifying instant, I'm sure it's a gun. And then I see the familiar cracked glass. My phone. She's taken my phone off the charger.

She waggles it in the air. "You really are the most predictable human being I've ever met."

"Lily." My voice cracks halfway through her name. I can't manage any other words at all. I am trapped, and she knows it. Our bedroom windows barely open. The side door is to her right, and the front door is behind her. The only way out is through her. And my phone isn't the only thing she's holding.

There's something boxy, square, and black in her right hand.

I recognize it in an instant. Her stun gun. I jerk, my body itching to run.

"Ah, ah, ah." Lily waggles that gun. "Don't move."

I do what she says, though my legs shake wildly. My throat is suddenly unbearably dry despite the cold sweat dampening my palms. Lily looks perfectly put together, her hair in a sleek braid. She's dressed in dark clothes—not cat-burglar black, but definitely clothes that would make her difficult to spot.

I glance around the kitchen, spotting George's dog bowls in the corner. Fear stabs at my heart. "Where is George?"

Lily tips her head to the side. "Out back. He was *delighted* to see me, by the way."

"You broke into my house," I say, my voice hoarse with shock.

She laughs. "Broke in? Honey, I've known where your spare key is since spring of last year. You showed me, remember?"

She's right. She didn't break in—she *let* herself in. She'd know where to park her car where the neighbors wouldn't notice and she wouldn't worry about cameras, because how many times have I complained to her about needing to convince Mom that getting them might be a good idea for two women living alone? Who would have thought Lily was the thing I needed to fear?

"Why are you here?" I ask.

Lily's smile is cruel. "I know you've been talking to people. Trying to look into my past."

Alarm flares like a fire in my chest, but I am so careful to keep that feeling off my face. She is not holding a revolver. It's a low-powered stun gun, one Lily isn't technically supposed to own, since she isn't quite eighteen. I only know about it because she had me research it at length before buying it through the online marketplace.

"I'm allowed to look into whatever I want, Lily."

"Really? I don't even know that you're allowed to leave your house." Lily's eyes are the picture of pity. "I've heard that you're a suspect in what happened to poor Mr. Droesch."

"You're the one who has an issue with Mr. Droesch," I say, and the feeling of panic is mounting. Maybe that stun gun couldn't kill me, but someone did kill Mr. Droesch. If Lily is that someone, how could I possibly be safe right now?

"I'm not the one with his name on my hit list," Lily says.

"We both know that isn't my list, so just tell me what you want."

"I'm here to tell you to stop dragging everyone else into your crimes."

My laugh is hard. "What exactly are my crimes, Lily? You know damn well that the folder in my backpack wasn't mine. That wasn't a real plan, so what's going to happen when they figure that out and start listening to my side of the story?"

"I think your former record speaks volumes. And that plan is just one piece to all of this, isn't it? What about poor Mr. Droesch?"

She holds my gaze with a cold, relentless stare. Is she somehow recording us? She has to be. Does she not realize how unhinged this would look?

"Funny how you don't have answers," she says.

"Funny that you're here as a friend, but you have a stun gun in my face. What the hell is wrong with you? There is no one here but us. So you can stop with the games."

She smiles, confirming my suspicions. I'd bet money she's recording this. So, fine, if she wants to play that game, I will. "Did you kill Mr. Droesch?"

She flinches. "No."

Her answer is fast but not fast enough. That pause wasn't an act or a strategic move—that flinch was human instinct. It tells me the Lily is not the perfect mastermind she's pretending to be. But it also tells me that she really might be a killer.

"You did, didn't you?" I whisper, my shock clear in my tone. "Lily, why?"

"You're crazy, Clara," she finally manages. "You can't pin this on me."

The way her voice trembles will work in her favor if she's recording this. She will sound afraid, but I know better. Lily isn't afraid of what I've said; she's rattled because it's true.

My best friend didn't just frame me. She murdered a teacher.

A chill runs up my back, and my eyes jump to that stun gun again. It won't kill me, but it would incapacitate me, and then what? My phone chimes in Lily's pocket with an incoming text. A reminder that it is not with me. That I am alone with a killer, and I don't know what her plan is.

"Where the hell does this end?" I ask. "Are you here to threaten me? To warn me? What the hell else are you planning?"

There's that flinch again. She masks it better this time, but as fake as our whole friendship might have been, I have spent hundreds of hours with her over the last year, and I have learned.

I know Lily. Maybe better than she thinks I do and definitely better than she wants me to. And I know her well enough to know that I hit the nail on the head again. She is planning something else. Whatever this is, it isn't finished.

"Who else are you going after?" I ask.

"I can't believe I'm hearing these things. I came here as a friend." Her face contorts like it's all deeply upsetting, like she is not accosting me in my own hallway with a stun gun. I feel queasy watching her expression.

"Why are you doing this to me?" I ask again. "What did I do to you?"

Her face hardens. "Maybe you should ask yourself some hard questions, Clara."

She fires the words at me like bullets, proving my suspicions right. She's upset that I don't already know why she's here. And that won't play as well on tape. She's slipping.

"I'm here as a friend," she says again, but the words feel

forced. "As your friend I wanted to tell you that you should be careful not to involve anyone else in these crimes."

"What goddamn crimes?" The words practically explode out of me. "I did not plan to do anything to those people. And I sure the hell did not kill Mr. Droesch."

She makes a *tsk*ing noise, the kind of sound you would make when a child is throwing a tantrum in the grocery store.

"That's not how the police see it," she says.

"The police don't see shit because there isn't shit to see!" I'm losing my cool. Feeling helpless. I look at the stun gun in Lily's hand. Weigh my chances.

She's watching me with pity now. I don't know how to wrap my head around an expression like this on the face of someone with a weapon pointed in my direction.

"Oh, Clara, are you sure about that?" Her voice is a sugared razor. "There are no do-overs when you mess up this badly. How do you know that you didn't leave something there? A few hairs or an earring?"

Her eyes move to the dining room chairs. "A jacket, maybe."

She waits for me to fill in the blanks. I stare at the back of the chair until I understand what's missing. My denim jacket. I suddenly have a crystal clear memory of tossing it into the back seat of her car. She still has it. She could have all kinds of things. And if they find something—if she *plants* something—I'm not just looking at a misdemeanor. I'll go down for murder.

"Maybe you understand me now? That you need to stop while you're ahead? Stop bringing our friends into this mess. Gretchen and Ava. You need to leave them alone. Especially Henry."

I tune back in when I hear her say Henry's name. She stops and smiles. "See, that *did* get your attention."

"You don't know what you're talking about."

"I know you've been seeing Henry," she says. "Don't you think it would be a shame if the police started looking too closely at him? What with everything with Mariana."

What happened with Mariana? The question must show in my expression because Lily stops, her face suddenly vibrant with delight. But I know she is looking for me to ask, and I will not give her that satisfaction.

"You should go," I say. "Unless you'd like to say hi to my mom."

"No, I'll go. I just hope you take my advice."

I look down at the floor, my face on fire. I have no idea what she's talking about with Henry. Maybe nothing. And it doesn't matter, because there's only one relevant piece of this conversation.

Lily isn't done. She has a plan, and more people are going to die.

THIRTY-TWO

Lily leaves through the front yard like it is any other day. She has her hood up, but otherwise, she walks like she doesn't have a care in the world, stopping at the edge of the sidewalk to toss something into my yard.

My phone.

I don't move for the door or the phone. I watch her head down the sidewalk, undoubtedly for her car, which I'm sure is parked nearby. She doesn't walk like a criminal or a villain. She walks like my best friend, an easy swing in her arms and a bounce in her step.

When she is out of sight, I rush to the kitchen, flinging the back door open. George is already on the stoop, eyes bright and pink tongue wagging.

"Thank God," I mutter.

George moseys in, completely unconcerned until he picks up on my nerves. Then he doubles back and pushes into me, his tail thumping.

"I'm okay," I say, though I'm crying now, relief rushing through me. I plop onto the floor, wrapping my arms around his neck. He smells like dog and the backyard, and I feel an overwhelming wave of affection, squeezing him close to kiss the top of his head. "I wish you knew what she really was. She tricked you into thinking she was nice. She tricked all of us."

George has no answer, but he's more than happy to let me cry. I pet him until my tears slow and then get up to offer him a full slice of American cheese from the fridge—a rare treat—and finally stop shaking enough to head out front to retrieve my phone.

When I come inside, I use the dead bolt on the front door and the security chain on the back. And even then, I force George into the hallway near me with a baby gate. I plug my still-dead phone into the outlet by the bathroom sink and shower while it charges.

When I am toweled off and tugging on sweatpants, I notice my phone is alive again. The screen indicates three missed calls, all in the last few minutes. Henry. I tug on a bra and shirt, and call him back.

My heart double-thumps as I dial.

"Hi, I'm sorry to have called three times."

I do not let him go on. "Lily was in my house, Henry."

He is quiet on the other end of the line. I'm half convinced that he hasn't heard me.

"Henry?"

"When did this happen?"

"When you dropped me off. She was waiting for me."

"Where is she now?" I hear a rustling. "I'm coming over."

"No, she's gone. I'm safe. She wasn't..." I shake my head, because I can't say she wasn't here to hurt me. It's pretty clear she's doing a hell of a lot of shit to hurt me. "She didn't attack me or anything."

"Then what did she want?"

"I think she wanted to warn me? She somehow knows I've talked to Gretchen and you." And now that I think about that, it sends a prickle of unease through me. What did she mean about *everything with Mariana*? I swallow down the urge to ask. "I don't know how she knows about me seeing you."

"Maybe because I left the new group chat. Or someone could have seen us at the restaurant. It's a small town."

I nod, trying to remember who was in Bon Gou. I don't remember anyone our age. No one I knew. Did someone know me?

"Or..." He sighs. "Shit, I'm sorry. It might be my fault."

"What are you talking about?"

"I talked to Drishti yesterday. I asked her if she knew of any reason why Lily might want to do something to you. She didn't know anything, so I didn't make a thing of it."

"You didn't ask her not to talk to anyone?"

"It's Drishti," he says, as if that explains it. And it sort of does. Drishti isn't a gossip. "I never dreamed she'd talk about it."

"But can you see her lying if Lily asked? Because I can't."

"Me either," he says. "I should have thought about it first."

"It's okay," I say, but the truth is, I don't know if it is okay. Wouldn't Henry know not to trust anyone with this?

Or maybe this little shadow of irritation passing over me isn't about him trusting Drishti; maybe it's about me trusting him. Was there something to what Lily said about Mariana? I've only been in this friend group for a year and a half. There are all kinds of things I might not know. Secrets and allegiances.

The questions swirl through my mind. Could Henry be hiding something? Why is he so eager to help me?

"Are you still there?" he asks,

"Yes. I'm sorry. Look, I should go. My mom's going to be home soon."

"Right, of course. But I called for a reason. I looked up the *Tusky Times* when I got home, the ones from right before last year's winter break."

"Okay, what about them?" I ask, because I can't fathom why it would be important.

"Well, I wondered if maybe something happened to Lily.

Maybe getting cut from a team or maybe something good happened to you that made her angry."

"Did you find anything?"

"No, not about you or about her, but I found something else. Something about Cadence."

I grip the phone tighter, feeling like I'm stuck in that night again at Cadence's house. Shivering and wet on the steps. Splinters in my palms.

"What about her?" I croak the question out.

"The newsletter right before winter break of our sophomore year—it announced Cadence's selection as the foreign exchange student going to Switzerland for the last ten weeks of the school year."

My heart thumps harder and faster. I think of the flags in Lily's room. "Do we know if Lily applied for that program too?"

"I'm not positive, but she's always talking about travel. Cadence would know."

"How?" I move from the bathroom into my bedroom, pacing a fast circle between my door and my bed.

"They had to go to interest sessions to apply, so she would have seen Lily. I could always ask someone like Ava. Or Mariana?"

"No," I say it too quickly. "No, I don't want them to know what I'm looking into because it could get back to Lily."

"Okay, so where do we go from here?"

I wince, because I know the next part isn't going to be taken well. "*We* aren't going to do anything."

There is a long pause on the other end of the line. Then he sighs. "I thought we talked about this, Clara."

"No, you talked and told me you were smart enough to make good choices about what's worth the risk."

"I did. And I am."

"Well, I'm smart enough to make good choices too, and it's my choice not to drag you any further into this. I need to do this on my own."

"I want to help," he says.

"I know that. And I'm not saying no. Not entirely. I'm just saying not right now."

Henry breathes softly on the other end of the line. I brace myself for him to fight me. To argue that I need help and shouldn't try to do this on my own.

"Okay," he says softly. "I hate it, but it's your choice."

"And you're okay with it?"

"Hell no. But I respect you."

I'm not sure anyone has ever said that to me before, and it leaves me on uncertain footing. Because I don't know what to say. In the end, I tell him I need to go. Henry and I agree to talk again soon, and I promise to keep him posted. Mom gets home as soon as we hang up. She puts her bag on the counter and crosses her arms. I can smell the bar on her tonight, that strange mix of deep-fried food and spilled beer. It's only three nights a week, but even that seems like too much, and it feels terrible knowing it will go on longer.

"You're back," she says, her expression pinched.

"Yes. I told you that I would be."

Mom rubs her temples. "Did you ever think that this maybe isn't the best time to go gallivanting around town by yourself?"

"I wasn't alone. Most of the day I was with Henry Toussaint."

Mom's brow scrunches. "Isn't he that boy you had a crush on a while back?"

"Yes, but that's not the point. Henry has been trying to help me."

"Help you with what?"

"*Mom.*" I'm pleading with my voice and the look on my face. Because I need her to not continue to ignore the elephant that's filling up every square inch of this kitchen. "I am trying to find some kind of proof that I have been set up."

"Do you think you're more capable than the detectives working on your situation?"

"No, I don't, but I think they believe this is an open-and-shut case. I don't think they're looking for proof that I didn't do this. I think they're looking for evidence to prove that I did."

George flops on the floor between us, and my mom relents, leaning back against the sink. "Clara, I think you need to seriously consider what you're doing here. What if the police came for you and you weren't here? What if they asked me about your whereabouts? What were you thinking?"

"I was thinking about the fact that you have the waitressing job because of what happened with Cadence. I was thinking about how expensive a lawyer is. I was thinking that I've worked really hard to make something better of my life, and I don't want to throw it all away because it's just easier to plead guilty."

She sits with that, letting my words sink in. "A better lawyer will give us a fighting chance. Right now, I need you to be smart. To keep your head low."

"There's more you should know," I say. "Lily was here."

I watch the words register, watch her face shift through confusion and shock before settling on fear.

"Lily was here," she repeats. "Here in our house?"

"Yes," I say. "She knows where our key is. She knows your work schedule. She knows everything a person would need to frame me. Which is why she's done such a good job of it."

"I'm calling the police," she says.

I thought about it too. I even pulled out Fleming's card, but in the end, I didn't think it would work. "What's the point?" I ask. "We don't have cameras. Our neighbors don't either. It's back to my word against hers, and we've seen how well that's worked out for me so far."

She exhales hard, her face wan with a lack of sleep. Her voice is small and unsure. "I don't know how to help you. I feel like calling the police is the only thing we can do."

"I think I'm close to having something better than that. Henry found something that might change help me."

"What is it?" Mom asks.

"It's something from way back, from before we were friends. I'm still not sure, but there are other people who've had similar run-ins with Lily. I need to talk to them."

"Are you saying Lily has done something like this before?"

"Not to this extent, but yes. And I'm starting to think her offer of friendship was strategic. Think about it. You told me more than once that you didn't understand what we had in common."

"I didn't," Mom says, and her expression reflects her concern about it now, her concern that maybe my claims about Lily's long game aren't so far-fetched. "I still don't."

"I didn't see it then. I thought we were friends. Real friends. Do you know how much she knows about me? How much access she has?"

"I do," Mom says softly. "I think that's one of the things that scares me."

"It scares me too, but I know her better than she realizes."

"Clara, it's possible you only know what she's letting you see."

My mother might be right. But I'm right too. "That's just the thing, Mom. When you're around somebody long enough, the truth slips out. Even if you're desperately trying to hide it."

THIRTY-THREE

Mom still wants to call the police, but I don't trust Detective Jones one bit, and this information would be going straight to him. Mom agrees to talk to John about Lily's visit first. When John doesn't answer, she sends an email, making it clear that if we don't hear by tomorrow at noon, she's calling it in. I agree and we let it go for now. We eat grilled cheese and clean up the dishes together.

Mom touches my arm. "I picked up a double shift tomorrow. I'm going in at six a.m., and I'll be out at ten p.m. It's double time, so it will cover the deposit on a new attorney."

"I don't—"

"Clara, this isn't a democracy. I'm your mom, and I need you to be safe."

"Does this mean I'm grounded?"

"No, you're not grounded. But I want you to be smart. I want you to be careful right now."

"And if I find something?"

"Then we'll have something to bring to the lawyer for them to look into. They'll gather the evidence, not you. Do you understand?"

I do understand. I hug her good night and head to bed by one thirty. On the edge of my bed, I plug in my phone and open a browser. It's next to impossible on a small cracked screen, and as the battery gets lower, that screen tends to glitch and freeze if I'm using it for too long.

But I need to be in my email. Because I need to talk to Cadence.

I log in carefully, half-afraid I won't remember my password, but it hasn't changed since I set up the account, so I'm in quickly. There's absolutely nothing of interest on the first page of my inbox. Sale reminders from stores I barely ever shop at. A tour notice for a band I no longer listen to.

I start a fresh email and find Cadence's name in my contacts.

My fingers pause over the subject line. Where the hell do I even start? What reason would she possibly have to answer an email? I'm the girl who ruined her life. I'm blocked from her phone number and all her social media accounts, and of course I am. Of course I am.

So what do you say to a person who has systematically cut you out of their life for completely justified reasons?

I type Question about Your Exchange Program in the subject line.

It sits on the screen cold and businesslike. I decide not to think about it much and start typing.

Hi Cadence,

I'm sorry to reach out like this. I'm sorry to reach out at all since I know my name isn't one you'd want to see in your inbox. You've probably heard about the trouble I'm in. I know I'm capable of doing terrible things. Every day, you live with a terrible thing I did, and I hate that I can't change that. But this new thing I'm being accused of is different. I really didn't do this. And that's where this email comes in. As strange as this sounds, I think this whole mess may have started with the exchange program last year. I heard that you had an amazing trip in Switzerland, and I'm so glad you had that opportunity. But do you remember who else applied? Was there anything strange about the application?

Anything you can remember would be appreciated. Sorry again for having to write, but I'm desperately trying to find answers to what's happening. And honestly, I'm running out of time.

Clara

I click to send the email, and my screen glitches. Freezes. Flashes to black. I sigh and put down my phone, changing into my pajamas. Every time it does this, it takes ninety seconds to unfreeze. And that's only if it's on the charger. Sometimes it never unfreezes off the charger, and I have to reboot the entire thing. It's a nightmare.

I slide my feet into my shark slippers and check my phone. It's still frozen, so I reboot, waiting for the slow, slow process. Icons bloom to life on the screen, and I navigate to email again. Click on Drafts and search for the first one, opening it with a double tap.

I can see in an instant that it's the wrong draft. I cannot believe I have to type this whole damn thing again. Then I spot something else—a cursor flashing at the bottom of the draft. Letters appearing in spurts.

"What the hell?"

My eyes skim the last paragraph. It's filling in like AI is on the job, spitting out line after line.

> Lily, I'm so sorry for everything. I see now the pain this caused, not just Cadence, but you too. I understand why you told your parents about the parking lot. I d_

The screen freezes.

I leap to my feet, my heart thundering in my chest, my head spinning and numb. Someone is typing a message from my email account.

Not somebody. Lily. Lily has accessed my email. She's in there right now, typing a message to herself. My hands are shaking so badly I can barely hold my phone. I have to stop her. I have to stop this. If she sends this—

My phone unfreezes. A miracle. I don't know what to do. What the hell do I do? I click on Settings and scroll down. General? Privacy? Where the hell is this? Display? I'm clicking desperately, struggling to see beneath the cracked glass.

Security!

I click it and maneuver to the Change Your Password section. My fingers mash the wrong keys. My palms are slick with sweat. I delete the screwed-up letters and try again. Turn on the option to let me see. Slow. Slow and steady.

I type my email password again, and then a new one, the first one I can think of.

GetHerOut1

I'm about to click to confirm when I realize I'm not done. I find the option to log out all other devices. And then I change my recovery email to my school email. Because I'm absolutely sure Lily doesn't have that password for one simple reason. It's set by the school, a random alphanumeric code that's now in my notes on my phone because it's impossible to remember.

I click Confirm, and the familiar loading icon begins to spin. And spin. And then my phone freezes.

I drop it on the bed and suppress a scream. I pace to my door and fling it open. I want to tell my mom. I *need* to tell her.

But something stops me.

No. Not yet. Not until I know if it worked. If Lily sent that email...

There are no answers for what I should do if Lily sent that email.

I retrieve my phone and hit the combination of buttons to reboot. It takes a long time, and I wait those long minutes the way I might wait for the worst news of my life. Or the best.

The screen loads. I navigate to my email. Follow the prompt, carefully typing my new password in the designated field. My inbox loads, the familiar stack of messages reappearing. I click to enter my drafts.

And there it is.

> Lily, I'm so sorry for everything. I see now the pain this caused, not just Cadence, but you too. I understand why you told your parents about the parking lot. I do. And I understand why you'll give them this email. But I'm not the only one who needs to pay for what happened to you. Mr. Droesch and M—

I close my eyes, relief washing over me. My bed is unmade, the covers pulled back invitingly. It's almost two in the morning, and I'm feeling the weight of every hour of this day. I sit on the edge of my mattress, shell-shocked and silent.

And slowly a flicker of triumph moves through me.

Lily didn't win. For the first time since I pulled that folder out of my bag, Lily's plan has come fully off the rails. I imagine what she's doing right now. What she's feeling knowing that I caught her. That I stopped her before she could finish the handy little confession she was whipping together.

All this time I've been thinking she's some sort of mastermind, but she's still Lily. She's seventeen, just like me, and she screwed up. And maybe this isn't the only thing she screwed up.

I navigate to the Drafts window. I leave that confession where it sits, because at some point, I will show this to my lawyer. To the police. I'll see if they can track my password change or maybe an IP address where my email was logged in. Maybe there is something.

But that's not what I'm worrying about right now. Right now, I still need to reach out to the last person who would want to help me. And unless that email sent by some miracle, I'm going to have to retype it. I check my sent items and slump in relief when I see the email sent to Cadence nine minutes ago.

I'm getting ready to close my email app when I pause. A slow chill creeps up the back of my neck, a terrifying whisper circling my mind. I felt nothing but relief when I saw that frozen draft, but what are the chances that I caught her at that perfect moment?

What are the chances that was the first time she logged in? The first time she sent an email pretending to be me? I click to the Sent folder in my email and scan the list that appears. My email to Cadence is at the top. Scrolling down, I see all the emails are messages I remember sending. My next breath comes easier.

But then I pause, one last possibility slithering through my brain. My finger hovers over the button to sign out, but paranoia wins. I change my mind, scrolling down on the navigation bar to find one folder I rarely check because I never delete anything, opting to archive instead. I click on the trash can icon and the screen changes as the folder opens.

Three sent emails appear on the screen. Each one is written to Lily. None of them were written by me.

THIRTY-FOUR

At a glance the emails seem mundane, but they're not.

TUE, APRIL 1, 9:23 PM

TO: LILY DALTON

SUBJECT: HAPPY NEW YEAR, LILY!

Yeah, yeah, I'm four months late, but Ava has been going on and on about her resolutions, and I'm so sick of it. So I'm going to make some of my own, even though it's four months later.

This year, I'm going to pick my top five colleges by May. I want to be ready to go for senior year application time.

This year, I'm also going to get a car and go on an epic road trip, and by the way, you're coming with me, because we've been talking about it for far too long.

And this year, I'm not going to let anyone stand in my way of success. Especially the trio you know I hate most. I've had enough of those assholes. If they mess with me, they'll be sorry.

Anyway, send me yours when you can! It's going to be an amazing year.

xo

Clara

FRI, APRIL 4, 6:41 PM

TO: LILY DALTON

SUBJECT: (NO SUBJECT)

Lily,

Ever since I had mono, I've been obsessed with poisons and pathogens. I've got to fill you in on this insane story of the teacup poisoner. It is unbelievable what he pulled off. Kind of impressive, really.

Anyway, I'm sorry I was so pissed off today. It wasn't you at all. Mr. Droesch gave me shit for being late to class. And Ms. Chang was such a bitch when I tried to explain why I had to leave early for the dentist. God, sometimes I can't with this place.

Anyway, I'm sorry I took it out on you. But I swear I didn't mean it. You're the only person in that school who actually matters to me. All the rest of them could burn.

Promise to be less of an ass when we talk tomorrow!

xo

Clara

SUN, APRIL 6, 11:26 PM

TO: LILY DALTON

SUBJECT: (NO SUBJECT)

Lily,

I know you don't want to talk about this, but I can't keep ignoring what happened. Now that I know the impact it had on you, it makes me hate myself even more.

I know you've forgiven me, but I can't forgive myself. And I can't forgive them either. I know I set this whole thing in motion, but you deserved that spot, and the three of them took it from you just as much as I did. They ruined your life, and they need to pay.

We all need to pay for what we did, and I'm going to make sure we do. Just give me time.

Clara

I save a screenshot of the Trash folder with all three items, and then I save each email as a PDF, knowing I will need to share them with an attorney. Even as I'm taking all these careful, precise steps, I know there's no proof that I didn't write these, let alone proof that Lily wrote them to frame me. They aren't incriminating enough to look like fabricated emails.

The one piece that does feel incriminating is that they are the only items in my deleted folder. Because Lily screwed up. She didn't empty the Trash folder. Or maybe she didn't think she needed to, figuring I wouldn't check it or wouldn't notice emails to her even if I did. Because she might not know that I don't delete anything. Not ever. I use the archive feature exclusively, an old habit born out of paranoia of deleting something I'll one day desperately need. Because you just never know.

I still don't know exactly how I'll prove that she wrote these, but I have them. And that's something.

I try to sleep but don't manage more than a few hours. When I wake, my windows are still dark, the sun still tucked under a bruised sky—5:02 a.m., but my mind is racing. I know trying to go back to sleep is a futile effort. I listen to my mom get ready for work and finally get out of bed when she leaves at 5:45.

I tug on clothes and pull my hair into a half-assed ponytail.

I check my email again at 6:00, and to my surprise, Cadence's name is at the top of my inbox.

Her reply is short.

Hey,

Stop by when you get up.

C

I don't think she meant at oh-dark-thirty in the morning, so I wait. I make coffee and feed the dog. I take a shower and brush my teeth. Finally, at 8:00 a.m., I decide it's late enough. Cadence was an early riser before; maybe she still is.

I ride to her house in silence, my mind dredging up plenty of terrible memories from my past. When I turn onto her block, it's like sliding back in time. I can hear Britt swearing, her shrill laugh rising in pitch because she spilled her hard seltzer straight down the front of her American Eagle dress. I can see Gretchen, twitchy and reluctant, her complaints ignored as we slipped left off the side street, walking through the narrow grassy path beside the river.

I turn right, onto Cadence's street, and the memories fast-forward. It is a blur of sensations. The frosty grass grazing my ankles. The fizzy cherry sting of the seltzer. The feeling of satisfaction when we broke the rusting screws loose from the gate latch. Then there was the burn of chlorine in my nose and the feel of the water, scorching and frothy. The laughter, the shoving, the bang of the back door flinging open.

And then, of course, the screams. The screams are with me always.

I push the sounds and smells away as Cadence's house comes into view.

It is the same as I remember. The house is the stuff of television shows. A wide front porch sits behind the shade of rosebushes. In the summer, those bushes are a stunning display of pink and white blossoms. A weeping cherry tree stands guard in the northeast corner, its long arms covered in buds and threatening to bloom any moment. The house itself is classic white with black shutters and a bright blue front door.

Since the front hasn't changed, I'm terrified to look at the back. What if it's the same too, the same steps leading down from the deck, the same security lights that came to life that night? The same hot tub with its kaleidoscope lights and shuddering jets. The same place where my poor joke ended with a broken leg and charges for assault and breaking and entering.

I park my bike on the sidewalk and check my phone. Two calls from Henry. I text him instead of calling back.

Me: Can't talk now. Call in 20?

Henry: Can you meet up? Or can I pick you up? It's important.

I think about what Lily said about Mariana again. But God help me, I also think about the quiet warmth of that too-long embrace in Henry's car. And I have no damn idea what to do.

Me: Let me call you in a few.

My phone freezes again before he responds. I pocket it and look up the driveway to Cadence's house. It's surreal standing here again, like slipping into a time machine. It's not quite 8:30 in the morning, and frost clings to the iron railing on the porch. I wonder if I should wait until 9:00. I wonder if there is a camera, and someone inside is already watching me. I wonder if her parents will open the door, and fear spikes through me the at the idea.

Her parents sat in the courtroom when I entered my plea, their eyes hot and angry, ready to pounce if I said anything they didn't agree with. They weren't happy that the charges were reduced, but I had things in my favor too. My spotless record. My tender age, a phrase my attorney turned to over and over. My obvious remorse. I cried through every court appearance, something my attorney loved, which made the tears feel cheap and dirty.

My hand is shaking by the time I knock on the door. I'm afraid to ring the bell. If I'm honest, I'm afraid to be here at all.

And then the door swings open, and Cadence is there. She is different and the same. She has the same brown skin and hazel eyes, but her hair is cropped to her chin, wild curls with streaks of blond. She meets my eyes, and I remember.

The last time I looked in Cadence's eyes, she was screaming. And I ran.

The reality of this situation lands like an unexpected punch. I haven't seen Cadence since I tore her world apart. And now I'm standing on her porch, because I need her to help me put my world back together.

THIRTY-FIVE

"Hi, Cadence," I say. "You look great."

"You look like you haven't slept," Cadence says. She isn't cruel or kind. There is a neutrality to her normally expressive face that is surprising. Or maybe not surprising at all. Really, I should be grateful she didn't open the door wielding a knife.

"It's cold out here," she says. "Come inside."

A beat of alarm rushes through me. Come in? It feels like a thing her parents would not allow. But she must see my hesitation. "They're at the gym."

I forgot how lovely Cadence's house is. We walk past a stairway with a wide oak banister and a hallway table with a row of matching baskets beneath. The living room on the left has the same dark blue couches, but the lemon-yellow wingback chairs are new. I follow Cadence into a large kitchen with a bank of windows above the sink. I can see the backyard from here, and it sends my stomach into freefall. You can also spot the edge of the deck from those windows. And from the deck, you can see the stairs where Cadence fell.

Cadence sits down at a familiar round table near the island. She doesn't offer me a drink or small talk. She launches right in. "Delaney called me yesterday, so I know why you're here. Or I did as soon as I saw your email."

"Oh," I say, deflating, because of course Delaney called. Why would I not think she'd call?

"There were six finalists for the exchange program," Cadence says. "Lily was a strong contender, but it was pretty clear she *thought* she was a shoo-in."

"What do you mean?"

Cadence shrugs. "Lily has the perfect high school resume: sports, clubs, and academics, right? The trifecta."

"I guess."

Cadence pushes the saltshaker on the table. There is a small scar on the left edge of her wrist. Did that happen that night too?

"Well," she goes on. "Lily has the opinion that she's always the best in the room, because she usually is the best in the room. But sometimes that confidence turns into something else."

"What do you mean?"

Cadence tilts her head to the side like she's weighing the

right response. "Something darker, I guess. Once you see it, it's hard to unsee it."

"Like what Delaney thought."

"And me too," she says. "Granted, Delaney had already warned me, so I knew to keep an eye on Lily during the process, but you know how Lily seems on the surface."

I nod. "Friendly. Funny. Beautiful."

"Yeah, pretty much perfect," Cadence says. "I never saw a different side until they awarded the exchange program to me."

"I don't really understand the exchange programs. How do they work?"

"There are lots of exchange providers, so it varies, but Tusky fully pays costs for one student each year. Mr. Droesch is the primary contact. He selects the exchange program each year, and he helps to evaluate the finalists. Or I guess he did."

I nod and drop my gaze. It's hard thinking of Mr. Droesch now. For me he was the guy with no sense of humor, the guy who lived to take points off of papers for dumb shit and found his only source of joy in handing out random detentions for things like being thirty seconds late to class. Now, this is a new picture. He chose to be a teacher. Not just for the pension or the summers off, but some part of him must have believed in it, and it had to have been that part that involved him in the exchange program.

"Did he do an exchange program when he was young?"

She nods. "He did one when he was in high school, and he said it changed his life. I think his niece did too or something. Whatever it was, it was a big deal to him, and he took it seriously. Though that's not saying much."

"Man took his erasers seriously," I say with a smirk.

Cadence snorts, and we make eye contact. For one second, it's like the days when we were friends. When we'd sit at this same table, playing euchre with Gretchen and Britt, and eating cold pizza from the fridge. The weight of what I've done feels impossible to carry.

"Cadence…"

She knows by my tone. I'm sure the pain is written all over my face. But she shakes her head. "We don't need to talk about it."

"But we never have."

Her eyes harden. "And we never will. There's no point."

"Okay. But since you said that, and I know I'll never have another chance, I want you to know that I'm sorry. I'm going to be sorry every single day as long as I live for what happened that night."

"I know. It just doesn't change much," she says, and though her words pinch, her tone is kind.

I stand up, the chair legs scraping the ground. "Thank you for the information about Lily. It really helps."

"I'm not done," Cadence says, but she stands up too. "Look, Clara, you and I can't be friends. I know it kills you what you did, and we both know you didn't mean it, and we also both know that it created the kind of damage we can't come back from."

I nod, blinking back tears. I'm not going to make her stand here and deal with my feelings about this situation.

"We can't be friends," she says again, and she sounds genuinely sad about it. But then her face changes, and she looks at me without that cool guard she's had up since she opened the door. "But I've known you since the second grade, and I know you aren't a person who bombs schools or murders teachers."

The feeling that washes over me is bigger than relief. It's big enough to reduce my voice to something small. "I'm not."

"But Lily isn't you," she says. "I don't think any of us knows what she's capable of."

"I think you're right," I say. And I decide to tell her the whole truth about why I'm here. "Lily called me the day winter break started, the day after you were awarded the exchange program, right?"

"I found out two weeks before that, but it was officially announced the day before winter break."

"Why such a delay?"

"Lily tried to appeal the decision. She said the evaluating committee was biased."

A shiver of unease runs through me. "Who was on the committee?"

"Mr. Droesch, Ms. Chang, and Paxton."

Alarm prickles through my mind. Lily's email—the one that she drafted posing as me—specifically mentioned Mr. Droesch, but she wasn't done writing. There was an *M*. Could that be Ms. Chang?

"You were in on the appeal?"

"No, but I heard about it. After I received the award, Lily begged to meet with Ms. Chang and Mr. Droesch about the decision. I was outside the room because I had an appointment to fill out the paperwork right after. And I could hear her in there. She was sobbing and desperate. Said they only chose me because I was a victim."

Cadence shakes her head as if she's trying to clear the memory from her mind. "It was over-the-top. And when she came out of that room, she took a long, long look at my stupid knee brace—that damn postsurgical one I was in forever—and I swear to God, I thought she was going to tear my eyes out. But she didn't. She never said a thing. But it felt like a crack in the mask, you know? I saw the monster beneath."

"Did she ever do anything else?"

"Nope. I always gave her a wide berth after that day, but she was sweet as could to be to me."

"But she called me a few days later. And I'm the girl who made you a victim in the first place."

Cadence doesn't reply to that. We wander back to her front

door, and I step onto the landing. The sun is up, and the frost is thawing on the railing. "Thank you for your help."

"Be careful with her," Cadence says. "We might not be friends, but I don't want to see… Well, just be careful with her."

I thank her again and watch her door close before I make my way slowly back down her driveway. At the street I pull out my phone, remembering that drafted email. Remembering, too, that Henry wanted to talk.

Henry has sent me one more text. Five minutes ago.

Henry: Call me. It's urgent.

The phone rings before I can call. Henry. I pick it up and hear him take a shuddering breath on the other end of the line.

"Where are you, Clara? Are you at home?"

"No, I'm at Cadence's," I say. "Why?"

"What…? It doesn't matter. I need to come get you."

"Why? What's going on?"

"I'll explain when I get there, but you have to get off the street right now."

"What is this about?"

"It's about Ms. Chang."

THIRTY-SIX

Henry picks me up at the corner of Dale and Shepherd. I hesitate for one second before I get inside the car. He takes off the second I'm buckled, darting into a neighborhood and heading east. Heading out of town.

"What happened to Ms. Chang?" I ask.

"She's in the hospital. There was an accident."

"What do you mean by *accident*?" I am gripping the seat beneath me now. Because somehow I know his answer is going to be bad.

"They aren't sure, but there are rumors. Her car was running in her garage."

"What? Why?"

"Sammy heard it from a friend of hers that's training with paramedics. She doesn't know much. Some people are thinking it could be a suicide attempt; others think someone else started the car while Ms. Chang was doing her spin bike thing."

I feel dizzy and sick. "Carbon monoxide. She had carbon monoxide poisoning."

Henry nods. My pulse feels too fast and too weak. "Is she…? Did she…?"

"No," Henry says firmly. "She is in the hospital. Sammy's friend said she was stable. Sick, but improving. Where have you been? Can anyone account for you early this morning?"

My chest squeezes. "I was with Cadence, but not until after 8:00 a.m."

Henry pulls to a stop light and twists until he's looking me full in the face. "Wait, what were you doing at Cadence's house?"

"I figured she would know about the exchange program, and she did. She said there was a committee that chose her. Mr. Droesch and Ms. Chang were both on it with Paxton Bryce."

"They should be able to look that up," he says. "That's got to be in some kind of school record. Clara, that's something your attorney can use."

I nod. "I know. Lily was in my email too, but I just don't know if that's enough. I don't think there's any actual evidence linking me to Mr. Droesch, so I'm counting on that to help my case. And I don't even know where Ms. Chang lives, so there wouldn't be evidence there either."

Henry flinches then, his grip tightening on the steering wheel.

"What is it?" I ask.

Henry doesn't want to tell me what he knows. But ultimately, what choice is there? He lets out a hard breath. "Sammy said the police were already there when they were loading Ms. Chang into the ambulance. They were bagging a denim jacket on the ground in her garage. It didn't sound like something she'd wear."

A denim jacket. Ice slides down my spine. Lily dangled that threat in front of me at my house not even twelve hours ago.

"It's mine," I say, my voice distant and strange, sounding like someone else.

"What?"

Anxiety rushes up through my middle leaving me shaking and cold. That jacket is mine. That is evidence—from me—at the scene of an attempted murder. Did Lily leave something at Mr. Droesch's house too? Will the police come to my house to get me? My chest feels too tight. I need to call my mom. I have to talk to her before the police come.

"I need to call my mom."

"Right now?" Henry looks concerned.

My voice is rising. "One of my teachers is dead, the cops think I'm involved, and now my principal is in the hospital, and my jacket is on the scene. And of course Lily is convincing everyone at school that I'm guilty too. I'm going to be arrested."

"Lily is saying it's you, but I think people are starting to question it. Sammy showed me a couple of things she heard. Gretchen apparently said something. Even Drishti urged people to stay out of it and not to assume things. I'm telling you not everyone is on her side."

I shake my head, feeling the tears coming fast. "It doesn't matter, Henry. There's evidence now."

"But when they know why she's doing this—

"I know why! It's all about that damn exchange program. Mr. Droesch and Ms. Chang were on the committee with Paxton to award the program to Cadence instead of Lily. Lily appealed the decision and was sure Cadence only got it because of what I did to her."

"See? That's good news! That means we have motive for her to do all this!"

"But I have motive too if you listen to her. And more importantly, I have a record and evidence at the scene of a crime. And let's not forget the most important fact of all."

"What's that?"

"People believe Lily, and they do not believe me."

"I want to go back to the exchange program. Does that mean Lily set this up to get back at you for Cadence getting the spot?"

"Lily is furious because she thinks she was owed that spot, and she's sure she would have gotten it if I hadn't hurt Cadence. I don't know why that's how the math works for Lily, but it is. She wants to take me down and it's working. She's doing it.

"Try to breathe," he says. "We have information to give to an attorney now. We can call the police. It's going to be okay."

But I shake my head. Despite his clear instructions, I can't breathe. "You don't understand. My jacket is there! That's physical evidence. The cops aren't going to listen to me when there is physical evidence linking me to an attempted murder."

"Slow down," Henry says. We're on a country road now, one of the rural highways that surrounds town. "You mentioned that email earlier. She sent you an email?"

"No, she was in my account! She sent emails to herself pretending to be me, showing that I was slowly getting close to this plan—she has thought of everything, Henry."

A sudden and intense wave of nausea moves through me. I might be sick. No, I'm going to be sick. "Pull over," I say. And then more urgently. "Please pull over. I feel sick."

Henry does, quickly, and I wrench open the car door. I'm sure I'll throw up, but the cold air rushes at my face, and it helps. I breathe in and out. I squeeze my eyes shut. The cold bites at my neck and cheeks, and slowly, slowly the nausea recedes. My eyes and nose are watering. I pull a tissue from my pocket and wipe my eyes.

Henry is right there in front of me. I didn't even hear him get out of the car, but he's here, crouched and ready to help. And something about the tenderness in his gaze is too much for me. I take a shuddering breath, and a sob comes out when I exhale. I can't have Lily's whispers between us anymore.

"What happened with Mariana?" I ask.

"What?"

"Lily said...she knows..." I take a breath, my words caught on the edge of a sob. "She knows we were talking. She warned me it would be bad if the police looked into you. Because of Mariana."

Henry shakes his head. "There's nothing with Mariana. There's..." He trails off, realization sparking in his eyes. Then he lets out a soft huff of a laugh. "It was a stab in the dark, but she was wrong. She's in your head."

I tense. Because he didn't stick with *there's nothing*. He amended it. Now it's a *stab in the dark*. "How can I trust that?" I ask, even though I am in his car. Even though he is crouched on the roadway staring up at me with nothing but patience in his gaze. "How, Henry?"

"Okay, I'll tell you." He takes a sharp breath. "Mariana broke up with me because of another girl. But things had already been weird with us. She was hiding something."

"Hiding something?"

His face scrunches. "I don't know what it was. I think something to do with a relationship she was ashamed of. Someone right before me, I think, but it wasn't a public thing. She was cagey and weird, but she kept turning that on me, getting suspicious. She was in my room, snooping, and she found some letters I'd written."

I let out a slow breath. "Mariana thought you cheated."

"I didn't, but she had reasons to be upset. My eyes were wandering. My eyes. My brain. Maybe a little bit of my heart. She found letters I hadn't sent that proved her theory."

"I don't get it."

"You don't?" he asks, voice low and eyes heavy.

Henry's gaze is electric. A car whips by on the freeway. My breath steams in front of me. He reaches for my face, but I hesitate. He looks so sincere and inviting. It's physically difficult to resist him, but I remind myself that Lily seemed sincere too. I can't trust myself on this. Not entirely.

I sit back, a little away from his reach. "Why would Lily think that a bunch of letters could matter to the police? She said it would be bad if the police looked into you."

He nods with a heavy sigh. "When Mariana found the letters, she kind of flipped. She had a moment about it, which I get. Went out with Lily and they dissected the letters. Tried to figure out who I was writing to. They decided I'd written the letters for this freshman."

"A freshman?"

He nods. "Lily took pictures of the letter and went through the yearbook and decided it was about a girl named CiCi Brent who I tutored in Algebra."

The idea is right on the edge of gross. "You're a senior, Henry. That's four years younger than you."

"The letters weren't written to CiCi Brent. The letters were written to a different CC. As in initials."

Realization hits me hard. His warm gaze and that softness in his mouth. I know who those letters were for.

"Do you understand, Clara Cutler?" He says my name slowly, emphasizing those first syllables, drawing the rest into something lyrical. Beautiful.

Traffic is flying past, and I think I hear Henry's phone buzzing with an incoming call, but we are utterly still. Trapped in this moment where I realize that this means. And why he's helping. Why I've found his eyes on me so many times. It wasn't my imagination. Henry was watching me as much as I was watching him.

Henry gingerly reaches toward me. He is steady and calm, but now, I am anything but. I fling myself at him without the slightest bit of grace. My shoulder is crammed under his arm, and my nose bumps into his chest, but his arms wrap around me like we've done this a thousand times. Like we know exactly the way we're supposed to fit together when we hug.

And then hugging is not enough, so I pull back enough to kiss him. I feel him freeze, my mouth slanted over his without warning of any sort. Too fast and too much, I'm sure. I try to stop, but then he makes a sound that drops my stomach into my knees. His lips part, and his hands are in my hair, and he is kissing me back. And his kiss fills in all the gaps and spaces between us—it shapes all the words he hasn't yet said.

After a long while, we part. I pull back, pressing my swollen lips together. His eyes are darker, now, a soft flush visible on his cheeks.

A semi whips by at that moment, offering a long honk of his horn. We startle and Henry's vision seems to clear. He stands up, the gravel on the berm crunching under his sneakers. "We should go. This probably isn't the safest."

He circles back to the driver's side and checks his phone. He frowns and drops it in the coin tray near the gear shift. Once we're both buckled, he pulls onto the highway. We look at each other, words feeling unnecessary. I don't know where we go from here. But when he inches his hand onto the console, I take it. Our fingers lace together, and my heartbeat slows.

"I don't want to go to jail," I whisper, the confession small and true.

"Not going to happen," Henry says, and there is a brightness to his eyes now. "She isn't perfect, and she's making mistakes. The proof is coming. Lily tried to plant those library books because she didn't know about your locker getting a new lock. And she got into your email but I'm betting she doesn't realize that they can check IP addresses of where your email was logged in."

I tilt my head, uncertain. "But we were best friends. I was at her house all the time."

"Not in the last week, you weren't. If the police see that last email was drafted from Lily's—"

I gasp, cutting him off. Because I'm suddenly remembering that last email. And what Cadence said about the international exchange program committee. Ms. Chang. Mr. Droesch. And one other person.

"Paxton." I practically cry out his name.

"What about Paxton?"

I swear softly, my hand going to my throat. "Oh my God, Henry. We need to warn Paxton. If Mr. Droesch is already dead, and Ms. Chang is in the hospital, that only leaves one person Lily really wants to hurt."

"I thought there were five people on the list."

I shake my head. "I'm starting to think that was an intentional misdirection. If the list only included those three, it might be easier to trace it back to Lily. But Gretchen has barely ever spoken to Lily, and Nate gets along with her pretty well. I don't think Lily ever planned to hurt either of them. I think the next person in danger will be Paxton."

"You think—" Henry cuts himself off when his phone begins to buzz again. "Can you check that?"

I turn over his phone and frown at the screen. "It's Mariana. You've missed four calls from her in the last fifteen minutes."

As I say it a text message comes in, popping into a box at the top of his screen. I read it out loud.

"She says I need to talk to you in person. It can't wait."

If I had to guess, I'd wager that 90 percent of men would

not call their ex in front of someone they just kissed, but to my surprise, Henry does. Even more shocking, he does it on speakerphone. "Hey, Mar, what's up?"

"Henry." Mariana takes in a shaky breath on the other end of the line. She sounds upset. "I'm sorry to call. But I don't have anyone else."

"What's wrong? Are you okay?"

A choked sob is all the answer she manages at first. Henry doesn't move his gaze from the road, but he tenses.

"I'm not. I need you to come over."

"What's this about? Are you safe?"

"I can't talk on the phone. Please, Henry. I'm scared. Please come. It's about Lily."

My skin goes cold. On the speaker, Mariana takes a sharp breath like she can't believe what she's said. And then in a rush. "I have to go. I can't talk about this here. Please come over. I need help."

Mariana hangs up before he can answer.

THIRTY-SEVEN

"We have to call the police," he says.

I'm already dialing 911.

"Do you know Paxton's number?" I ask, while I wait for them to pick up.

He shakes his head. "I'll try to get Sammy—she knows everyone."

"Nine one one, what's your emergency?"

"Yes, I need to report a threat against a resident. His name is Paxton Bryce, and he's a student at Tuskegee High School."

"Slow down. You're saying there's a threat at the high school?"

"No, I think a high school student is in danger. His name is Paxton Bryce."

"What kind of danger is he in? Is he with you now? Is he injured?"

"No, it's not like that. I don't know where he is, but I think someone wants to kill him."

"Ma'am, is Paxton being attacked? Is someone with a weapon approaching him?" The dispatcher sounds confused. Maybe frustrated.

"No, I don't think so. But I can't be sure. I'm not with him."

"Can you see the situation you're referring to? What is your location right now?"

"I'm… I don't know. I think I'm on a state route, but I'm not the one in danger. My location doesn't matter!"

"I'm going to need you to calm down. Is this an emergency situation?"

"Yes!"

"Then I need a location to send—

My phone glitches. Freezes.

"Damn it!" I throw it on the seat beside me.

"I'll call them back," he says. "But I need to get to Mariana. Something's not right there."

"You're right. And I need to talk to Paxton," I say. "The police don't get how it's an emergency."

"Wait, I think Sammy just got his number. Try to call him."

I take his phone and collect my own from the seat. Still frozen, so I start the process of rebooting it.

I dial the number Sammy texted on Henry's phone. I try it again. No answer either time. "He isn't picking up. Do you know where he lives?"

Henry starts to shake his head but then pauses. "Actually, wait. Yes, I do. We had a couple of pool parties there freshman year. It's a couple of blocks from Mariana's."

"Go there. You drop me at Paxton's and go to Mariana."

We're already back on the outskirts of town, and Henry hits the gas. We peel off the main drag almost immediately after entering town, winding into a neighborhood I know very well. This is the other side of Lily's neighborhood, one with sprawling houses and towering shade trees. I try the phone number two more times and get sent to voicemail on the third attempt.

"Damn it."

I start a text from Henry's phone, but a low battery warning flashes on the screen.

"Your battery is at two percent."

"Shit, it didn't charge last night. There's a cord under the radio."

I find it and plug it in as Henry is pulling up to a curb. "It's that big two-story there with the door set back behind those hedges."

"I'm going in. Call 911 again. And get to Mariana."

Henry starts to dial, and I race up the driveway. It is eleven in the morning, the kind of blue-skies sunny day that begs for long walks in the park. It feels surreal to be sprinting up Paxton's steps, my fist banging rapidly on the door to get his attention.

I see motion in the window beside the door. Just for a second.

I knock again and listen hard. There is a muted shuffle. He is here. He is watching me.

I knock again. "Paxton, it's Clara. Are you home?"

A louder thump inside. Something scraping. A voice maybe? I can't be sure.

I know he's home. I'm hearing him in there behind the door. But of course he isn't answering. He either hates me or he's afraid of me. Maybe both.

I sigh. "Paxton, I know you don't trust me, but I promise you I did not plan to bomb the school parking lot. I did not kill Mr. Droesch or hurt Ms. Chang, and I definitely don't want to hurt you. But I know who did, and I think you're in danger."

Paxton flings the door open so suddenly that I jump back, nearly slipping off the porch. I don't know what I was expecting, but it is not this. Paxton looks horrible. His skin is beyond pale, and he's soaked in sweat. His shirt is stained, and he smells of vomit.

I pause. The stain covering his shirt *is* vomit. He's sick.

The odor I detected is intense now that the door is wide open. It permeates the air in his house. Behind him, I think I see something on the floor. Did he retch right there? I feel queasy at the evidence on and behind him.

"Clara?" Paxton says my name like a prayer. He reaches for me, his eyes wide with terror. There is foam in the corners of his mouth.

"Paxton, what happened? What's wrong with you?"

He is beyond answering me, his head lolling forward. He holds his stomach with one hand and groans in agony. His eyes are rolling.

I fumble for my phone. Still dead. Something scrapes inside the house. A door? A chair? "Who's home with you? We need to call the ambulance. Do you have a phone?"

Paxton says something I can't make out, his voice dissolving into another groan. I look up at the house. I heard something. I'm sure I did.

"Are you alone?" I ask.

"No."

What does he mean he's not alone?

He groans again, and his knees buckle. I catch him by the arms. "Help! Someone help us!" I call out. Paxton is bigger than he looks. Heavier. I ease him down, letting the doorframe help us as he slumps.

"I need your phone." I give him a gentle shake. "Do you have your phone?"

His hand drops, and it's there. He has his phone gripped like he's terrified to lose it. The screen is bright, and I try to pry his fingers loose.

A text message comes in. There are two other message notifications above it.

911: Are you located at 6412 Ridgeway Drive?

911: We are sending paramedics.

911: Are you still able to respond?

I pull the phone from his hand and see that the last message came in four minutes ago. They're coming.

"You did good," I say. "The ambulance is on its way."

He grips my arm, looking up at me with dark, desperate eyes. "Help."

"Help is coming. The paramedics are already on their way."

Paxton shakes his head, his sweat-slicked hair clinging to his forehead. He gurgles out another word. "Mariana."

I go cold, sure I've misheard. Sure he must have said something else.

"Did you say *Mariana*?"

"Please." His face is desperate.

Inside, I hear something else. I'm sure of it this time, and it chills me. If someone is in the house, why are they not here with us? Why are they not helping? Or is Mariana in there for some reason, and sick too?

I freeze, looking up. Looking into his house. It's beautiful like Cadence's and maybe even larger. Brass sconces light the long hallway, which opens into a bright kitchen. There is an arched opening on the left revealing what I would guess would be a living room. But this room is completely empty. There are divots in the carpet where furniture must have been and a couple of end tables against the walls, but the couches, coffee table, TV—everything that feels like it should be in this room is missing.

I hear the soft sound of a door closing. The back door? Chills chase each other up the length of my spine.

"Mariana?" I call.

There is no answer. I follow the hallway, noticing another room—maybe an office—that is also entirely empty. A single cardboard file box, but no desk. No computer. Are they moving or renovating? What the hell is going on in here? I move into a wide kitchen. There are gleaming white countertops, but things look wrong here too. A broken faucet. Three cracked floor tiles leading into the dining room.

I see a dark folding table—the kind of cheap table you'd imagine in a college apartment, not a huge house with a sprawling backyard. Folding chairs are placed around it, and two matching coffee cups are situated on the table.

Paxton retches again behind me, but there is nothing left to bring up. His body contorts. I should go back to him, but there is something about this scene inside that is pulling me closer.

Sirens wail from a distance. They're almost here. I rush back to the door, making sure Paxton is still breathing. He is slumped sideways, but he's awake.

"Just hold on. I can hear them."

Paxton's fingers clamp onto my wrist, nails digging into my skin as he pulls me closer.

"Lily!"

Paxton is dragging harsh breaths. The sirens are growing closer. He squeezes my wrist until it hurts, and alarm bursts in the center of my chest.

"I'm going to check the house," I say, yanking myself free.

As I return to the kitchen I see something moving through the back window. A slight figure. Slim shoulders. Black jacket. Long pale braid swinging behind her.

Lily.

I sprint down the hallway to the dining room window as she disappears down the back stairs. Paxton's house overlooks a hill, so I cannot see his yard, just the edge of the grass that borders the woods behind their property. But I know that was Lily I saw. Mariana's hair is too dark.

Paxton said both of their names. Mariana called Henry for help. Lily is running through his backyard. What the hell is happening here?

I look at the table again, at the two coffee cups. And now I see that two chairs are moved away from the table. One is pushed out like someone just stood up. And the other is on its side with only the legs visible from where I'm standing.

The sirens are on the street now. And then I see her again. Looking out the window past the table and the two cups and the deck, I see Lily is moving up the back half of Paxton's yard. She is going to slip into that forest, and the paramedics will arrive to find me standing in Paxton's kitchen. I don't know what was in those cups, but one is clearly untouched. I'd bet a thousand dollars Paxton drank from the cup that's half-empty.

Outside, Lily is running up the slope of his yard to the line of trees. She is going to get away with this. Rage rushes through me at the idea of it. At the reality of all the things Lily has already destroyed.

And then my instincts take over. I don't think at all. I sprint for the back door.

THIRTY-EIGHT

I fly onto the deck. The stairs are on the left, and I take them two at a time, racing into the backyard. The pool Henry mentioned is in shambles, the cover sunken in and covered in algae. Broken lawn chairs litter the area near the pool house. This house is crumbling.

Lily is already inside the tree line, her blond braid flying behind her. I run trying to catch her, but she's in better shape, and it immediately shows.

"Lily!" I scream her name like I have nothing left to lose, because I don't. She flinches, but she does not stop. She bolts through a line of evergreens and into another neighbor's yard. I follow, breathing hard. I know we are in her neighborhood, but I don't know these houses, not from the back. Is she trying to run home? Does she really think she can just go home?

My lungs are burning, and my legs are rubbery with exhaustion. Lily is slowing too, but she is still faster than me. She is pulling ahead. I recognize the house to our left now, a towering Victorian with a turret on the back. This house is on Lily's street. I had no idea she and Paxton lived so close to each other.

"Lily, you can't just go home," I scream. "Paxton is going to tell."

She stumbles. Rights herself and keeps going.

"You can't keep running! Paxton is alive. He called 911. He knows what happened!"

She makes a sound, and I realize with surprise that she's crying. Sobbing.

"Just stop!" I scream. "Why are you doing this? Why would you do this to Paxton?"

I'm already guessing at what she did. All I have is the two coffee cups on the table and a distinct memory of Lily and her fascination with the teacup poison killer. Those toxicology books clearly weren't for show. She used them. She killed Mr. Droesch with opioids. She tried to kill Ms. Chang with carbon monoxide, and I don't know what she used on Paxton, but my money says she sat at that table, watching until it kicked in. Waiting until she knew she had finished the job.

Her backyard is not even thirty yards from us now, but my body is done. My knees buckle, refusing to let me continue. My chest burns like fire with every breath, and my voice is ragged when I speak.

"He's going to live, and he's going to tell, Lily. It's over."

Lily stops, whirling to face me. She looks truly unhinged, mascara smudged and wet beneath her eyes, her lips chapped. She is still wearing the clothes she confronted me in at my house. She has not slept. Has she even been home?

"You were in Paxton's house, Clara!" she screams. "They won't blame me because you're the villain. They know you did this. They know you killed Mr. Droesch. They found your jacket in Ms. Chang's garage! No one will believe you!"

But this time, her threats fall at my feet. I watch her carefully, her wild eyes and heaving chest. A day ago, I would have been terrified of her. Now, I think I'm more terrified *for* her. Because this isn't how it will work. It is not my word against hers anymore. There will be a different story—Paxton's story. And then? The real investigation will dig deeper.

"They'll believe Paxton. They'll believe the IP address you tried that email from. They'll believe the DNA they find on those cups."

Lily's eyes widen as she registers my words. She whines and goes pale. Some part of her knows that it's over. I can see that. And just as quickly, I can see the other part of her, the part that refuses to give in. That part of her laughs in my face.

"It's too late to stop me," she snarls. "This is already over, do you understand?"

I do not understand, but she does not wait for an answer. She races into her yard, and I let her go. I open my phone, which has finally rebooted.

It's time to call the police. This time I will have all the details they need. This time I know exactly what to say.

I have missed six calls from Henry. I have no doubt he is frantic. I call him and can hear him breathing hard. "Where are you, Clara?"

"I'm near Paxton's. I'm outside." I'm still panting from the run.

"You need to get to Mariana's. She told me everything about Lily. It's bad, Clara."

"I know. I think she poisoned Paxton."

"Poisoned? What? Where is he?"

I can hear Mariana is with him. She is nearly shrieking. Asking what happened. I can't keep up.

"The ambulance is with him. He was conscious."

Mariana screams something. I've never heard her like this. She's usually so quiet, I barely hear her at all.

"We're on our way back," Henry says.

"I'm not there. I'm by Lily's house, and I have to call the police. I have to go, Henry."

"I'm coming to you," he says.

He disconnects, and my fingers hover over the keypad to call 911. But I change my mind. I reach for the card in my back pocket, the edges now worn. Officer Maya Fleming is on the front, but handwritten beneath *Officer* is *Detective*.

Detective Fleming picks up on the second ring. "Fleming here." She sounds like she's driving. Maybe fast.

"This is Clara Cutler."

"We've been by your house, Clara. We've been trying to reach you."

"I'm not at home. Please listen. Paramedics just picked up Paxton Bryce. He was poisoned, and Lily Dalton did it. I saw her in his backyard. I chased her. She's inside her house."

"I need to know where you are. Do you see Lily? What is your location?"

I think of the handcuffs heavy on my wrists, and Detective Jones, who brushed off everything I said, so convinced of my guilt. Is there any possible way this will turn against me too? Because as crazy as it feels, some part of me still worries that Lily might spin this. That she'll find some way to convince them all.

But then I remember Paxton's terrified eyes. And I give Detective Fleming Lily's address.

"I'll be on the corner near the house," I say.

"Keep your distance. Do not approach her under any circumstances. You'll see me sooner than you think."

Detective Fleming hangs up the phone before I can ask her what she means. I am making my way down the sidewalk when Henry's car appears on the street. He must see me, because he jerks the car to the curb and leaps out, sprinting for me.

I am in his arms and off the ground before I can say his name. He squeezes me hard, breathing in my hair. "God, Clara, I thought something happened. I thought..."

He doesn't finish. He just squeezes me tighter and then eases me gently back down to the ground.

"Where's Mariana?" I ask.

"She's with Paxton," he says.

"Wait, why?"

"They're together," he says. "It's a long story, but they're together."

"What kind of long story? And how did Mariana know Lily was going to—"

"Lily has been saying weird shit to Mariana too, stuff about a secret."

"A secret? What does that even mean?"

"Mariana thought it was something else, even after the plan came out and you were arrested. She was waiting for Lily to talk to her—to tell her what this big secret was."

"So what was it?"

"Framing you. Killing Mr. Droesch. Lily never told her outright, but Mariana started putting together the pieces after Mr. Droesch. That's why she was at the Y—she wasn't there to get a job. She was trying to warn Paxton that the list was real."

I take a sharp breath that feels like knives in my throat. "Why did Paxton let her inside then? Why didn't he listen?"

"I don't know. Mariana didn't know all of it, just enough pieces to scare her."

"But she didn't say anything?"

Henry's face twists with pain. "She and Lily had something terrible in common. They both had something they were really ashamed—" Henry cuts himself off with a shake of his head. "What matters is that she called me when she figured it out. She wanted to do the right thing."

"Why didn't she tell the police? Why did she let this happen to me?"

The anguish on Henry's face tells me the answer is more than he can put words to right now. He shakes his head again, horror shadowing his expression.

A cop car flies past us. No lights. No siren. Another one is close behind. We whirl to watch them go past. They are heading for Lily's house.

"Are they here for her?" he asks. "For Lily."

"Yes."

The cars lurch to a halt in front of Lily's house. A third pulls up from the alley. Six officers emerge in unison, guns drawn and black protective gear covering them head to toe. Detective Fleming arrives next. She's fastening the straps on a Kevlar vest when she opens her car door. She scans the scene, and her eyes catch on me. I raise my hand in greeting, and she raises hers as well, her palm jutted toward me in a crystal clear gesture.

Stay where you are.

Henry laces his fingers with mine and pulls me close. I do not ask any more questions when the police circle the house. I do not speak when they pound on the door or when they pull the battering ram from one of the cruiser trunks.

The door gives way easily, and the officers pour inside. The shouts from the house are muffled but urgent. Two officers outside are on their radios in an instant. There is a sharp, high-pitched scream from inside the house. Banging. I gasp.

"What was that? Was that a gunshot?"

Henry pulls me closer. "It's okay," he says. "I think it was a door slamming open. Just breathe. Just breathe."

And that's when I realize I'm crying. I swipe at the tears and try to nod. Try to agree with him. But it doesn't feel okay. One person is dead. Two others are in the hospital. And I'm standing on a sidewalk watching the police descend on my best friend's house. Nothing feels like it will ever be okay again.

I lean into Henry's shoulder and let myself cry. And we wait long minutes for something to happen. Officers emerge. Ambulances arrive. Two paramedics enter with a gurney, and I stiffen, watching them move.

"Why aren't they rushing?" I ask.

"Maybe whoever is hurt is stable," Henry says, but he doesn't sound convinced.

A few minutes later, a flurry of activity erupts at the front door, several officers exiting. There is a paramedic tool kit by the baskets full of flowers. There are dirty smears on the white front door.

A van pulls up, and I remember it from a few days ago when it pulled to the curb beside my house. Crime scene processing.

The same people that pawed through my drawers are stepping out of that van, snapping on blue nitrile gloves and pulling out black boxes full of equipment. Back at the house, the door is pulled wide, and I see the gurney emerge.

I suck in a deep breath and hold it. A white sheet hangs down over the edge of the gurney, but the wind catches the edge, lifting it up. Just enough to give me a glimpse. Just enough that I see the black body bag peeking out.

THIRTY-NINE

Time slows to a chilling crawl as I watch the paramedics roll the gurney down the long walkway. They do not rush to the ambulance. They do not check pulses or work machinery. There is no work left to do, because whoever is on that gurney is beyond saving.

And I know who is on that gurney.

Lily.

I feel a hot rush of tears, my heart torn. She was my only friend. And she was never my friend. She saved me and she ruined me. All those hours and hours together. So many memories before all of this. Something in there must have been more than the person who slid that folder into my bag. Something in her had to be real, didn't it?

But it doesn't matter now, because all the parts of her are gone.

A sob escapes me, and I pull in a shuddering breath. Henry wraps his arm around me and pulls me close. And then the front door opens again. Two officers emerge, and there is someone between them. Someone small. I see her feet first, and then her tear-streaked face. And then I see the long blond braid trailing behind her.

It is not Lily in that body bag, because Lily is being walked down the sidewalk toward a police car. I hold my breath, sure she'll see me. I'm sure she'll look.

But they turn her toward the cruiser, and I watch her from behind, her arms pinned at her back, handcuffs gleaming on her wrists.

~

I don't know how many times I've been to this police station, but this is the first time I've been seated in a conference room. The chairs are cushioned, and there are water bottles on a little tray in the center of the table, and while it's still not exactly my favorite place, it sure beats where I was supposed to be today. My arraignment—now canceled—was supposed to be held later this afternoon.

My mother is with me again, but John Pruitt isn't here. No new lawyer either. All charges have been dropped, and I'm not here to be interviewed. At least...not for my own crimes.

Detective Fleming comes in alone. I imagine Detective

Jones is with Lily. I haven't seen Lily since she was tucked into the police cruiser. And I still don't know who was in the body bag.

Mom holds my arm tightly. She's been crying since she arrived. She's apologized so many times I've stopped counting. And it's clear she's as eager for answers as I am.

Fleming smiles and sits down at the table. "How are you both holding up?"

"I'm okay," I say. Which is ridiculous. I'm not even in the same universe as okay.

Mom leans forward. "How is Paxton? And Principal Chang? We're trying to find out what's happening. Clara said someone died at the Dalton house."

"Yes, someone did. I will give you some answers, but I need you to be patient with me. I have some important questions. Let's start with Ms. Chang and Mr. Bryce. I'm happy to report they are both recovering well."

"Thank God," I say, feeling relieved. But the relief doesn't last. She still hasn't explained what happened at Lily's house. "Who died?"

"I need to ask you a few questions first, Clara. Did you ever notice anything concerning in Lily's family?"

"No, not really. I mean, sometimes they were protective. She didn't always get along with them."

"With both of her parents? Or just one?" Fleming asks.

My heart pounds. I think of that sheet rippling up and the body bag underneath. Did something happen to one of Lily's parents? I think of her mother's shortbread cookies. Her father's easy laugh. Lily couldn't have done something to them, could she? My face feels numb.

"I..." My voice cracks. I clear my throat and try again. "I don't know. I guess she sometimes thought her mom was flaky. She spent more time with her dad because of tennis."

"Did she ever talk to you about her dad? Did she ever talk about how she felt about him?"

There is something in Detective Fleming's tone that makes me deeply uneasy. "No, not really."

"Did you ever have any uncomfortable interactions with Mr. Dalton?"

My body goes cold. My mom and I exchange a look, and I can see stark horror gathering in her eyes. Suddenly, memories are filtering through me. Lily's flinch when he called her name. Her blank expression when he squeezed her shoulder. Mariana said Lily had it hard at home.

What did she mean by *hard*? Was something happening with Mr. Dalton?

Suddenly Henry's words come back to me. Lily and Mariana were both ashamed of something. I think of the endless afternoons at tennis. At Lily's desperation to leave town. Her presentation, trying to convince her parents about Finland.

Oh my God. What the hell was Lily trying to escape?

"Was her father...?" I can't say the words. I imagine this tall strapping man with his wide shoulders and thick hair. Lily was so small. She wouldn't have stood a chance if he wanted...

Horrible thoughts fill my head. Mom grips my hand, and an anguished noise comes out of me.

"Was he hurting Lily?" Mom asks. She sounds every inch as horrified as I feel.

Detective Fleming's face softens. I can see real pain in her eyes as well. She nods, her voice gentle. "We don't know anything for sure."

But she does know. Her voice tells me all the things her words do not.

"Did she kill him?" I ask, my voice cracking.

"We don't know that yet."

"But he's dead." My breath shudders in and then back out. "That's what I saw, isn't it? It was him on that stretcher."

"Yes. Yes, it was."

Lily's face in the woods comes back to me, tear-streaked and furious, her words a desperate shriek.

It's too late to stop me. This is already over, do you understand?

The world tilts precariously. I grip my mother's hand and think about the seventeen and a half months I was near this man. Seventeen months that I was Lily's friend. How did I not see this? How did I not know someone was hurting her?

Is this why she was so desperate to go away that first year? Was that exchange program her one chance at escape?

Mom is asking about Lily's mother, and Detective Fleming is talking about how easy it is for terrible things to happen right beneath people's noses.

When they turn to me, I tune back in. "We're trying to piece things together," Fleming says. "I know you have questions, and I know this is a lot to process, but I still need more information from you if you think you can do it."

"When did you figure all this out?" I ask.

Detective Fleming opens the file in front of her. "We began to suspect abuse when we discovered that Lily may have been framing you. We confiscated your computer and phone, Clara, and our technology task force has been assessing things since. It took time, but some pieces started to take shape yesterday afternoon. Have you been in any of your online accounts?"

"Yes. I reactivated an old phone, so there's that. I also signed into my email from the library and from my phone a few times."

"And did you see anything that stood out?"

"There are three emails that were sent from my account that were not written by me. I only found them because I was writing an email and found a draft that was being created as I was watching."

"Someone else was in your email account?" She jots a note.

I nod, feeling chilled. "Lily was. She's the only one with the password. The email was some sort of confession to murdering Mr. Droesch. And more."

"And what did you do when you saw this?"

"I changed my password right then and forced all devices to sign out. The draft is still there. And there are three other emails. She deleted them from my Sent folder, but they're still in the trash. She didn't empty the trash."

"That all lines up with what Ms. Dalton shared with me just now," Fleming says. Then she closes the folder. "And it lines up with our research. I checked the IP address for your email log-ins and checked your attendance records at school. The library books as well. At least two of the messages were sent from the Daltons' house when you were somewhere else. That's what tipped us off. And then of course, there is the confession now."

"Lily confessed?"

She nods. "It's difficult to deny something like this when there are survivors who can testify. And once she confessed to murdering her father, I think the rest of it didn't feel like it mattered."

"How?" My voice is very small. "How did she kill him?"

"I..." Detective Fleming seems uncertain.

"If she confessed, it will be all be public record soon, won't it?" Mom asks.

Detective Fleming relents with a nod. "According to Lily she used the same method on Mr. Droesch as she did on her father. She obtained high-dose opioids, crushed them, and replaced supplements in Mr. Droesch's medication organizer. She did something similar with her father, replacing the contents of a series of capsules he took each morning with crushed barbiturates. She did this after leaving Ms. Chang's house and before going to Paxton's."

Mom begins to softly cry. She pulls me in, and I feel myself going slow and numb. "I'm sorry, Clara. I'm so sorry."

It is her grief that opens my own. I know that Lily was never really my friend. But I was hers. And losing her like this is more painful than I could have imagined.

Mom and I sleep in her bed that night, with George on our feet and the TV playing old reruns of our favorite shows. When we wake up, Mom calls off of work. She declares that she will lie around until she can't stand it anymore.

"You should rest too," she says. "You look completely exhausted."

She's right and I am, which is why I'm not sure how she'll take what I'm about to say. "Actually, I called Henry this morning. I think he's going to take me to see Paxton."

Mom watches me for a long moment. "Are you sure?"

"I am."

I expect her to argue, but I'm wrong. Instead, she drives me, and Henry meets us. I ask Mom to wait in the car, and Henry takes me up to the sixth floor. Sammy—who seems to know everyone and everything—found his room number, so we navigate to the right one and knock softly.

"Come in."

I push the door open, spotting a plump older blond with swollen red eyes in a chair at the foot of Paxton's bed. She's wearing a pink sweater set, and she's crocheting something in a bag on her lap.

"Hi, Henry. Hi, Clara."

It's Mariana who speaks, perched on a second chair just beside Paxton's bed. They have a deck of cards out on the rolling table, and Mariana's fingers are laced with Paxton's on a pillow. He makes a move to pull away from her, but she squeezes his hand, giving him a sorrowful look. Something lovely passes between them, and I feel intrusive bearing witness.

"You're Clara." Mrs. Bryce says my name with reverence. It's strange seeing this woman who looks so much like Paxton watching me with such naked gratitude. She puts her crocheting bag down and gets up. "You saved my son's life."

I don't know how to react, so I duck my head. "It was lucky timing. And he was the one who texted 911."

"It was a miracle," she says, her voice breaking. "You're a miracle."

"Mom." It's Paxton's voice. He sounds groggy but much more like himself. "Can we have a minute?"

"Of course. I'll go see about a decent cup of coffee."

I inch my way past her to the foot of Paxton's bed. He is still pale, and his lips are chapped and cracked. There are red speckles around his eyes, burst capillaries from so much vomiting, probably.

"Hey," I say.

"Hi."

"How are you feeling?" I ask.

"Well, I was poisoned, so not great."

He smirks and I laugh, and it occurs to me that I haven't had a civil conversation with Paxton since the pill bug races. It's weird and maybe a little nice.

"I'm glad you came," he says. "I wanted to thank you. Obviously."

"It really was just lucky timing. It would have been the police if I'd done a better job explaining it to 911."

"Maybe. But it wasn't the police who showed up first. It was you."

I sit on the very edge of one of the chairs at the foot of his bed. He looks at Mariana, and Mariana looks at him. They seem calm and open and when Henry squeezes my shoulders, I can't keep the question in.

"Can I ask how this happened?" I ask, gesturing to their clasped hands.

Mariana and Paxton look at each other, and Mariana flushes.

"Oh, you don't have to answer. That was rude," I say, feeling awkward.

"It's a long story," Paxton says, and I can see that Mariana looks uncomfortable. She's biting her lip.

"It's not," she says softly. "Not really. But I should explain how I'm involved in this mess."

"Mariana," Paxton says.

She shakes her head gently. "No, it's okay. I can talk about it. I need to talk about it." And then she looks at me. "Two years ago, I was a sophomore. I…made a stupid decision. I got involved with a teacher."

I feel my mouth drop open and force my lips to close. I nod slowly, trying desperately to keep my face open and gentle.

Mariana gives a bitter little cough of a laugh. "Yeah, I know. It's gross. He was young. Mr. Bowman. Do you remember him?"

I do remember him. A first-year teacher who worked part-time in the art department my freshman year. I barely knew him, and he moved to a different school district as soon as he got a full-time gig.

"He went to NYU and knew a lot of alumni. He was kind of a big deal there, I guess." She shrugs. "I don't know. It was dumb, but it happened. And he shouldn't have, obviously. I know that. But I wasn't unwilling."

"So you never told anyone?" I ask gently.

"No. I was completely embarrassed. And he set me up with

all these interviews and recommendations afterward. He's part of the reason I got into NYU on early acceptance. I thought if people found out, they'd assume I didn't deserve it."

"You do deserve it," Paxton says.

She offers him a small smile.

I wait, trying to be patient and still feeling confused as to what this has to do with Lily. But I don't wait long.

"Lily knew. We had this French project, and I worked really hard on it, but Lily wasn't doing great. She kind of blamed me and then told me it was her father. She told me—"

Mariana cuts herself off, sniffling. Paxton pulls her closer, and she situates herself on the edge of his bed, curling her feet beneath her. After a moment, she continues.

"She told me some of what her father did. I tried to get her to say something, but it was so messed up. He swore it would destroy her mother. That he'd lose his job and their home, and he made it out like she was twisting the truth—imagining it or whatever. He messed with Lily's head so much, and she felt like getting as far away as possible was the only answer."

"So she applied for the exchange program," Paxton says. "I actually voted for her, but our votes are confidential, and the teachers were impressed by Cadence after everything she'd been through."

"Everything she'd been through because of me," I say, letting out a slow breath. "Lily felt like I took away her one chance at escape."

Mariana nods. "She was furious, so I didn't know why she then turned around and became friends with you. But she and I had this connection too. Along the way, I told her about what happened with Jeff. With Mr. Bowman, I mean. And we were close. When she mentioned having a secret last month, I figured she'd tell me. I thought she might be planning to run away on her eighteenth birthday. I had no idea the secret was anything like this."

"Until Mr. Droesch. And the text messages," Paxton says. "We read them together and could both see she was just too over-the-top."

"She doesn't know about Paxton and me," Mariana says.

"To be fair," Henry says with a grin. "No one knows about Paxton and you."

"Now that I'm the emperor with no clothes, I'm not the top choice with that crowd, you know," Paxton says with a smirk.

The emperor with no clothes? I think of his empty house. The broken-down pool. Was Paxton ousted over some kind of family money thing?

"Did they really push you out of the group?" I ask.

"They didn't push me out. I pulled away. It's humiliating. And despite that, I was a dick to you because they were nice to you. I'm not proud of it."

"I'm not proud of spending seventeen months believing an absolute lie," I say.

"I think I win the not-proud game," Mariana says, her smile rueful.

Henry trails off shaking his head. "I didn't help either of you. Mar, I never even asked you about what you and Lily really talked about. And I know Lily's dad is weird. I saw them once at a stoplight. It was just a little thing—I totally blew it off, but I saw him kind of grab the back of her neck. It just...It wasn't a thing a dad would do, but I never gave it a second thought."

"She hid it well," I say.

Mariana nods, looking grave. "He had her totally convinced that he was unstoppable."

"I understand how that can happen," I say, thinking back to my own belief that Lily was unstoppable when she was framing me.

But I still hate the part of me that never saw what was happening with Mr. Dalton. All those private tennis lessons. All the nicknames and the hugs, and I should have known. God, why didn't I know?

"I wasn't the only one who suspected something was wrong with Lily," Mariana said. "She told me that Mr. Droesch had once point blank-asked her if she was safe at home—if there was anyone hurting her. Of course she said no."

"And he believed her?" Henry asks, but I just nod, feeling numb.

"It's Lily," I say. "Doesn't everyone believe her?"

FORTY

Henry drives me to the station so I can pick up my phone and laptop. We drive from there directly to a Five Guys, where I order an enormous burger and a huge bag of fries that I immediately douse in vinegar.

"God, it will be good to have a functional phone," I say, unplugging my returned phone from the charger in his car. It powers up, the screen bigger and beautifully crack-free.

Henry frowns and leans over. "No, I don't think that's quite working yet."

"It isn't?"

He takes the unlocked phone and quickly taps away on the screen. When I take it back, I see I'm in my contacts looking at a new addition. Henry Toussaint. With a single red heart after his name.

I smile. "I guess that side-of-the-road kiss was a real winner."

"To be fair, I didn't plan on you crying the first time we kissed."

"I'm not crying now," I say.

Henry twists in his seat, his hand on my arm and then the side of my neck. "No. No, you aren't."

His kiss is much softer this time, and we both taste like the salty fries we've been eating. He slowly pulls away, leaving me wanting more. But instead of leaning back in, he straightens, clearing his throat.

"That's all I get? I was a fugitive twenty-four hours ago," I complain.

He arches a brow. "Well now you're a high school junior again. And you have your AP Chem test in five days. You should crack open that laptop so we can get to work."

I laugh and do as he says, pushing the seat back to prop my laptop on my knees. The strip mall's Wi-Fi kicks in, and I open my browser, all of my tabs reopening from a week ago. Like nothing ever happened.

My stomach catches looking at these tabs. There are the concert tickets Lily and I were considering last Monday. The email from John Carroll. The classroom website with the chemistry test scores. It's as if the whole last week didn't happen.

And then there is the last tab. My personal email. I click on it to close it down and freeze when I spot a new email at the top of my inbox.

APRIL 12, 10:05 A.M.

LILY DALTON

SUBJECT: YOU WERE RIGHT.

"You look like you've seen a ghost," he says.

"I sort of have. I can't read this. Will you?"

I offer him my laptop and watch his face shift when he sees the email. He opens it with a click and begins to read.

Dear Clara,

I guess it's my turn to be the criminal. Do you think anyone will believe it? If they don't, I hope you'll tell them. Tell them I was nothing like the sweet little girl they all believed me to be. I hope you'll tell them that I killed a monster they can't imagine. Because I've never needed their approval and I've never been afraid to be evil. All I've ever needed was the freedom to survive. Now that he's dead, no one will ever take that away from me again. And if they call me evil for that, I'll wear that title with pride.

I guess you'll have to be good enough for both of us now.

Lily

Henry closes my laptop and slides it under his seat. Then he scoops me up onto his lap where we sit, heads pressed together in silence.

"It's not true, what she wrote. She isn't evil," I say. "It's not that simple."

"None of us are completely anything, right?" Henry says. "We're good and bad and a whole lot of other things, and somehow we've got to sort it out."

I nestle my head under his chin and breathe deep. I will think no more of good or evil tonight. I will breathe in and out. I will do it again. And somehow, in this strange world, I'll do just what Henry said. I will sort it out, and I will find my own way through.

THE END

ACKNOWLEDGMENTS

Lots of people say writing is a solitary business, and that's true. The rest of the truth is that writing isn't possible without an incredible supporting cast.

A huge thank you goes out to my brilliant editor, Wendy McClure. When I lose my way, which is often, Wendy is the wise voice who leads me back to the story I'm trying to tell. And thanks to the Sourcebooks Team (Karen, Emily, Caitlyn, Lia, Thea, and so many others I'm not recalling in this moment) who make every part of the author experience wonderful.

To my wise and wonderful agent, Suzie, along with Olivia and Sarah and the rest of the New Leaf Team. You handle all of the red tape and confusing language so that I'm still able to write the stories, and I'm so grateful for your support. And of course to my awesome readers. Your notes, emails, and kindness make every tough day worth it—thank you!

To my dear friend, Jonathan, for some helpful injury discussions and his beautiful wife, Lori Ann, for offering up his surgeon smarts! Much love to my brilliant and talented writing friends Margaret, Lisa, and Edie—your friendship is a buoy in stormy waters. And to Jody who has been a beacon through my darkest moments, writing and otherwise. And of course to Ben, who makes every part of my life better and easier—I owe you lots of chocolate chip cookies for this one.

And of course, all of my love and gratitude goes out to Ian, Adrienne, and Lydia. The story of your lives will always be my favorite. And the stories I write will always be for you.

ABOUT THE AUTHOR

Natalie D. Richards is the *New York Times* bestselling, award-winning author of several young adult thrillers. She lives in Ohio where her writing is inspired and supported by her wonderful family and her enormous dust mop of a dog, Wookiee, who served as the inspiration for George in this novel. *Two Perfect Lies* is her eleventh novel for young adults.

sourcebooks
fire